DEDICATION

For Caitlin, the inspiration for Chase and one of the loveliest young people I've had the honor to know. And Sophie, her big sister, who loves Caitlin for everything she is.

Undeniable

—— Always Book 3

LEXXIE COUPER

The characters and events portrayed in this book are fictitious. Any similarity to real persons, living or dead, is purely coincidental and not intended by the author.

UNDENIABLE
Copyright © 2015 by Lexxie Couper

ONE

"Lots of people talk to animals. Not very many listen though. That's the problem."
~ Benjamin Hoff

Chase

Caden O'Dae could bite me.

Not literally of course. The proximity of the annoying Australian's mouth to any area of my body was an essential part of the problem I faced.

No, he could bite me because, no matter how hard he tried, I refused to fall for him. It was not happening. Didn't matter how cute he was, with his blue eyes, sexy Aussie accent, ridiculously endearing passionate need to care for wounded animals, beard that made me want to . . .

Wait. What? Where was I going with this?

Ah, that's right. Me not falling for Caden or his shtick.

For one, I didn't do the romance thing any more. I'd learned my lesson last year and frankly, it was a lesson learned well.

For another, I'm defective, and defective people like me don't make for good "romantic" entanglements, no matter what the movies tell you (learned in part from that lesson I already mentioned).

So, yeah, there we go. Didn't matter what Caden O'Dae did, me and him were *not* going to happening.

Once you've had your heart ripped out and stomped on, once you've had your defect thrown in your face as the *reason* for the decimation of your heart and any Happy Ever After you'd planned, you know it's just better to be *that* girl. You know the one? The prickly, stand-offish, sarcastic girl who never dates and spends her time scoffing at the ridiculousness of the world. I'm that girl, with the added bonus of being defective.

The thing is, I'm okay with the *defective* bit. I was born that way.

I overheard my father call me that when I was twelve. I'm using the term *heard* in an ironic way, of course, given the reason I'm faulty. I have profound sensorineural hearing loss in my left ear and moderate conductive hearing loss in the other. Or to put it more simply, I'm completely deaf in one ear and can hardly hear with the other. The "officially" recognized term is Hard of Hearing.

I was born with the profoundly deaf ear, thanks to a serious case of being premature and Mom being rushed into an emergency C-section that almost went horribly wrong. The almost-but-not-quite-working ear came about thanks to some nasty, nasty reoccurring ear infections as a result of being premature. Essentially, my pressing need to get into this world earlier than planned kind of fucked me over somewhat. Go figure.

Sometimes I wear a hearing aid in the ear that almost works, but it irritates the hell out of me, and frankly, the second people see it pity fills their eyes. Have you ever been looked at with pity? Yeah. Not fun.

My hearing, or lack thereof, also means I tend to tilt my head a little to the left when people talk, so that I can pick up their voices, even as I watch their lips move. I also get annoyed when people don't look directly at me when they're speaking, which – what with the hypnotizing power of cells phones and the seeming inability of the average person to exist for more than five seconds without looking at one – happens more often than you realize. We really are, as a species, becoming enslaved by the ubiquitous devices.

I'm amazing at reading lips. Amazing. I can also sign, and do so whenever I want to swear or tell my sister something I'd rather not share with the world when we're with company, but I don't rely on it for communication. Because the moment someone realizes you're deaf, they treat you differently.

That sucks.

It's never stopped me or slowed me down, my defect. It's never really bothered me. Sure, going to the movies is a pain (it's just too damn loud for me, which is also ironic when you think about it), and getting treated like I'm sub-human and intellectually deficient, or fragile and helpless, has a way of bringing out the bitch in me if I'm not careful, but it's never stopped me from living the life I want to.

Most times, I should point out, I'm *not* careful. That helps deal with the people who treat me like I'm less than them. Keeps them at arm's length. Keeps them wondering. Keeps them on guard. When people are on guard enough they tend to eventually move away from you.

I'm good with that.

Essentially, I don't do people. I don't do relationships. I definitely don't do romance. Not any more. There's nothing romantic about someone whispering sweet nothings in your ear when you can't hear them. They get antsy when you don't whisper something back. (I'm not good with whispering. Unfortunately, it's a volume thing I've never gotten the hang of.)

The few times I tried to do romance when I was a teenager ended with the intended recipient of my affections giving up and finding themselves a date with someone who *didn't* have to wear a hearing aid in one ear; who *didn't* ask them to repeat themselves when they whispered said sweet nothings in said ear. Who didn't get irritated in crowds and parties, and snarky with people trying to communicate with her when she couldn't decipher what they were saying.

The one time I got really serious about romance, the only time I sincerely believed the person I was with loved me for everything I was, including the faulty hearing, ended up with me sobbing ugly tears in my closet and dropping out of college.

Apparently, dating me is hard *and,* according to Professor Douchebag, an inconvenience. Have you ever been told you're an inconvenience, not just by a stranger who doesn't like how long you're taking to order your coffee at Starbucks, but by someone who you've given your heart to? Have you been told an integral part of what makes you *you* is an inconvenience? It freaking rips your emotions to shreds and makes you feel like shit. As a result, I stopped dating.

No dating. No falling in love. No decimated heart. It was a win-win for everyone concerned, right? I just needed Caden O'Dae to get with the program and stop being so . . . so . . .

Damn it.

Why had I agreed to pick him up from the airport again? I knew what he was going to do – see me through the crowd, grin, wave, weave his way toward me with an emotion in his eyes I didn't want to acknowledge, even as my tummy tight-ened at the sight of it.

Every time I'd collected him from LAX to date, my tummy told me my body liked the way he looked, and the way he looked at me. Every time I told my tummy to tell my body to get a grip. Every time, my body refused to comply.

Stupid body. Hadn't it learned its lesson with Professor Douchebag? Apparently, I was as defective in the head as I was in the ears.

I didn't need an annoying Australian making my life complicated with his sexy accent and smiling eyes and relaxed laugh that vibrated through me regardless of how little I could actually hear it. I didn't. I didn't need anyone. Not in that way.

I had my family, who I love beyond words. My mom (she of the witty sarcasm and addiction to running marathons) and dad (he of the over-protective coddle-swaddling and zero tact), my big sister Amanda (The best sister ever, even if she does like Coldplay) and her husband Brendon (The Wonder from Down Under, with a heart as big as his biceps, which is saying something), and my nephew Tanner.

Tanner is my world. A fighter to the nth degree, at the age of three Tanner has already fought and beaten leukemia, learned to say g'day like the half-Aussie he is, and spent more time in hospital and tolerating doctors and needles than any adult should, let alone a child.

But apart from those people, and a friend or two here and there, I don't do human interaction. It's easier. Less frustrat-ing. Less exasperating.

Less . . . painful.

Caden, however, has refused to read my fuck-off-and-leave-me-alone vibes.

Didn't matter how many times I ignored him, or rolled my

eyes at him or swore at him (signing, of course – I figured if I sign at him enough he'll do what everyone who's not my immediate family do when I'm signing and get all uncomfortable and weird and just go away), he seemed hell-bent on not taking the hint.

Didn't matter that the one time we almost kissed, I damn near sprinted from the room and pretended I was asleep in Tanner's bed. Seriously, the guy can't take a hint.

If it wasn't for the fact he's so freaking smart, I'd think he was stupid. He's definitely not stupid. Stubborn, yes. Obstinate, yes. But stupid? No. You can't be top of your class at college and be stupid.

Caden O'Dae is far from stupid. Caden is . . .

Jesus, why am I talking about him so much? I don't want to talk about him. I've said my piece. I was not – repeat not – falling for him, no matter what he did.

I'm not talking about him any more.

For now, let's concentrate on me. (Hey, what twenty-two year old doesn't want to do that, right?)

I'm a college dropout, something my university-professor father is horrified about. By the way, Professor Douchebag is not my dad, I should make that clear. Professor Douchebag is the *reason* I'm a college dropout, but no one apart from he and I know that.

Of course, Dad thought I'd dropped out to irritate him and I happily let him go with that.

Don't get me wrong, I love my father. I really do. He's just . . . a perfect example of academic pretentiousness wrapped up in over-protective righteousness with a safety-harness of elitism attached for good measure.

So I'm a college dropout who's deaf in one ear, partially deaf in the other, who drives a metallic purple Volvo station wagon with a neon green Chinese luck dragon painted along each side. My hair changes color regularly (it's currently an awesome aqua-blue) and until last week I wore it in dreadlocks. Now it's short. Short and aqua-blue.

I've got a tattoo of Buddha eating pizza just above my right butt cheek, but don't tell Dad. I'm pretty certain I'd get kicked out of the house if he knew.

Currently, I'm working in a pet store that specializes in exotic animals, which isn't anywhere near as exciting as it sounds. No matter what part of the world the animals come from, their poop still smells the same. Cleaning out the terrarium of an Australian bearded dragon is no different from cleaning out a terrarium of your common, garden variety Green Anole lizard, and no matter what the movies tell you, macaws from Rio are not anal-retentive germophobes, but rather big-ass birds who drop their shit wherever they happen to be perched. Oh, and they *don't* sound like Jesse Eisenberg.

Despite all that, I genuinely enjoy working there. My boss is more anti-social than I am (who knew that was even possible?), leaves me alone most of the time (win!) and the customers on the whole know what they want.

I've only ever had to put my bitch hat on twice since working there, once to stop a stupid parent buying her child a snake, a gift that would have inevitably resulted in the child, or the mother, in the morgue.

The second time I had to convince a father that the Sydney Funnel Web he'd illegally smuggled in from Australia did not make a "cool" present for his son's graduation from elementary school.

Safety tip for future reference: Sydney Funnel Web spiders are the most deadly, venomous, dangerous spider on the planet. They are *not* like tarantulas. They are *not* suitable for young children as pets. Yes, they look cool, all shiny and black and hairy, but they *can kill you*. In fifteen minutes. Like most things from Down Under, America is not physically, medically, psychologically or emotionally prepared for them.

The same warning goes for that country's Taipan snake, Eastern Brown snake, Red-bellied Black snake, and Caden O'Dae.

Shit. I didn't mean to say that.

Back on track.

More about me (that's what you're here for, right?) . . .

So, college dropout with unconventional hair, awesomely talented artist doing little but doodling nowadays, second daughter to parents with parenting issues, totally dedicated and fabulous aunt, proud Volvo owner (FYI, I call my car the Speeding Dragon) and exotic pet shop worker. I'm a card-carrying geek who would run away with Loki at the drop of a hat. (Google him if you don't know who I'm talking about. Tom Hiddleston . . . sigh) I still live at home (yeah, that one needs some attention), love movies but really don't like going to the movies, generally want very little to do with most people, and have zero plans of ever being in a relationship that requires any kisses except the Hershey kind.

You still with me? You haven't decided to dump me yet?

Okay, that's good.

So Caden O'Dae, Brendon's cousin, comes back and forth to San Diego as often as his studies will allow. Usually those visits are only short trips. I can deal with that. But this next trip he's staying for three weeks.

Three weeks. How am I meant to deal with him being around for three weeks?

He was planning to spend those three weeks with Amanda and Brendon, true, but I doubt I could avoid him for the entire time. I also knew he was going to be bringing all manner of gifts for everyone, and try as hard as I might, standing in the Arrivals section of LAX waiting for him, I couldn't help but wonder what he was bringing me.

The first time he came back, after Tanner's successful bone marrow transplant, he'd presented me with a bright purple and green sock puppet dragon. He'd made it himself. He does this weird thing where he makes sock puppets. I will never tell him this because then he might get the stupid opinion I actually *like* him, but they are adorable. If his intended career as a veterinarian fails he could make a living selling sock puppets on Etsy. Not a good living, I'm sure. Not compared to what he could make as Dr. Caden O'Dae, Animal Doctor, but a living all the same.

The *last* time he visited, he gave me a Thor sock puppet. Except Thor wasn't wielding his mighty hammer, but a can of Foster's beer. And he was wearing board shorts covered in flowers.

"Cause he's actually Australian," he'd said as I stared at the puppet in my hand. "Not Asgardin."

That was one of those moments where, no matter how hard I tried, I couldn't help but laugh. Our eyes had met for a moment. My tummy did one of those unsettling tightening things. Thank God he said something low enough that I couldn't quite make it out, something that was probably lovely and sweet, because it gave me a reason to get grumpy and stomp off.

(By the way, I'm sure most people think I'm a brat. Given how anti-social I am, I'm fine with that. I am guilty, however, of sometimes behaving less than exemplary to cover the fact I'm feeling awkward. I'm not a fan of feeling awkward. Who is?)

I didn't see him for the rest of the time he was here.

I didn't take him back to LAX, which was my normal

routine. Instead I sat at home, glaring at the clock in my room when his plane was due for takeoff.

My phone pinged at me once five minutes after, but when I grabbed it out of my bag, my heart beating faster than it should, I discovered it was a text from Professor Douchebag.

The text –

No, let me start that again.

The *professor*.

Professor Douchebag was my Art History professor when I was still a college student. Insanely sexy and hugely popular, he had this amazing ability to make students feel like they were the most important thing in his world with just a look.

When I joined his class, he'd commented about my hair (purple at the time) and suggested my father – who he knew quite well – was probably not a fan. Straight away I'd felt like he understood me.

After just one month I lived for his lectures. Hurried to them, eager to see his face. To have him see me.

Those classes . . . oh wow. He'd hang on every word I said. He'd call on me to answer questions, ask my opinion on the topic at hand. That may not seem like a big deal, but when you've gone through the education system with teachers who handled your hearing impairment by either pretending you didn't exist in their class, or shouting the most basic of questions at you just so you can feel like you're included, to be treated like a normal student is huge. And I so desperately wanted to be treated like a normal student back then.

When I look back, that desperation really messed me up. But I was only eighteen. That's my excuse and I'm sticking to it. Eighteen and angry with my father for making it obvious he was disappointed with me.

On some weird, subconscious level, I suspect the fact

Professor Douchebag taught at the same collage as Dad was an added bonus.

Whatever the reasons, I fell hard. Took out my heart – that moronic organ I'd spent eighteen years guarding like it was the One Ring – and gave it to him.

He took it. And for ever so long I was happy. Why wouldn't I be? He worshipped me. Adored me. Spent long hours exploring my body with his hands and lips and tongue. Made me feel normal. Like a *real* girl, not the defective one I'd grown up believing I was.

I should have wised up to the fact he didn't consider my heart as precious as I did when it became clear we were never to be seen in public together in any capacity other than that of student/teacher.

But I was in awe of this intellectual, sexy, popular god with more than one New York Times Bestselling art book to his name. I was in love with him.

Love is stupid.

And it makes you blind, which is not ideal when you're already damn near completely deaf. Functioning on three senses is tricky at best.

Ending it hurt more than it should have, for a variety of reasons. But the thing with Professor Douchebag? He figured out very quickly he'd got under my skin. And for every *No, I'm over you* text I sent in reply to his *I need to see you now* texts, there were shamefully just as many *Okay, I'm coming* ones.

Under my skin. Didn't matter what I did to try and exorcise him, he was under there. And when we were alone together at his place, or in his car, or his office . . . when he was touching me, looking at me, listening to me . . . I forgot how the us that existed behind closed doors wasn't the us I wanted beyond them.

So when I got the professor's text asking me to come to his place, as I was sitting on my bed with the knowledge Caden O'Dae was once again gone from my life, I went.

Was it self-punishment for refusing to acknowledge that Caden O'Dae was the first guy to *ever* make me feel like my life was actually fine the way I was living it? I don't know.

I still don't.

Thankfully, I stopped myself from doing something completely stupid and drove away from Professor Douchebag's place before I could get out of the car.

I went to a friend's house and we got drunk on tequila, and watched *Daredevil* on Netflix, and while Charlie Cox beat up bad guys with brooding, angst-ridden intensity I was wondering if maybe this time, *this time*, Professor Douchebag was going to take me out for dinner in public, hold my hand in public, say he was wrong for breaking my heart. Apologize for hurting me . . .

And then it wasn't the professor I was thinking about but Caden. Caden and sock puppets, and his laugh, his grin, his eyes. Caden and his ability to make me forget I was defective. His ability to make me realize when I *did* remember, that it was okay . . .

His ability to make me smile . . .

I passed out before the last episode of Season One began. My friend let me crash on the couch, which was a good thing. I couldn't have faced whatever disappointment I'd find in Dad's eyes if I went home, and if I'd gone to Amanda and Brendon's I would have told my sister about *everything* and I wasn't ready to deal with that either.

Being messed up about who you are and what you want is *really* messed up.

Caden and I hadn't spoken or been in contact since the Thor sock-puppet incident. I'd seen what he was up to on

Facebook, of course. And Instagram, where he posts pics of him and the animals he cares for at the RSPCA on the weekends (the RSPCA – the Royal Society for the Prevention of Cruelty to Animals – is the Australian equivalent of the ASPCA). Facebook is mainly dedicated to his social life.

Most of his Facebook posts involve him and his university friends being twentysomething-year-old students doing the kind of things twentysomething-year-old students do. There are lots of images of him and his friends in crazy costumes no doubt for crazy college parties. Lately, there have been a few posts involving the celebrity veterinarian he's interning for in Australia.

I'm not jealous. Honest. It means nothing to me that she's tall, blonde and stunning, with teeth so white my brain hurts. It really doesn't. But seriously, people were going to talk soon if he wasn't careful. I mean she's older than him for starters. And she tags him all the time. And you should see the way she leans into him in all the photos she has posted on—

". . . incoming flight . . . delayed."

I blinked, frowning at the crowded airport around me. What was that announcement?

The noise of the place – an incomprehensible, muffled cacophony that grated on my senses and made my head buzz – seemed to swell around me. Because I was grumpy, I hadn't bothered to charge the battery of my hearing aid, which meant it was just another thing I was carrying around that I didn't need. I rarely wore it, because it irritated the hell out of me. Noises were either too loud when I wore it or too confusing, and the second people saw it they treated me differently.

So no hearing aid, just a lot of noise in my head.

And now an announcement I'm almost certain was about an incoming flight from Melbourne, but because I couldn't hear it clearly I could have been completely wrong.

That happens. More than I like, unfortunately. There are ways around it, of course. Services provided for the "hearing impaired" (I don't know why, but that term grates on me just as much as the noise of a crowd). All I needed to do was seek out one of those services and problem fixed. Or do something as simple as go check the arrivals board again.

I didn't do either. Common sense and I weren't on speaking terms at that point in time.

Instead, I held my ground, glared at the flow of tired-looking people ambling into the arrivals section, and waited until Caden came into my line of sight.

He didn't.

Instead, someone else did. Someone I did not want to see.

"Shit," I muttered, turning away.

But not before Professor Douchebag saw me. Not before he smiled at me.

Shit.

And as much as I hated the fact, my throat grew tight and my belly fluttered.

Shit. Again. Times three. God, where was Caden O'Dae when I needed him?

Caden

What was a good Aussie boy like me doing falling in love with a prickly, feisty, snarky American girl, you ask?

Good question.

The answer? Hmmm . . . not sure if there is a good answer. Just a brutally honest one. And in love – and war – brutal honesty is paramount.

The second I saw Chase Sinclair I fell in love with her.

I'm not embarrassed to admit it. Okay, I didn't admit it to

anyone but myself, and begrudgingly to start with. I wasn't in the market for the love of my life, and if I had been, I'm one hundred percent certain I wouldn't have been looking for an American girl who seemed convinced I was trying to kill her sick nephew with the sock puppet I'd made for him. But the heart wants what the heart wants, as the saying goes, and the moment I laid eyes on Chase my heart wanted her. It was only later the logical problems of that love sank in. Things like her being in the Northern Hemisphere, and me being in the Southern Hemisphere. Things like me being twelve months away from finishing my doctorate at the top of my class in Veterinary Medicine at Melbourne University. Things like the fact I was an intern for Australia's most distinguished and respected vet, with the offer of joining her practice when I finished my studies.

None of those logistic complications mattered when I first saw Chase. I fell in love with her instantly.

She, however, didn't want a bar of me.

I was jet lagged when I first saw her. Jet lagged, sleep deprived and over-caffeinated. At the best of times I'm . . . how should I put this? Exuberant. I've been called a prat, a dickhead, accused of never taking anything serious, dumped more than once for that very reason, labeled a joker and – in that weird way Australians appropriate American slang – a jackass. Jackarse just doesn't have the right sound to it, I guess.

I'm probably all of these things, truth be told, but the one I'll gladly own is the not-taking-things-seriously label. I don't. Not really.

Unless it's important, and when my cousin Brendon called and told me he had an eighteen-month-old son he'd only just found out about in America, and that son had leukemia and was likely to die if a suitable bone marrow match wasn't found . . . yeah, that falls into things-that-need-to-be-taken-seriously.

I hopped on the first flight to the US.

Almost three hours after touching down in the country and walking into Tanner's hospital room, I met Chase. For a second I kind of forgot why I was there. She took my breath away.

When she jumped up and snatched the sock puppet out of my hands, spraying it liberally with disinfectant before giving me permission to "give it to her nephew" I was gone. Just like that.

Hook. Line. Sinker.

All over, red rover.

It wasn't the electric-blue dreadlocks, the eyebrow piercing, the Iron Man T-shirt that did nothing to hide the fact she had a bloody awesome body that would look even more awesome wrapped around mine. All those things – and more – sank into my consciousness later.

It was the protective way she guarded her nephew. The fiery, fierce instinct to look out for someone she loved. The unabashed accusation I was fucking things up and she was going to stop me from doing so.

And before you say, *Really? That's why fell in love with her?* remember the reason I was in the States to begin with: my cousin had called and told me he had a sick kid. I could hear how fucked up he was about that – and Brendon Osmond didn't do fucked up – and I knew I had to go be there for him, regardless of cost or uni lectures or assignments due. He was family; I loved him, and he needed me, whether he said so or not.

That was me. And I saw that part of me in Chase.

That's why I fell in love with her.

I had a lot of contact with her during the next few

months. I was in the States a lot, due to a bone marrow transfer that changed everyone's world. But even if I didn't need to keep coming back to San Diego for Tanner and Brendon, I couldn't have stayed away.

A little bit about me before I continue, just so you get an idea of who I am. It's probably good that you get some backstory, because I'm pretty certain you're going to want to hit me at some point in this tale and tell me to wake up to myself.

I'm a fourth-year student at Melbourne University studying a Doctorate of Veterinary Medicine, with the end goal of opening up my own clinic. As part of my degree, I'm currently working as an intern at Briny Phillips' vet clinic. Briny Phillips is a celebrity vet with her own television show, and one of the best vets I've ever met. I've learned a lot from her, particularly how to deal with stressed pet owners. There's an art to it, a fine line to walk. I haven't always been able to walk that line, but I'm getting better at it, thanks to Briny.

I'm an only child, but not a spoilt one. My parents are divorced, not because they grew to despise each other, but because they were grown-up enough to recognize they just weren't compatible, and when I was twelve they did something about it.

It was amicable. They didn't rant and rave at each other. In fact, I never saw them get angry or slam doors and fight during the demise of their marriage. They were calm. Dad joked about it with a relaxed good nature I remember as a kid not understanding, but emulating.

If my parents were shouting at each other, if they weren't getting angry with each other, it meant I shouldn't either.

So as angry as I was – and I *was* angry – I joked. Laughed. Made fun at my own expense. Didn't ruffle anyone's feathers, including my own. When Dad left and never came back, I joked about the fact I needed to change my deodorant.

Laughing at life proved to be an effective way to deal with whatever life threw at me, and I've lived that way ever since. Getting ruffled, angry doesn't achieve anything. I've had girl-friends in the past, hence being dumped for not taking things seriously, but none I've fallen in love with. Two had the audacity to tell me to get rid of my beard.

I love my beard. Don't ever, ever, ever tell me to shave off my beard.

I play rugby union on weekends, despite the fact I'm built more like a tennis player.

I plan to one day own a rescue mutt of indecipherable parentage and call him Puss-Cat, just to mess with people's heads.

Every uni break, I fly to San Diego. Originally, this had been to see my cousin, who is like a brother to me, and Tanner, to see how the champion kid was doing, to be a part of his life. Trust me, if you knew Tanner, you'd want to be a part of his life as well.

That's about it. At least, that's all that really matters.

Which brings us to Chase.

Chase has never asked me to shave off my beard. What she *has* done is told me she doesn't like it, told me to get the damn thing away from her, used it as a way of throwing me to the floor in a wrestling match that somehow got completely out of hand, spread honey through it while I was dozing after one particularly brutal red-eye flight from Melbourne, and once, during a midnight movie marathon while we were babysitting Tanner, combed her fingers through it, her breath warm on my lips as she studied my face, confusion warring with desire in her eyes.

That was the night I realized Chase felt for me what I felt for her.

It was also the night I fully accepted she was going to fight it harder than she'd fought anything in her life. And Chase Sinclair is, if nothing else, a stubborn pain in the butt when it comes to backing down.

Chase holds the world at bay. At arm's length. She's had a lifetime of being treated differently because of her hearing, of being dismissed by people for being dumb or rude, of being cossetted by her father in a misguided attempt to protect her from whatever he thinks might bring her pain, and unfortunately, of being disconnected from normal life by something she has no control over. The first week after meeting her, I could see it bugged the hell out of her. I could also see she hid all her anger and dejection behind a wall of snark, unlike any I'd encountered.

And there was something else. Something I couldn't quite figure out. Like a secret in her eyes, that were filled with a pain darker than any I'd experienced.

What I wanted to do more than anything else from that very first week, was to show her she didn't need to be defensive with me. That I got her. That I would protect her from whatever crap the world threw at her.

Not exactly an easy goal to achieve.

The closest I'd ever come was during that midnight movie marathon in Brendon's living room almost five months ago, as Simon Pegg dealt with his zombie stepfather Bill Nighy on screen.

I caught her laughing, really laughing. Before I could stop myself, I flicked her ear so she'd look at me, see my lips, and told her she had an awesome laugh.

She studied me, silent, and then brushed her fingers through my beard, drawing closer to me, so close my heart tried to smash its way out of my chest via my throat, and . . .

That's when Tanner toddled out to us, in perfect three-year-old interception, and asked for a drink of water.

I've never seen a person move so fast as I saw Chase move that night. Up off the sofa and across to the door where her nephew stood, rubbing his eyes, his Transformer PJs as crumpled as his crazy blond Mohawk was messy. She scooped him up, snuggled him against her chest and told him she would get him a drink.

A quick glance over her shoulder told me she was unsettled. I didn't realize how unsettled until she didn't come back from Tanner's room after putting him back to bed. I found her there thirty minutes later, asleep beside him, a frown on her face.

She didn't talk to me the next morning. She kissed her sister on the cheek, muttered something about not being hungry and left before anyone could say a word.

Brendon had looked at me with a raised eyebrow. "What did you do?"

True to form, I answered him honestly. "Made her acknowledge she has a thing for me."

That was my reason for this trip to San Diego. To make Chase acknowledge she liked me, and that we'd be good together.

Actually, it was more than just making her acknowledge she had a thing for me, as undeniable as I had for her. I was here to help her see that she didn't have to face the world alone. That I was more than happy to face it with her. That I was willing. And able. And ready.

So when I entered the Arrivals hall of LAX, duffle bag slung over my shoulder, tired and dry-eyed from my thirteen hour flight but full of the upbeat optimism my family is known for, my heart thumping fast as it always did when I knew I was about to see her, and found a man cupping her face with his palm, a man standing so close to her I could barely make out any light or space between their hips, I kinda felt it in my gut.

Actually, *kinda* is an understatement.

I felt it alright.

Hard.

A visceral reaction to the sight of Chase interacting with a man clearly older than her, in a way that was clearly beyond platonic.

I stumbled to a halt, my grip on my bag's strap loosening. My fingers didn't seem to have any strength in them. Neither did my legs to move forward. It was taking all my brainpower to process what I was seeing, even as my brain fiercely rebelled against it. A few of my fellow arriving passengers bumped into me, my abrupt stop taking them by surprise as they hurried toward their waiting loved ones.

I didn't mumble out an apology as they flicked me exasperated looks. All I could do was stand motionless and watch as Chase looked up at the older dude mauling her mouth with his thumb.

Alright, *mauling* might be a slight exaggeration, but fuck a duck, was he ever going to move his thumb away from her bottom lip? Was she ever going to make him?

I narrowed my eyes, watching them through the crowd. My fingers had found their strength again, now curling around the strap of my duffle bag with almost painful force. My pulse smashed in my throat and my ears, a pounding *thud-thud thud-thud* that drowned out the noise of LAX.

The dude lowered his head closer to Chase's. I couldn't miss how perfectly combed his dark hair was, nor how chiseled his jaw. His clean-shaven jaw. His chiseled, clean-shaven jaw with its square lines and cleft chin. Not a hint of a beard on that chin and jaw.

I didn't miss the sprinkling of gray at his temples, nor the impressive width of his shoulders. Nor the clothes so artfully bohemian they must have cost more than my semester uni fees.

I saw his lips move as they drew closer to Chase's. I saw him say something but couldn't make out what. I saw him lower his hand from the side of her face, down the smooth column of her throat, until he was trailing his fingertip down her chest to the beginning of her cleavage.

My pulse turned to a cannon in my head.

And then I saw Chase flinch. A little. Barely noticeable, but as you may have figured out by now, when it came to Chase Sinclair, I was almost an expert.

She flinched, the slightest of frowns pulling at her straight eyebrows. The tiniest of frowns making the piercing in her right eyebrow dip.

She flinched and turned her head a fraction to the side.

I moved. Not a run, but a purposeful stride. She wasn't happy about the situation, and I was going to bring it to an end.

I'm all about being protective. Brendon reckons that's why I decided to become a vet: to protect those that need it most. I think it was because animals don't complain like people do, but hey, maybe he's got a point?

Grin in place, I reached Chase's side just as Mr. Dude was about to do something to her ear with his lips.

Without hesitation – or contemplation, when it came down to it – I slid my hand over the small of Chase's back, dumped my duffle bag at my feet and let out a very loud, very exhausted sigh. "Christ, that was a long flight," I said, louder than even Chase needed me to be.

Loud enough Mr. Dude and his trendy clothes straightened away from her with a startled hiss, jerking his hand from her throat with the same abrupt speed.

Chase swung her stare at me and locked on my face. Her eyes widened. Her lips parted. "Caden?"

God, I loved the way she said my name. Even stunned, she made it sound like a promise of something she still refused to admit.

I smoothed my hand from her back, and with a quick glance at Mr. Dude – a glance that said *I have no idea who you are but I'm already bored by you* – signed *Hello gorgeous. God, I've missed you* to Chase.

Her eyes widened until she was gaping at me. She'd achieved maximum gape and she still looked amazing.

Gorgeous. She truly was gorgeous. I don't know when she'd cut off her dreadlocks, but her new pixie-short hair only made her more so.

I like the new hair, I signed. *It looks good on you.*

She studied me, her expression unreadable. And then she lifted her hands in front of her chest. *You learned to sign?*

"Chase?"

At Mr. Dude's confused utterance, both Chase and I swung to face him, me with a wide smile stretching my lips.

"Donald," she said, that distinct inflection in her voice unique to people who'd grown up without the luxury of complete hearing. "This is—"

"What did he say to you?"

I couldn't help but smile wider at the agitation in Mr. Dude's voice. He couldn't sign. Which meant no matter what he thought he felt for Chase, he wasn't legit. He might think he was, but he wasn't.

Nor could I help but feel a warm buzz of delight at the fact Chase didn't move away from me when she turned to him, but instead touched my chest with her hand and drew closer to my body.

Mr. Dude puffed himself up as much as he could. He was

as tall as me, and to be honest, probably a little more built. He slid his gaze over me, down to the thongs on my feet – Hey, I'm an Aussie on a long-haul international flight, what else would I be wearing on my feet? – and back up to my face.

"G'day." I stuck out my right hand. "I'm Caden. Just flew in from Australia."

His eyes slitted. He looked at my hand, and then back at Chase, touching her cheek with the tip of his index finger. To say I wanted to smack his hand away was an understatement. I bit the inside of my mouth instead, refusing to be ruffled.

"I'll call you later, babe," he said, the last word louder than all the others.

My gut clenched. Babe?

Chase nodded, a strange little up-and-down of her head I'd never seen her make before. "Okay," she said, the single word almost a mumble.

With that, Donald the Dude gave me an oily smirk, ran another inspection over me – this one very clearly designed to make me feel insignificant – and then pivoted on his heel and took off through the thinning crowd.

I watched him walk away, my heart thumping a crazy beat in my throat. Of course he'd be one of those guys that didn't wear socks. I was surprised he didn't whip out a Trilby and plonk it on his head before draping a cashmere scarf around his neck.

You know what else would have looked good around his neck? My—

"When did you learn to sign?"

At Chase's question, I turned a relaxed smile on her. Relaxed. Not Ruffled. "On the flight over."

She rolled her eyes, stepping away from me a little. I wanted to snag her wrist and bring her back to my side. In fact, I didn't just *want* to do that, the craving to do it was almost painful, a fierce tugging on something deep in my body. My soul? Was that possible?

"You still think you're funny, I see?"

I preened. "Hell yeah."

She opened her mouth, an acerbic gleam in her eyes, but closed it again when I held up my finger and shook my head.

Hell. Yeah. I signed, finishing with a flourish of my wrist my signing teacher had called a "quirky accent".

Chase pulled a face, closed her fingers around my wrists and held my hands still, her stare fixed on my face. "Why?"

"Why did I learn to sign?"

She nodded.

I grinned. "So I could scare off creeps in international airports."

I'd intended the smart-arsed remark to make her chuckle. Instead, the slight smile on her lips faded. She dropped my hands and stepped back from me. "Come on," she said, her eyes sliding away from my face. "Let's get going."

As she turned I stopped her with a gentle grip on her wrist. This was seriously overstepping our unspoken interaction rules. As much as I hungered to hold her, touch her – and *hungered* isn't hyperbole, trust me – the only time Chase and I touched without her initiating it was the night I flicked her ear during *Shaun of the Dead*.

But I couldn't help myself. Not now. I'd just flown halfway around the world on the pretense of seeing Brendon and his family when what I was really here for was to make Chase see what I already knew – that she liked me. Like, *liked* me liked me – and the guarded sadness on her face before she'd turned away ripped at my heart.

She held my gaze now for a heartbeat before she let out a ragged sigh. "You can let go of me any time you like," she said. "And I don't need you to protect me against creeps in international airports. Or against anything else, for that matter."

I shook my head. "Not until you tell me who Donald the Dude is."

Her eyebrows shot up. She let out a wry snort – almost but not quite a laugh.

"Well?" I asked.

Until that point I can honestly say jealousy wasn't something I felt often. In fact, I think the last time I was jealous about something was when my best friend at uni managed to drop the last can of Red Bull in the dispensing machine when we were both pulling a pre-exam all-nighter. Man, I'd really needed that hit of extra-leaded caffeine.

What was twisting and threading through me right now though left that feeling for dead. Cold and hot and tight all at once, it filled me with a dark sensation I didn't like at all.

Chase studied my face, her gaze searching my eyes. I didn't move. Nor did I drop her wrist.

"Chase," I finally said, "you know why I'm *really* here. You do. And you know it has nothing to do with Brendon and Amanda and Tanner. So you've gotta tell me, who's Donald the Dude?"

A shaky breath left her and, with an expression the very definition of ambiguous, she looked away. "Donald is – was – my Art History professor at college."

My gut clenched. I *knew* where this was going and I liked it even less than the unexpected jealousy snaking through me. He was a snake. I could see that after barely a minute in his company. How could she even give him the time of day? Why?

She looked back at me, caught her bottom lip with her teeth, and shrugged. "Do I need to tell you any more?"

"You were seeing each other?"

God, how sour did *that* question taste in my mouth?

She finally laughed, but there was no humor in the sound. "You could say that."

I swallowed, controlling my rising agitation. "Is it over?"

"You could say that as well."

"Doesn't look over."

She drew in another slow breath, her gaze moving to where Donald the Dude had moments ago been standing before her. Was she imagining him there again? And if so, why?

"Chase?" I prompted, keeping my voice loud enough for her to hear but calm enough not to make those around us curious. Chase doesn't like attention. Which is ironic when you consider they way she looks and the car she drives.

With another wobbly breath, she returned her focus to my face and smiled. "Come on, O'Dae. Time to get you to San Diego."

TWO

"Dogs have a way of finding the people who need them."
~ Unknown

Chase

I could have solved my Caden O'Dae problem there and then. In the busy LAX terminal, with a muffled cacophony of noise in my head and my heart hammering in my throat and defective ears, I could have solved it once and for all.

Sure, we're still seeing each other, I could have said. *Yes, I still love him. He's incredible.*

I have no idea why I didn't. The opportunity was there, and I didn't take it.

Maybe it's because my mom raised me not to be a liar. Maybe it's because the idea of saying I *loved* Donald made me feel sick. What I felt for Donald – or should I say the effect Donald had on my ability to actually use my brain – was unsettling, but it wasn't love. It *had* been, and much to my shame I'd thought more than once it was again, but *thought* is a misguided thing sometimes. It can be like planting a feather in the hopes of growing a chicken.

Instead, we walked to the Speeding Dragon side by side, neither of us speaking. Caden's hand swung perilously close to mine. All I would have needed to do for our fingers to brush against each other was move the tiniest bit to the right. The muscles in my arms and legs actually began to do that very thing before I caught them. Forcing my hand to *not* draw closer to his was harder than it should have been.

The trouble was, even as I walked beside him, so very aware of him on levels I hadn't wanted to acknowledge before, the sound of Donald calling me *babe* flayed at my sanity.

Babe. He'd only ever called me that when we were in bed. Or in his office, alone . . . and semi-naked. Or in the back seat of his Porsche. I'd always thought of it as a term of endearment, but after he'd ripped out my heart I'd recognized it for what it really was: a misogynistic form of sexual control, designed to make me feel special when I wasn't.

So why was I affected so much by him saying the word now? What the hell was wrong with me? The Douchebag had torn out my heart. He was a prick. A deceptive bastard. He'd reduced me to the lowest I'd ever been, destroyed any sense of self-esteem. He'd made me question everything about who I believed I was.

He'd done all that and so much more. I hated him. And yet he'd once made me feel more special than anyone ever had. He'd made me feel cherished. He'd made me feel intelligent. He'd given me a sense of worth I'd never really felt before. Hell, Dad sure hadn't made me feel like I was walking the right path in my life, but Donald had.

At the start, and despite how we'd ended, I'd still find myself thinking of him, of our conversations, when a partic-

ular movie came on HBO, or when an art gallery ran an exhibition by an artist we both admired.

Those things were hard to forget. Hard to dismiss. And
here he was, calling me *babe* again?

The very fact my heart skipped a beat when he'd said he
was just back from attending a Salvador Dali opening in New
York only highlighted how significant he'd been in my life.
We'd spent one entire lunch break in his office discussing
Dali's influence on the art world. A lunch break that had
finished with him going down on me beneath his desk, his
muffled voice listing Dali's works between swipes of his
tongue.

I'd tried to tell my skipping heart to remember that tongue
of his had found someone else to swipe over a few short weeks
after that lunch, but my heart hadn't wanted to listen.

And now here he was calling me *babe*, and as much as I
didn't want to react, I had.

Christ, was I truly that broken?

Or was I just stupid?

Stomach clenching, chest tight, Caden silent at my side,
we crossed the parking lot, heading for my Volvo. We were
two steps away when Caden's fingers threaded through mine,
bringing me to a halt. I turned and looked up at him, a frown
pulling at my eyebrows, my heart beating fast. Try as I might,
it was impossible to deny how much I liked the feel of his
hand holding mine. How safe and right and genuine it felt.

God, why hadn't I told him Donald and I were still a thing
back in the airport? It would have made this so much easier. I
didn't want to hurt him, but if we kept going the way we were,
I would. How could I not? When I was so fucking weak?
When at just a *word*, Donald had me so damn flustered and
confused? Why hadn't I—

Caden kissed me.

There was no warning, no smartass comment, no doofus grin. Nothing to prepare me for the unexpected sensation of his lips brushing mine. My body reacted instantly. It was as if I'd suddenly become a live wire of charged energy, thrumming with an elemental power I couldn't fathom.

His lips lingered on mine for a sublime moment, just long enough for my parted lips to fit perfectly against his with an infinitesimal hint of pressure. A strange whimper vibrated at the back of my throat. I'm very attuned to vibrations, one of the perks of having a hearing problem. *This* vibration was new to me, however. As was the funny flip-flopping in my tummy. And the prickling sensation in the junction of my thighs.

Holy Christ, Caden O'Dae was kissing me.

And then he wasn't.

Just like that, he lifted his head and his lips were no longer on mine. Another whimpering vibration tickled the back of my throat, this one born from dismay. Before I could register the sound I was making it was out there, for Caden and his perfectly working ears to hear.

He released my hand, and as with the loss of contact of his lips, a soft moan of disappointment escaped me. I frowned, channeling my confusion into a glare directed at him. "Why did you do that?"

He didn't cup my face in his hand or smooth his palms up over my hips. He didn't tug me to his body, or brush the back of his knuckles over my cheek. The movies had taught me that's exactly what he was meant to do in a situation like this.

I've come to realize movies lie. A lot.

Instead of being incredibly romantic and predictable, he hitched his bag farther up his shoulder and grinned. "So you'd stop thinking about Donald the Dude."

A lump didn't just fill my throat, it damn near choked me.

My mouth fell open. A wave of guilt rolled over me, as unsettling as my reaction to his kiss and equally as unnerving.

Guilt. Of all the emotions I'd experienced in my twenty-two years, guilt wasn't really one of them. Snarky, sarcastic, almost-deaf girls have no use for guilt.

And yet, here I was, feeling it. I didn't like it. Not at all.

Narrowing my eyes, I crossed my arms over my chest. "And it's your opinion I should be thinking about you instead?"

His grin stretched wider. His hands and fingers moved in front of his chest. *Hell. Yeah.*

"Stop signing," I snarled, snatching for his hands.

Caden was quicker. He snared my wrist and drew me closer to him, not close enough for our bodies to touch (I refused to acknowledge the hot disappointment bubbling inside me at the fact they didn't), but close enough I could smell *him*: the unique, distinct, subtle scent of Caden O'Dae that I'd often find myself thinking about when he wasn't in the country.

"Tell me why I'm here, Chase," he said.

His voice wasn't low enough for me to need to watch his lips move, but I watched them anyway. There was an emotion in his eyes I wasn't prepared to deal with at the moment. His words, however, left me no other option.

Why was he here? To make me do that which I'd adamantly sworn to myself I wouldn't.

"To be a pain in my ass?" I answered.

Yes, I was aware he still held my hand. Yes, I was aware I was doing nothing to remove it. Yes, I was very aware I was leaning closer to him, as if taunting him to kiss me again.

I wasn't. I don't think . . .

He laughed. As always, when he laughed I wanted to join

in. As always, I countered that unnerving, unsettling reaction with a surly glare at him.

"Close," he said, lips moving carefully around the word. Damn it, how the hell was he so good at making it so easy to understand him? ". . . but no cigar."

"I know," I shot back. "You're here to make me want to smack you."

My stomach was doing more of that weird flip-flopping. I knew what it meant but didn't want to admit it. Damn it, he was making me enjoy myself with him. That wasn't right. That wasn't playing fair. That was—

"Smacking?" A devious light gleamed in his eyes, detonating a thoroughly filthy want in me I'd never experienced before. "That comes later. After you've accepted what I already know."

"I am not going to fall in love with you, O'Dae."

"Yes, you are."

More flip-flopping in the tummy. More prickling in the spot between my thighs, the place my mom referred to as girly bits and that I called *Temporarily Out of Business*.

"Says who?" God, was I five?

And if I was, no five year old should feel so . . . so . . . goddamn it, so horny. The irritating pain in the ass was making me hot and horny and flustered and—

My phone vibrated to life in my back pocket, Pink's 'Walk of Shame' playing loudly along with it.

I didn't need to look at my cell to know who the caller was. I sure as hell wasn't going to answer it though. Screw him.

Caden frowned, no doubt waiting for me to do just that though.

A second later Pink stopped singing. My heart hammered fast in my throat, anticipating what was going to happen next.

"Is everything . . ." Caden began, his frown deepening.

Pink started singing again.

Yanking my hand free of Caden's, I shoved it into my pocket and pulled out my cell, fixing him with the fiercest glare I could as I raised it to the one ear that could actually receive sound. "What?" I snarled.

From the beginning of our "relationship", Donald had this weird habit of calling me immediately after I didn't answer his first call. When I asked him why he did so, he told me it was in case I hadn't heard my phone ringing the first time.

I'd been foolish enough to think it sweet when I was under his sway. Now . . . now it just pissed me off.

"Dinner?" his voice came from the cell's small speaker, faint but still there. "Tonight. My place."

I would have been able to hear him better if I had my hearing aid in (my cell was compatible with the damn thing after all), but in all honesty, I don't know if it would have made any difference to the way I reacted. A hot blade seemed to trace a path up the line of my spine. It was a jarring sensation, given that at the same time all the blood from my face seemed to drain down to my sex.

Before I thought about what I was doing – and when it came to Donald, that was my *modus operandi* – I pivoted on my heel and hunched my shoulders as I presented Caden the barrier of my back.

I could feel his eyes drilling into me. It competed with the self-disgust churning in my belly and the contempt twisting in my chest. And the wrong wrong *wrong* ache Donald always brought out in me.

"Why?" I asked, doing my version of a murmur (which is probably a little louder than most people's).

"Why do we need to eat dinner?" Donald asked. The velvety smooth timbre of his voice did what it always did to me, which only tightened the contempt in my chest more. "Because we need sustenance for what comes after."

An image flashed through my head of exactly what Donald was alluding we'd need sustenance for. In that image I was naked. Donald wasn't. Even when we were together, Donald was rarely naked. It wasn't until later, as the wounds on my heart and my psyche were finally beginning to heal, that I realized he kept himself semi-dressed for a fast getaway.

Truth be known, I'd probably realized it before then. People can be masochists sometimes. Or was it just me?

"I'm not having dinner with you, Don," I answered. He hated when people called him Don. Almost as much as when they called him Donny. His preferred form of address was Professor Perry. He'd even asked me to call him that once while we were mid—

Jesus, why was I still talking to him now?

"Yes, you are, babe," he countered, that smooth arrogance that had been my undoing from the beginning slipping through the phone. "You've missed me too much. And I've missed you. I've missed my Chase, missed my hunt."

I closed my eyes. My head was roaring. My heart was thumping in my chest like a goddamn cannon.

And all the while I could feel Caden's gaze on my back. Feel him standing there, watching. Waiting.

Waiting to take my hand again and look into my eyes and make me feel the way I'd promised myself I'd never feel again.

Fuck this.

"Let me chase you down, babe," Donald crooned.

Once upon a time, when I'd been his star-struck student, in awe of his talent and intelligence and knowledge of art history, that cheesy pun on my name had rendered me weak at the knees and wet at the junction of my thighs. Now it turned the disquieting sensation blooming low in my belly to a churning, conflicted mess of contempt and wretched want.

Christ, how was I not over him already? After what he'd done to me?

"My place. Nine pm. Let me show you how much I've missed you."

Another image flashed through my head. Donald's head buried between my legs, his hands smoothing up my thighs . . .

"Let me show you how much I know I hurt you." His voice dropped an octave, low enough I almost had trouble hearing him. Almost. "Let me show you I know I was wrong."

I was wrong.

I squeezed my eyes shut. Damn it, why hadn't he uttered that last line an octave lower?

Heat washed over me like a wave of fire ants, biting my skin. "Nine," I said, hating the word as it scraped at my throat. Hating what it meant. "I'll see you at nine. But only to talk."

"Bring your toothbrush," he said, smug triumph in his voice.

"We're not having—"

He ended the call before I could tell him it wasn't a booty call. A classic Donald Perry move: don't let the person telling you something you didn't want to hear finish saying that thing. I'd seen him do it to other professors at college, other students. He'd done it to me more than once since our relationship moved from together-in-secret to whatever you'd label the fucked-up mess it was now.

Opening my eyes, I stared at the neon green Chinese dragon on my car and tried to fathom what the fuck was wrong with me. I'd just agreed to walk back into Professor Douchebag's house. I'd just agreed to put myself back in his sway. After everything he'd done to me, I'd just . . .

What. The. Fuck. Was wrong with me?

"So, the thing you've got with Donald the Dude isn't really over then, eh?"

I turned at Caden's calm observation, shoving my cell into my back pocket as I did so. Our eyes clashed for a split second before I looked away. I'd expected him to be angry, but he wasn't. There was no judgment in his expression, no censure, just regret.

What he was regretting, I don't know. The fact he'd come all this way to convince me to fall in love with him and I'd just arranged a dinner date with my ex (huh, ex *so* doesn't begin to cover it) right there in his presence? Or the fact even he could see I was being an idiotic imbecilic of epic proportions who seemed to *want* to be hurt all over again?

Let me show you I know I was wrong.

Donald's words clawed at me and I let out a ragged sigh. "Please don't try and think you get me, Caden."

That sensation of sour guilt lashed at me again, but I shoved it away. At least, I did my best to shove it away. My best wasn't that good, however, which pissed me off.

Stomping past Caden without another word, I yanked open the passenger door of the Speeding Dragon. "Well?" I said impatiently, hand shoved to my hip.

He studied me, his expression enigmatic, and then let out a chuckle I heard despite the distance between us. "I get you, Chase Sinclair," he said as he made his way toward me and the open door. "When are *you* going to get you?"

Before I could tell him to bite me, he tossed his duffle bag into the backseat, dropped himself into the passenger seat, and grinned up at me. "Coming?"

Sometimes, Caden's unwavering good humor drove me crazy. Right now was one of those moments.

Temples throbbing, I slammed the door shut with as much force as I could muster and continued my stomp around to the driver's side. I refused to look at Caden as we exited the parking lot. In fact, I refused to acknowledge he was even there. I switched on the radio, gripped the steering wheel and pretended I was in the Speeding Dragon alone.

The ruse lasted all of fifteen minutes, when Caden flicked my ear.

I turned my head, ready to tell him to fuck off, but the words died on my lips. He was holding something up for me to see.

"I made this for you," he said, lips twitching. On his hand sat a small bearded dragon lizard, made from wool. A knitted bearded dragon, no bigger than his palm.

I blinked.

His grin widened. "I thought I'd branch out from sock puppets."

I blinked again, then jerked my eyes back to the busy LA-congested street in front of me. But not before I noticed the knitted lizard seemed to be wearing a Wonder Woman's costume.

Jesus. How the hell was I going to survive the next three weeks?

"Thank you," I muttered, clenching the wheel. My knuckles ached. A hot, thick lump in my throat was doing everything it could to choke me.

Silence stretched for a moment before, out of the corner of my eye, the knitted reptile appeared on the Volvo's dash.

I tried not to look but I couldn't help myself. Yep. It was a Wonder Woman costume. A tiny Wonder Woman costume.

"Did you make the costume?" I asked. Damn it, wasn't I trying to pretend he wasn't there?

"I did."

Playful pride danced in the answer. I could see the smile on his face without looking at him.

"I'll make an excellent wife someday," he said.

I rolled my eyes and grinned, despite myself. Damn him. Seriously, damn him. "God help anyone foolish enough to marry you," I said, shaking my head and returning my attention to the road. I tried to muster up anger at him but it was frustratingly absent.

"I'm the full package," he said loud enough for me to hear him without needing to follow the words on his lips with my eyes. "I can cook, make awesome sock puppets, knit, sew, and I don't snore. Oh, and I have no issues whatsoever with animal feces, so when we get a dog I'll pick up all its poop."

I arched an eyebrow at him, even as a picture filled my head of him in Mom and Dad's backyard playing with a puppy that looked suspiciously like the one Amanda had been forced to give away because of Tanner's leukemia. "What's this *we* business? I've told you before, you and I aren't happening."

He studied me from behind his black Ray-Bans. "You could do worse," he replied.

I rolled my eyes and focused on the upcoming on-ramp to the 105. "Drop it, Caden."

He did.

I don't know why, but I wished he hadn't. Was I just fishing for an excuse to pick a fight with him? To make him lose his temper? I could justify being grumpy with him if he'd snarled or snapped at me. What would an angry Caden O'Dae be like?

I didn't know. Did anyone? Did the guy ever crack?

We merged onto the 405 South, the Speeding Dragon eating up the miles, getting closer to San Diego by the minute. When the traffic got bad, I cut across on the 710 to California's famous Highway 1. It ran along the coast, and I figured we both could both do with the peaceful views to decompress from the airport incidences: Donald's unexpected appearance, and Caden kissing me in the parking lot. Not exactly the most auspicious beginning to his three-week stay here.

It was a long while before he said anything to me again.

Not that he was silent for all those miles.

Caden sang along with whatever song came on the radio. When he didn't know the lyrics, he made them up. He turned an Imagine Dragons song about everything being fantastic and turning to gold, into a song about having a cold.

I did my best not to react to him, but it was damn hard. His relaxed sense of humor was infectious, damn it.

The upside to his singing was I'd completely forgotten about my insane decision to agree to Donald's dinner invitation. In fact, I'd completely forgotten about Donald. *That* fact had just registered as we neared the junction of Highway 1 and Interstate 5, when Caden suddenly lunged forward in his seat.

"Stop!" he shouted, his head snapping to the right.

I hit the brakes. I'd never heard such distress in Caden's voice before. A choir of car horns sounded behind me, although by the time my faulty ears and startled brain registered it, the cars were blurring past me.

"What the hell?" I damn near shouted, as I pulled up onto the shoulder, pulse wild.

"Don't go anywhere," Caden shouted, before flinging off his seatbelt, shoving open the door and leaping from the passenger seat.

I sat and blinked at the empty seat, before the unmistakable sound of tires screeching and car horns blaring sank into my discombobulated brain.

I looked up. "Jesus!" Caden was hurrying across the road, arms held up and palms out toward the oncoming cars, his head swinging from them to something I couldn't see and back again.

I scrambled from behind the wheel out into the dry Southern Californian heat. More car horns blasted the air. More tires screeched. Someone in one of the cars yelled something at Caden I'm glad my bad hearing didn't allow me to make out.

"Yeah yeah," he shouted back, not looking at them. He was slowing down, arms still held out in an attempt to divert cars traveling in excess of fifty miles an hour, his attention now completely focused on . . . what?

I fidgeted beside the Speeding Dragon's tailgate, squinting into the sunlight. Caden was now almost squatting in the middle of one lane, one arm still up to ward off traffic, the other drawing closer to . . .

My heart smashed up into my throat. A dog. A big black dog lay on its side in the middle of the lane, its head raised toward Caden, its long tail thumping weakly onto the asphalt. Caden half squatted in the middle of the highway, one hand held up to divert cars, the other resting on the side of the dog, that had obviously been hit by a car, given the blood seeping onto the road.

Jesus.

For a second I didn't know what to do. I was struck frozen. And then Caden swung his face to me and I sprang into action.

Fast.

Caden

No, I didn't want Chase to come to me. The second she moved, terror gripped me. What if a car hit her? Fuck, I hadn't been thinking. I'd seen the injured dog and I'd just reacted. I was such a fucking idiot. How the fuck could I protect her if she was running through speeding cars?

Keeping my palm gently on the dog's side to track his shallow breaths, I couldn't tear my eyes from the girl I was deeply and irretrievably in love with, as she risked her life to get to me. I wanted to yell at her to stop, to go back to the safety of the side of the freeway, but I knew she wouldn't be able to hear me. All I could do was stand and make myself as visible as possible to the oncoming traffic and hope to fuck they saw me and hit the brakes. But if they swerved into the other lanes, Chase could be right in the way—

Fuck.

At my feet, the dog whined. The heat from the bitumen radiated up through the soles of my thongs, hot enough for the vet part of my brain to know the dog would not only be getting overheated, but that the blood flow to its skin would be increasing, putting a strain on its already stressed heart.

All those things passed through my brain as I frantically watched Chase run to where I stood.

All those thing vanished as a bright red car sped into my line of sight, its tires screeching as Chase ran directly into its path.

"No!" I screamed, throwing myself toward her.

I still don't know how the car missed her. She ran straight past me, grabbing at my wrist and dragging me back to the dog.

"Quick," she yelled, not looking at me but behind me, as she waved at the oncoming cars. "Pick him up."

I did as she ordered, fighting to contain the anger boiling up in me. As quickly as I was prepared to risk, without knowing how extensive the injuries were, I slid my arms under the dog and lifted him off the road. My brain registered the fact that he only had three legs; his left back leg was a deformed stump.

He yelped as I straightened completely, writhing in my arms as he tried to bite me. The word *rabies* slashed through my mind, a heartbeat before Chase's hand found my forearm and her worried gaze found my eyes through my sunglasses.

"It's okay," she said, her hand moving from my arm to stroke the dog's shoulder. "It's okay, Caden's got you."

The dog whined again, and I felt its tail thump weakly against my hip.

"Let's go," I said, raising my voice so Chase could hear me more clearly over the sound of the car horns and tires.

She nodded, and then moved between me and the traffic, arms out, palms up. I followed, hurrying for the car, the dog whimpering in my arms. I wanted Chase off this maniacal stretch of road ASAP. I needed her safe so my heart and brain could actually start functioning properly again. If I didn't love her so much I would have killed her. Didn't she have any clue how dangerous her actions had been?

What had felt like a mere couple of yards when I'd been running *to* the dog, had now somehow stretched into miles and miles of never ending bitumen and speeding cars. Chase crooned to the dog, stroking its shoulder with one hand as she held up the other at the oncoming traffic.

By the time we made it to Chase's Volvo, I was furious. I gently placed the dog on the ground on the other side of her car, in a miniscule strip of shade away from the madness of the freeway. I glared up at Chase. "What the hell were you thinking?"

She blanched. The second she did, something cold punched a hole in my chest.

"I *was* thinking," she answered, her voice ripe with an emotion I couldn't decipher, "I wanted to help you."

"You could have gotten yourself killed," I yelled back, making sure to emphasize the words and movement of my lips.

She narrowed her eyes and then signed at me, her movements sharp and jerky: *You don't have to fucking shout at me.*

"Fucking hell, Chase," I snapped, my voice was getting louder by the syllable. "You make it hard to keep you safe. You weren't even looking at the cars! What if you didn't hear the horns? What if you didn't hear that red car's horn?"

At the word *hear* she grew still. Her face shut down, devoid of emotion.

That cold sensation punched at my chest again, joined by a sickening knot in my gut.

"I don't need to *hear* everything to understand what's going on," she snarled. "And clearly there are things I *hear* that are not really there. Like you *getting* me."

Fuck. I'd fucked up.

"I don't need your protection, O'Dae," she went on. Pain warred with anger on her face. Pain and betrayal. "And I'm not your little girl to shelter from the world. I can take care of myself."

My breath left me in a whoosh. On the ground before me, the dog whined. "Chase," I began, "I didn't mean—"

"You're not my father," she said, contempt now in her voice. "Nor are you my boyfriend. You don't have the right to yell at me and treat me like an helpless baby." She scrunched up her face and shook her head. "My God. How could I have been so—"

The unmistakable sound of a police siren whooped into life behind the Volvo, drowning out the rest of her words. The dog whimpered, and writhed under my hands that were gently pressed to his ribcage.

Chase winced, swinging her glare from me.

Fuck, could I have fucked up any more? I turned my attention to the dog, my thoughts a wild mess. I needed to concentrate on the animal. I needed to make sure it he was okay.

I needed to calm down.

I was ruffled. No good came of being ruffled. None. I laughed at life. Didn't take it seriously. That's what I did.

But shit, was I angry.

It sounds weird, maybe even wrong, but I used the dog's injuries as a means of meditation. Meditation is all about centering, and finding a peaceful calm within oneself. My cousin Brendon meditates daily. He sits on the beach at dawn, in the typical Buddha pose, and does nothing but focus on his breathing. He's one of the most relaxed, positive people I know, regardless of the nightmare that might one day claim his son's life.

I meditate daily, but in a completely different way. I meditate via my interaction with animals. There's nothing as harrowing in my future as Brendon's, but I was beginning to discover my plan to make Chase acknowledge she was in love with me wasn't going to be as easy as I'd hoped.

Especially as I had to open my stupid bloody mouth and shout – *shout* – at her. My mind was a hot mess.

Crouching at the dog's side, I tuned out Chase and focused on the muscles and bones and form of the animal. He was a big dog, a mixed breed. Doberman, definitely, mixed with maybe Great Dane and a bit of German Shepherd. His front right shoulder was shattered. Under his fur – short, smooth and healthy, although long overdue for a wash – the bone structure of his right shoulder was almost as big a mess as my head, and I estimated at least three broken rib bones, maybe four. He had internal injuries that needed to be tended to ASAP. Surgery might save his life. Might. If time was on our side.

I drew a slow breath, noting the abrasions and wounds in his flesh. Moving my hand down to his rear leg, I gently moved it enough to ascertain the knee joint was dislocated.

"It's going to be okay, mate," I murmured, returning the dog's leg to a position I knew would be less painful. He whimpered as I tenderly ran my fingers over the injury, his limpid brown eyes watching me with a trust so implicit I could hardly breathe for a second.

Animals do that to me: rock me to my core. I know almost everything there is to know about animals: their anatomy, their behavior, their psychology. I've studied them to a clinical level beyond what was expected in my degree. I've operated on them in my internship, reconstructed their insides, saved them from dying by car and cancer and carelessness. I've rehabilitated animals so callously mistreated by their owners I've contemplated taking the law into my own hands and showing them what it feels like to be kicked, starved, burned, tortured. I've made my life about animals, but they still surprise me with their trust.

An animal will trust you when it knows it can. That simple. Doesn't matter if it's a mixed-breed dog like my friend on the road before me, or an elephant caught in a poacher's trap in South Africa, or a tiger caged by a cruel circus owner, an animal will trust you when it knows you are trustworthy. It may be only for a fleeting second, before the opportunity to flee presents itself, but in that fleeting second, you make a connection with that animal that will change you on a level I've yet to find a word to describe.

I wasn't prepared for the sudden feel of a firm grip on my shoulder.

"Sir, step away from the animal, please."

All the calm I'd found tending to the dog evaporated at the brusque tone of the police officer. The dog whimpered, twisting beneath my hands in an instinctive need to escape. I looked up straight into a pair of mirrored sunglasses, and saw myself and the dog in their reflection. Chase stood in my peripheral vision.

"Are you aware that it's illegal to obstruct the flow of traffic?" the cop asked, his grip on my shoulder loosening. Loosening. Not releasing.

"Are you aware this dog would have died on the road if I hadn't?" I answered. It wasn't until later I accepted that antagonizing a California Highway Patrol Officer probably wasn't a good idea. "If not from his injuries, than from having his internal organs crushed by the tires of another car running over him? Are you aware how painful it would be to have your intestines compressed like a balloon before rupturing in a spew of—"

"Caden."

Chase's admonishment stopped me before I could continue. Suffice to say, *that* was a good idea. By the look on the cop's face, I was already in enough trouble to get me deported. Or imprisoned.

"What's your name, sir?"

Still crouching beside the dog, I smoothed my hand over its neck. I needed to find my calm again. I'd destroyed any ground I'd made with Chase by shouting at her and being worried for her safety – something that clearly pissed her off – and now I was about to go ballistic on a cop more worried about traffic flow than an animal in pain. "Caden O'Dae," I answered, hoping to hell my face didn't show my impatience and irritation.

"Where are you from, Mr. O'Dae?"

Frustration flared through me. "Melbourne, Australia.

Look, this dog needs urgent medical attention. Are you going to get it, or am I going to have to do it myself?"

The cop's grip on my shoulder released. Yay.

He raised his hand to the mic attached to the front of his shirt and turned his head a little, mirrored lenses still trained on me. "Dispatch, this is Gibson. I've got a situation on southbound Highway 1 near Dana Point."

Not yay. So not yay.

I shot Chase a quick look. She stood in the space between me and the cop, her teeth gnawing at her bottom lip, worry eating up her face. God, I hated seeing that. Hated it even more that I was responsible for it. I should have protected her better, regardless of what she'd said about not needing it. I should have made sure she was safe and out of any harm before running to the dog.

I'd been foolish, and she'd almost paid the cost.

It's going to be okay, I signed. I don't know why I did. I could have said the words aloud, but at this point, I was not in a . . . let's go with *stable* headspace. *But if I'm arrested, can you bring me a cake with a jar of Vegemite baked into the middle, please?*

It took her a while to put together the letters I'd signed for Vegemite – there's no American sign-language shortcut for the iconic Australian spread – but when she did, she did exactly as I hoped she would.

She rolled her eyes and let out a snort that was so close to a laugh it made my heart thump faster.

Dropping my attention to the dog, I stroked its neck gently. "It's going to be okay, mate," I reassured him. I wasn't just talking about its injuries.

"Okay, Mr. O'Dae?"

I jerked my head up to discover the cop was now

crouched opposite me, mirrored lenses gone. Compassion and concern filled his eyes.

"What do we need to do?"

I blinked at his question. Having already decided I was going to be arrested and thrown into a US prison, my mind was having difficulty dealing with this sudden shift.

He smiled. "Thought you were being arrested?"

I frowned.

His smile turned to a grin. *She told me*, he signed, nodding his head toward Chase.

A gust of air left me in what I hoped sounded like a laugh but was probably more a relieved gasp.

"You sign?"

"Deaf sister," he answered. "It would come in handy when she'd bring boys home I didn't like. I'd tell her exactly what I thought of them, and most of the time they were clueless about what I was saying."

"Know how that works," I said, remembering Donald the Dude's reaction to my signing to Chase in the airport terminal. I did *not* like that guy. Have I mentioned that yet? But I wasn't going to let Chase see that. Better to not let her know I was ruffled.

Rubbing at my face with one hand, I returned my attention to the dog and the police officer opposite me. "Okay, we need to get him to an emergency vet ASAP. Do you know of one?"

The cop stroked the dog and frowned. "The closest is in Laguna Niguel, back toward LA. From here, it's safest to keep going south, then get on the 5 North."

I nodded. "Let's get him there, pronto. Do you mind if I sit in the back with him? That way I can monitor his breathing and heart rate. There's not much more I can do in the car, but hopefully it'll keep him less stressed at least."

"Do I mind?" The cop shook his head. "Hell no. I was going to ask you to. Your girl okay with meeting us there?"

My girl.

I lifted my gaze to Chase, a disquieting sense of anticipation unfurling through me at her reaction to the cop's mistaken term. She stood watching us from the Volvo's tailgate, too far away for her to hear his question, and not at the right angle to see his lips.

"We have to get to a vet. Back toward LA," I said, loud enough for my voice to travel to her over the busy freeway noise.

She nodded. "Figured as much."

"You okay to follow us back? Meet me at the animal hospital?"

She arched an eyebrow. "I don't know if I like you *that* much."

The cop chuckled.

My chest tightened. She *did* like me that much. I just had to make her admit it.

Of course, almost getting her killed on the busy freeway and then shouting at her about her hearing probably wasn't the best way to go about it.

Oh man, things were not going the way I'd hoped.

Fuck a bloody duck.

THREE

"Until one has loved an animal, a part of one's soul remains unawakened."
~ Anatole France

Chase

Flashbacks can knock you off your feet.

The second Caden had yelled at me on the side of the road back on the freeway, the *second* he'd shouted that I hadn't heard the red car's horn, I'd been flung back to the moment when my father had yanked me off my new bike – the bike I'd been so excited about receiving – and yelled at me on our driveway about almost being struck by a car.

I was six.

He'd shouted at me for so long that morning. I can still feel the heat in my cheeks, not just from the baking summer sun, but from my shame. My daddy was yelling at me. Outside. About being deaf and almost dying and making him need to run after me.

I remember crying. I remember Mom coming out and

yelling at Dad. I remember Amanda scooping me up and taking me inside as Dad continued to yell. I was too far away to hear the words clearly, to know what he was shouting at Mom, but by the way Amanda was shaking, they weren't happy words. Or relieved words that his little girl hadn't be struck by a car.

They were angry words.

Amanda had taken me to her room and hugged me on her bed. She'd done her best to make me smile. She'd wiped the tears streaming down my cheeks. She'd even wiped away my snot with the cuff of her shirt. I remember that so clearly.

The tears had started to slow down by the time Dad entered her room.

He'd stood in the doorway, hands on his hips, the light from outside reflecting in his glasses. I couldn't see his eyes. But I could see his lips. His lips formed words like "dangerous" and "irresponsible". His lips formed sentences like "Don't you know you can't be normal, Chastity?"

I cried all over again. Sobs that tore at my heart and my tummy. Amanda held me and finally shouted at Dad to stop. Mom came in and dragged Dad out of the room.

I remember being glad I couldn't hear the fight continue out in the living room. I knew it had though. I could see it in Amanda's eyes, in the way she flinched and hugged me tighter.

The next day, when I went out into the garage, determined to show my father I could be a "responsible" girl, a "careful normal girl" my bike was gone. I never got it back. I've never ridden a bike since.

That moment hit me hard when Caden yelled at me about not hearing the car. I was that little girl again, being yelled at about needing to be protected, about being "irresponsible". Caden didn't mean all those things, but it still hit me. Hurt me.

It was a good thing Officer Gibson was so lovely. If he hadn't been, who knows what would have happened between Caden and me on the side of the road. Who knows what I would have said.

I'm not a believer in Fate, but some higher power had a hand in placing a highway patrol cop who could sign on the road that day. Whatever higher power that was, they/it saved me from doing something embarrassing in front of Caden: cry.

To the best of my knowledge, only two people have seen me cry since I was that little girl. Brendon, when it looked like Tanner's body was going to reject Caden's bone marrow, and Mom, but I was only fourteen at the time, and it was over a boy who was so not worth it.

On a side note, if you ever in your travels meet a guy called Crick Wallace, punch him for me, okay? He was the first boy to break my stupid heart. Promised to take me to the Homecoming dance and then was a complete no-show on the night. I sat on the bottom step of Mom and Dad's house, dressed up fancier than I ever had in my young life, watching our road for any sign of his folks' car. As it turns out, he went with Taisy Benington, the most popular girl in our year. The same girl who used to walk up to me at school and pretend to talk to me, all the while just mouthing the words without making a sound while her friends giggled behind her.

Taisy was the reason for my first real trip to the Principal's office. There are only so many times a girl who's Hard of Hearing can watch someone poke fun at her before she decides to grab said someone by the exquisitely braided pony-tail, yank her head down so her ear is level with her mouth, and shout "What? I can't hear you!"

I was angry that day in the school hallway. I was angrier now.

That hot fury had simmered for the entire drive back to Laguna Niguel.

I want to say I was angry at Caden, but it was more than that. I was angry at being that six-year-old little girl again.

I was angry I'd *allowed* myself to be her again.

I'd refused to be that little girl for sixteen years. I didn't need to be protected. I could look after myself, damn it. I knew I had limitations and I worked with them. Hell, a person walking the street wearing earbuds stood a higher chance of getting themselves run over than I did. I wasn't an idiot, I was hearing impaired. I knew how to be careful and how to keep myself safe. But I also knew how to live.

In fact, when I got back to San Diego, I was going to buy a bike and ride it. Ride it. And after I finished riding it, I was going to find the busiest street around and run across it. Over and over. Screw it.

Who was going to stop me? Caden? Huh. No. I wasn't going to let him.

It was a good thing he was in the car with Officer Gibson and the dog or I'd tell him that. And then tell him he was going to stand on the side of that busy road and watch me do it. And he wasn't allowed to say a word.

Yes, I was being childish, but what six-year-old isn't?

Pulling into the animal hospital parking lot, I sat behind the wheel, staring hard at the place. I felt churned up. Unsettled. I didn't like being unsettled. I was detached and disinterested Chase Sinclair.

I was also Chase Caden-Doesn't-Mean-Anything-To-Me Sinclair. I needed to remember that.

I'd just got myself settled and calm when my cell pinged and vibrated in my pocket.

I flinched, my heart jumping into my throat.

Pulling it free, I read the incoming message: *I'm looking forward to tonight. D.*

My heart tried to hammer its way farther out my body. Donald. Damn it, why was he suddenly texting again? Nothing for three months and then BAM, he's bumping into me at the airport and calling me *babe* and inviting me to his house . . .

The thought he was jealous about Caden scraped at my unsettled mind, followed by an equally unsettled notion that I had no idea how I felt about it if he was.

Whatever I was feeling, I ignored his text, shoved my cell back into my pocket and climbed out of the Speeding Dragon. At this point, the only thing I wanted clarity on was Doofus.

Yeah, I'd named the dog on the way here.

It took me two steps into the animal hospital for my churned up feeling to be overwhelmed by an entirely different one. The one that made me remember how much I've had my fill of hospitals.

At twenty-two I've spent more time in them than anyone should. I've lost count of the visits Mom and I made to the hospital and hearing specialists as I was growing up. Monumental treks involving test after test, result after result, disappointment after disappointment. Exploratory operations on your ear canal aren't anywhere near as fun as they sound, and given they don't sound fun at all, you can imagine how much I enjoyed all those trips to the hospital.

When Tanner was diagnosed with leukemia I spent a lot of my days and nights in his room with him. Whenever Amanda couldn't be there, I was. By that stage Professor Douchebag and I were spending less time together and my college class attendance was beginning to wane, so as much as

I hated hospitals, there really was nowhere else I wanted to be than with my nephew.

However, watching your nephew die from leukemia is even less fun than exploratory ear canal surgery, no matter how wonderful the staff at the hospital. Watching your sister cry day and night tears you apart.

There was also the time Caden himself was rushed to hospital, just after the bone marrow transfer. I spent the night beside his bed, convincing myself I was there because I was worried something was going to happen to the only person on the planet who had bone marrow compatible with my nephew's, knowing the whole time it was for a completely different reason I didn't want to acknowledge. Of course, that put me in a very bad mood, which increased my dislike for hospitals even more.

No, me and hospitals have had our time and I was more than happy never to step foot in another one again, thank you very much.

I didn't realize until I walked through the doors of Laguna Niguel Animal Hospital, that my self-established embargo included animal hospitals. Who knew? But the second I crossed the threshold into the cool interior of the building and was confronted with the distinct smell of disinfectant, I was flung back to all those painful tests, all those post-op let-downs, all those days and nights spent with Tanner watching the bitch that was leukemia devour him from the inside out.

I wanted to turn around and run out into the warm after-noon. I wanted to take great big gulping breaths of non-disin-fectant-tainted air. I wanted to stand in the sun and have my face warmed by it, not stand under white fluorescent lights with the artificial temperature set to chilly.

If it weren't for the fact Caden was in there somewhere, with a broken dog and a cop who could sign, I would have done just that. My heart was thumping faster than it should. I didn't want to see the dog die. I'd had enough of that kind of bleakness in my life lately. I also didn't want to see Caden get in trouble for his insane actions on the highway. He would though. No amount of Australian charm could save him from a citation at the very least. In fact, we were both likely to get a citation, but unlike Caden, I wasn't a visiting tourist from another country. Who knew what the consequences were? I didn't. I didn't think he'd be deported, but what did I know?

Despite the fact I was angry at him, that he'd made me feel like that wounded little girl I'd swore I'd never be again, I understood exactly why he'd done what he'd done. The trouble was, that made me like him more. Goddamn it. Which actually made me angry with him for an entirely different reason than my original reason for being angry with him.

Wait. My original reason for being angry with him *today*, not my *original* original reason, which was because he was trying to make me fall in love with him.

How did he have this unique ability to piss me off, confound me, irritate me, and yet make me smile and feel contented all at once? Bastard. He was so going to get it when I saw him next – injured dog and citation-delivering cop or not, I was going to give it to him.

Yes, I'm aware I was not exactly in a stable state of mind at that point. Trust me, it didn't get much better when what happened next . . . well, happened.

Doing my best to ignore the rush of hospital-induced unease, I crossed to the front counter and leaned on it. The receptionist was a girl about my age with some serious brunette roots belying the platinum-blonde status of her hair. She didn't look up from the paperwork on the desk in front of her, and mumbled something. Something a person with normal hearing would be able to hear.

My stomach tightened. Oh boy, here we go.

"I'm sorry," I said, doing my best to keep my voice casual. A part of me was kicking myself for not wearing my hearing aid today. Stupidly, I'd been thinking of what I looked like that morning before leaving San Diego for LAX, of the first thing Caden would see when we came face to face in Arrivals. "Can you say that again?"

Little Miss Regrowth let out an exasperated sigh. I didn't hear it, but I know she did it. I read body language very well. Another one of those perks I spoke of earlier. Her chest and upper back lifted with a drawn-out inhalation, followed by a slump that screamed *OMG, why do I have to be subjected to this kind of annoyance??*

I wanted to reach across the counter and shake her. Not a good start to this social interaction for sure.

What felt like an eternity later, she finally raised her head and bestowed on me a smile of infinite patience. Oh, this was so going to be fun.

"Can I help you?" she asked, with a quick glance over my head. Trust me, I didn't miss the slight curl of her top lip when she got to my spiky aqua-blue do.

"I'm with the cop and the Australian that are here with the injured Doofus." I shook my head. "I mean, the injured dog."

Little Miss Regrowth frowned with confusion, and then realization flooded her face as it dawned on her why I sounded the way I did.

Yeah, she'd figured it out I was Hard of Hearing. Oh joy.

Just in case you don't know, or I haven't mentioned it yet, I have that very distinct speech pattern that most people with major hearing problems have. There's no real way to explain it – slurred sounds, missing sounds, a kind of smudginess to the words being formed – but it elicits a response so typical it makes me want to roll me eyes.

I could tell the instant the word *deaf* shuffled through the receptionist's head. Pity filled her face. And then gratitude. It's the last one that pushes my buttons the most – the relief when it dawns on the person I'm speaking to how lucky they are not to have my problem.

Tapping the tips of my fingers on the counter, I raised one eyebrow. "The Australian?" I repeated, slower this time. Louder. "And the cop. And the dog?"

I deliberately signed that last one, as if the action was subconscious. I've noticed some people get really excited about sign language. I've also noticed some people get really excited about Justin Bieber. As I've said before, people are weird.

Fuck her, my brain grumbled as my fingers made the form for dog. *Let's give her something exciting to talk about later when she's with her friends sipping frappuccinos at Starbucks.*

"You're deaf?"

I gave her my patented *Are you kidding me?* face.

Consternation and sympathy rippled over hers. "I'm sorry. I mean, *I'm sorry*."

Yep, she shouted the last part.

Sometimes, when people say "I'm sorry" to me when they find out I'm Hard of Hearing, I wave off the apology. Today was not one of those times. I was worried about a dog that wasn't mine and an Australian who equally did not belong to me. That added up to Snarky-Chase. Besides, Little Miss Regrowth had curled her lip at my hair. I love my hair.

"That's okay," I shouted back, so loud she flinched. "I forgive you. You didn't know what you were doing. My lawyer will be in touch, however. Can you tell me your name?"

She blinked and stiffened in her seat. Her mouth fell open. I didn't need to be good at reading facial expressions to know the thought *What? What what what?* was screaming through her head. Her eyebrows danced in abject terror and confusion. She blinked again.

I waited, tapping my fingers on the counter.

Before either of us could contribute further to her psychological massacre, a door behind the counter swung open and the cop who'd come to Caden's aid on the freeway – Gibson, his name was – stepped through.

Little Miss Regrowth swiveled around, her sigh of relief so fierce it made her lips wobble.

Gibson smiled at me.

"She's deaf," the receptionist told him in a high shout, pointing at me with impressively acrylic nails. "You'll have to speak loudly."

Gibson's eyebrows shot up before he frowned at me.

I rolled my eyes and shrugged. "It happens," I said.

Giving our not-so-helpful friend a small smile, he pushed his hand against the door behind him, opening it. "Caden's in here."

My heart did a weird little skip at Caden's name. Stupid heart.

"Thank you," I said, moving around the counter.

"You're welcome," Little Miss Regrowth shouted.

Both Gibson and I paused long enough to give her twin looks of disbelief.

As the door to the inner workings of the animal hospital closed behind us, the pungent odor of animal poo and disinfectant was heavy on the air. Gibson touched my arm. I looked at him. When this was over I was going to thank him for knowing how to treat a person like me, and maybe ask if I could meet his sister, but for now I was anxious to get to Caden and Doofus.

"The dog is being operated on," he said as we walked along the corridor. "Your boyfriend is in the operating room with the veterinary surgeon."

Remember how I'd said my heart did a little skip at Caden's name? That was nothing compared to what it did at the word *boyfriend*.

Throat thick, I shook my head. "He's not my boyfriend. We're just . . ."

Acquaintances? Relatives by marriage? Was there actually a term to describe us? He was my brother-in-law's first cousin. What did that make him to me?

". . . friends," I finished. For some reason, my head was roaring.

Gibson didn't look convinced. "Then your *friend* is totally enamored with you. Just thought I should let you know."

I scowled. And then did something I'm not really proud of. "What? I didn't hear what you said."

Gibson laughed. An honest-to-goodness laugh. If he was going to say anything else, the arrival of Caden stopped him.

Stopped me, as well. In my tracks.

He stepped through a door on the right. He hadn't seen us. At least, I don't think he had. He stood in the middle of the corridor, staring at the floor, shoulders slumped. His chest rose and fell in that way chests do when someone is sighing, and then he buried his face in his hands.

My stomach dropped. Everything about him screamed distress. Disappointment.

Oh no. Doofus.

Before I knew what I was doing, I was hurrying toward him. My hand found his upper arm first, my fingers sliding around it. A distant part of my mind noted his biceps and triceps were far more sculpted than I'd thought, and then he was jerking his face in my direction, confusion in his eyes.

"Caden," I said, a heartbeat before smoothing my arms around his waist and hugging him.

There was no thought or contemplation in what I was doing, just an undeniable need to take away some of the pain I knew he was feeling. To let him know I was there for him.

For a moment, he didn't move in my arms. I could feel his heart thumping against my cheek, a fast rhythm that journeyed through my body and into my soul. What would it sound like, that beat? What would it be like to *truly* hear it? What would it be like to lay my head on his naked chest and close my eyes and just hear it with my ears?

Strong arms wrapped around me, warm hands buried into the hair at my nape, and suddenly Caden was hugging me back.

Holding me. Close.

I closed my eyes and breathed him in, felt his heat seeping into my body.

I don't know how long we stood that way. Maybe a few seconds? Maybe a year.

It wasn't until I felt him shift his feet and clear his throat – a hesitant sound I heard as well as felt – that it sank in what we were doing. What *I* was doing, hugging a guy I knew wanted me when I had no intentions of wanting him back? Especially when said guy seemed to forget I was totally capable of taking care of myself and didn't need to be treated like I was a fragile flower, despite the fact he kept saying he *got* me? If he *got* me like he claimed he did, he wouldn't have yelled at me about not hearing the cars.

Right?

Shit.

I pulled away. "Sorry," I muttered.

"Don't be," he said.

I watched his lips form the words, too nervous to make eye contact.

Rubbing my palms on the top of my butt, I took another step backward. "Is Doofus . . . the dog, I mean . . . is he . . ."

"Dead?" Caden finished what I couldn't. Even I heard the harrowed dismay in his voice. "No. But the vet doesn't know if he can save him. His injuries are severe."

I swallowed. And hugged my elbows to stop myself stepping back closer to Caden. I've never been much of a touchy-feely kind of girl, but for some reason I desperately wanted to smooth my hands up Caden's arms. The thought of *not* touching him at that moment in time was horrible. And goddamn confusing.

"When will you know?"

At the deep male voice at my shoulder I let out a little squeak of surprise. I'd totally forgotten our friendly Californian Highway Patrol cop was still with us.

I turned to him, my shoulder coming to rest against Caden's chest. His hand found my hip, with a gentle pressure that drew me closer to him.

I should have removed his hand, should have put some distance between us. I didn't. I don't know why.

"It's going to be a while," Caden said. There was a husky quality to his voice that made the words hard to catch. If I wasn't so close to him I would have missed half of them, I suspect.

So close . . . I was so close to him . . .

"A few hours at least."

"Have the owners been contacted?" I asked, turning back to Caden.

He shook his head. "The phone number attached to his microchip goes to a disconnected number, the address is now a gas station, and he wasn't wearing a collar. There's no way of knowing who he belongs to, but it seems he's been abandoned."

Once again, I had an overwhelming compulsion to press my cheek to Caden's chest and just stand there with him, our arms wrapped around each other. My heart ached for Doofus. How cruelly the dog had been treated. Had his owners abandoned him because of his malformed back leg? Because he was defective? How could any one just abandon something intended for love?

The thought lashed at me, as did the memory of Donald Perry ending our relationship. I didn't need to be an English Literature student to acknowledge my mind had turned the dog into a metaphor for my own state (Although Dad would have loved it if I *were* an English Lit. student. He still had yet to forgive me for studying art. And let's not talk about his absolute disappointment at the fact I hadn't even finished such a woeful course).

"So what happens now?" I asked, shutting down the thought of Professor Douchebag's douchiness and my father's perpetual patriarchal dismay.

Caden's answering smile tore at my heart. He was genuinely upset about a dog he'd never known existed until today. I knew Caden was all about animals, but seeing this . . .

Damn it, it was doing things to me I wasn't prepared for. Things that made me question *everything*. Like how much I was letting Donald fuck me up, and how much I was letting *me* fuck me up.

"Now, I wait," he answered, smoothing his palm up and down my back. I'm not even sure he was aware he was doing it, but I didn't stop him. I couldn't. It was too nice. Too natural. Too *normal*. "I'm sorry I've messed up your day. I'm pretty certain there's a train I can catch to San Diego from around here, right?"

"I'll wait with you."

There you go. It was out there. I was waiting with him. Staying with him. Being with him. Not leaving his side.

He regarded me with a steady look, something in his eyes I couldn't read. Hope? I held his gaze, my palm on his chest, his heart beating against it.

The sound of a throat clearing loudly made us both jump.

"I hate to do this to you, Mr. O'Dae," Gibson said, "but I'm afraid I'm going to have to give you a citation for obstructing traffic."

Caden laughed. I didn't just feel it, I heard it. A low, good-humored chuckle that tickled my palm and sent warm fingers of emotion into my core.

"Yeah," he said, his palm still stroking my back, "figured you might. Still, better than being deported, 'eh?"

Gibson let out his own laugh, although his was far more apologetic. "True."

"Give me a sec to see how things are going in there, and then we can move out to the reception area," Caden said.

Before Gibson or I could respond, Caden turned and slipped back through the door on the right.

I studied that closed door for a second, not entirely sure what I was feeling. Empty? Adrift? Finally, I gave the waiting police officer a smile. "Thank you."

"For giving your boyfriend a citation?"

I frowned, even though I knew he was teasing me by his deliberate use of the term *boyfriend*. "You know, as a comedian, you make an awesome cop."

He winked as he reached into his back pocket for his citation notepad. "You better believe it, Chase Sinclair."

I could only assume he'd run my plates on the trip back

here. It was that or the fact he and Caden had talked about me during the journey. For some reason that made my cheeks fill with a heat I didn't want to analyze.

By the time Caden returned, Gibson was writing up his ticket.

"Sorry about this," he said, handing it to Caden.

Caden took it with a shrug. "I made a mistake," he said, with a glance at me. I didn't need to be a genius to know he wasn't just talking about his mad run across the freeway.

I went searching inside me for the anger I'd felt for him earlier, after he'd shouted at me, but could only find a muted feeling of disappointment that he really didn't understand me like I'd thought he did.

I also found the lingering pain from my memory of the bike incident, along with the almost constant churning unease that came whenever I thought about Dad's opinion of me. That latter one had messed with my head and heart for so long now I almost forgot it was there . . . until Dad and I were in the same room, that was. Hard to forget it when it's in his eyes, his expression, his demeanor, every time he looks at you.

Laughably, I tried to muster up my anger with Caden again. It was easier to remember I didn't want to like him when I was angry at him. Maybe if I focused on how he was trying to protect me from . . . from . . . life? From Donald? Maybe then I'd be angry at him again?

A long whistle jerked me back to the hospital corridor. Even though it was muffled, I knew who it belonged to. During the months since Caden entered my Hard-of-Hearing life I had become attuned to the sounds he made. I wanted to be grumpy about that. Tried to be grumpy about that. I wasn't always successful, but I wasn't ready to admit *why* that was the case.

Sometimes being a snarky, stubborn girl can really be a pain in the ass.

Frowning, I looked at Caden and realized he'd just gotten a taste of what California Highway Patrol fines were like.

"Ouch," he said. I didn't hear him, but I didn't need to. The word was plain on his lips and face.

Gibson gave him an apologetic frown. "Sorry."

Caden looked up from the citation and shrugged. "It is what it is."

Gibson turned his attention to me, his smile knowing. "I'm going to leave this insane Australian in your capable hands now, Chase."

In my hands.

An unnerving image flashed through my head at the words, one better left undescribed at this point in time. One that made my belly flutter and the bits between my legs . . . do things. I scowled at my body's reaction, and crossed my arms over my chest.

Gibson had the nerve to laugh. Turning back to Caden he offered his hand. "You've got my number, Caden. Let me know how the dog is doing when you can."

"I will," he replied, taking Gibson's hand and giving it a shake.

"Doofus."

They both swung puzzled looks at me.

"I've decided his name is Doofus," I said, tilting my chin at them.

Gibson lifted his eyebrows. Caden smiled. "We'll let you know how Doofus is going."

I didn't miss the *we* in that statement. And like the wholly pornographic image that had filled my head at the notion of Caden being *in my hands*, my body reacted again. Maybe even more powerfully than the first time.

Great. Awesome.

Fuck.

Caden

We stayed at the animal hospital for the next hour, sitting in the waiting room out the front. I slumped in the hard plastic seats, exhaustion and jetlag doing their best to render me catatonic.

I'm afraid to say I was mentally, physically and emotionally drained. I'd been awake now for over twenty-four hours. I hadn't slept on the flight over, instead binging on the latest season of *Game of Thrones* in an attempt to stop my mind stewing on Chase. For what it's worth, it didn't work. If you asked me what happened in the show, I couldn't tell you. I think there was a dragon . . . maybe? And a guy with a sword? And some snow? I think . . .

While I slumped in my seat, Chase paced the small area, arms still crossed over her chest, her frown growing darker by the second.

She kept flinging glances at the door behind the reception counter. It didn't matter how many times I told her the doctor working on Doofus was going to be a while, that the dog's injuries were extensive and the procedures needed were time-consuming, she seemed to be affronted he hadn't strode out yet to tell us Doofus was going to be okay.

The receptionist behind the counter watched Chase like she was some kind of curious caged animal. I noticed she often stared at Chase's ears. I wanted to tell her to stop it. Had, in fact, stood up at one point and walked over to the counter to do just that, but had stopped myself before opening my mouth.

Chase had accused me of treating her like she was a little girl back on the freeway. She'd informed me I wasn't her father or boyfriend and therefore had no right to protect her.

I wasn't protecting her, not at *this* point in time at least, but I *was* thinking if she caught the receptionist constantly looking at her ears she might snap. I hated the idea of her feeling shitty about her hearing, but knew Chase would hate that kind of attention being brought to her hearing impairment more. So instead, I'd returned to my chair, slumped in its hard plastic seat and told her it was going to be okay – even as I prayed to God that Doofus would pull through.

Doofus. The fact she'd named the dog stirred something inside me, made me love her even more. It occurred to me right then I was a closet romantic. My mates at uni – the guys I played rugby with on the main lawn during lunch, who constantly told me I should hit on Dr. Briny Philips – would be laughing their heads off at the notion I was all mushy over a girl naming a stray dog that may or may not die. But there you go, I was.

As I was fond of saying, it is what it is. And what it was with Chase was too profound for me to deny.

I had three weeks to make her see that. Three weeks starting in a veterinary hospital, surrounded by the smell of sick animals, disinfectant, with the memory of Donald the Dude niggling away at me.

I closed my eyes, unable to keep them open.

"Doofus is going to be okay, gorgeous." My fried brain told me I'd mumbled it, but I didn't seem to have the strength or ability to repeat it louder. My fried brain also told me I'd called her *gorgeous*, but that was lost in a fog of heavy nothingness.

Suffice to say, I fell asleep.

I woke sometime later to a soft nudge on my arm. I did

that slow, uneven, bleary-eyed blink/squint thing you do when being woken unexpectedly from a deep slumber in the middle of the day. Harsh white light stabbed at my dry eyes as I peered up at the receptionist bending over in front of me.

I mumbled "Yes?" at her.

Before she could respond I felt a warm weight on my lap. Dropping my still-fuzzy gaze, I found Chase curled on her side on the seat beside me, her head resting on my thighs. Her eyes were closed. My hand was lying on her shoulder, my fingers loosely cupping its finely curved shape. It moved gently with her breaths, breaths steady and slow enough to tell me she was asleep.

A hot, tight ball filled my throat. I'm ashamed to say, my cock twitched in my jeans, an eager rush of excited blood pumping into its flaccid length.

It wouldn't be flaccid for long. Not with the enthusiastic way my body was reacting to Chase's proximity to my groin. Seriously, anyone would think I was fifteen with the way my dick was behaving.

"Are you deaf too?"

At the question – asked with part curiosity, part frustration – I lifted my eyes from Chase and fixed them on the receptionist. "And if I was?"

She blinked.

I don't do anger *that* often – I'm the guy who smiled and laughed all the way through his parent's divorce, remember – because getting angry doesn't help anything. But this girl was rubbing me the wrong way, and I don't think it had anything to do with being tired or jetlagged.

Shifting a little in my seat, I dragged a hand through my hair – though not the one on Chase's shoulder – let out a choppy sigh and offered her an apologetic smile. "How's Doofus?"

Another one of those blinks answered me.

"The dog?" I said. "The reason we're sitting here?"

"Oh, it survived."

Relief rushed through me like a wave.

"Dr. Adams wants to talk to you about it, though."

Unsettled tension polluted that wave. A cold lump replaced the hot one in my throat.

"Okay," I said. "Thanks."

She regarded me for a moment, as if unsure what to do, and then made her way back behind the counter.

It was my turn to blink. Was she seriously wearing stilettoes in a vet clinic?

Returning my gaze to Chase, I allowed myself a moment to take in the beauty of her face. There was no frown pulling at her eyebrows, no guarded tension. Just a relaxed peaceful expression I longed to see all the time. If only she'd let me . . .

Heart racing, I brushed a fingertip over her cheek in a gentle stroke, before tracing the line of her ear. She moaned, the sound low and thick with sleep, and then shifted about on the seat a little, her head doing the same on my lap. Her eyes didn't open. Nor did she wake.

I did it again: cheek, then ear. Stupidly, I whispered her name. I'm chalking *that* one up to jetlag and exhaustion.

Her eyelids fluttered a few times and then, with a soft little hitching noise that sent purely male blood into that purely male organ between my thighs – that purely male organ currently *right next to her face* – she opened her eyes and smiled up at me.

For a split second I don't think she was aware of what she was doing. A split second of raw, ungoverned emotion. And then realization of what she was doing, where she was laying, hit her and she scrambled up so fast she clocked my chin with the back of her head and rammed the heel of her palm into my groin.

Pain. Instant pain. Whoa. Trust me when I say, getting a semi hard-on whacked with a floundering palm is not fun. I winced. Couldn't help it. Tried. Failed. I winced, concertinaed into a groaning U shape and winced again, when the back of her head smashed into my chin once more.

My beard didn't buffer the contact. I saw stars.

Chase let out a pain-laced "Fuck".

I've never heard her swear. Not aloud, at least. Sure, she'd signed profanity at me a few times, but I've never *heard* her curse. For some reason, it made me laugh.

I reached for her, my groin aching, my dick rapidly shrinking in agony-induced retreat, my balls throbbing in both pain and desire, and my chin just throbbing in pain. Before she could fully right herself on the seat beside me, I took her in my arms, grinning, and kissed her.

I wasn't really thinking. I just did it. The second my lips touched hers I realized what I was doing. We both snapped frozen. And then Chase moved. She let out another sound, infinitely more sexy than that slumberous one she'd made earlier, and she was cupping my face in her hands and kissing me back. A crazy hot kiss that involved tongues touching and teeth clinking. It lasted a lifetime and sent me insane. It was incredible. My cock decided it was over its pain and flooded with eager, happy blood. My heart thumped hard and fast and wild in my chest, my throat, my ears.

And then the kiss was finished. As surprisingly abrupt as it had begun, it was over.

Chase jerked away from me, her eyes wide. Her mouth was open, her lips shiny. My chest tightened. That was my saliva on her lips. Mine. Not anyone else's. Not Donald the Dude's. Mine.

Time ceased for a moment, and then I rose to my feet.

We were in the waiting room of an animal hospital. We were sharing the space with pets and their owners, and a receptionist who seemed to look upon Chase as an oddity. As much as I wanted to kiss her again, as much as I wanted to talk to her about the truthfulness of our unexpected kiss, we weren't alone. This was not the place to continue what was the best moment of my life.

This was the moment to find out about the dog we'd saved.

She watched me stand. Confusion swam in her eyes.

"I'll be right back," I said.

With a shake of her head, she jolted to her feet beside me. "I want to know what's going on too."

I couldn't miss the scratchy quality to her voice. Nor the wavery quality to it either. As wrong as it sounds, a part of me was happy she was as affected by the kiss as I was.

Deciding to ignore the contemptuous look on the receptionist's face, I took Chase's hand and we walked together around the counter to the door. She didn't try to squirm her fingers free of mine. Another thing I was happy about.

Actually, ecstatic is probably a better word.

I'd just pushed the door open, the biting smell of animal feces and disinfectant attacking my sinuses instantly, when I heard the receptionist mutter "Deaf freaks".

Without letting Chase's hand go, or slowing my pace, I flicked her a smile. "And proud of it."

The door swung shut behind us before the shock finished forming on her face.

"Proud of what?" Chase asked as we made our way along the corridor toward the surgery.

"How freakishly good-looking I am," I answered.

She rolled her eyes . . . and adjusted her fingers so they threaded through mine.

I'm not sure I can adequately describe how amazing the feel of her palm against mine was. It sure as hell affected me as much as her palm against my crotch had earlier. In a whole different way, true, but with the same impact.

I couldn't have been happier, holding her hand there in one of the least romantic places to hold a girl's hand.

I grinned.

She smiled back at me. And then wrinkled her nose and sniffed. "Nice smell," she said with a grimace.

I squeezed her hand a little more. "You get used to it."

The smell of vet clinics is very distinct. It's not the same as a hospital smell. At least, not to me. A vet clinic is undercut with the musky odor of animals and all the smells they produce. It's not essentially a pleasant smell, but one *I* found great comfort in. I guess it takes a particular kind of person to be a veterinarian, and I was one of them.

What kind of person *is* that?

My animal ethics lecturer at Melbourne Uni will tell you one of great compassion, patience, empathy and intelligence. She's adamant a vet is more talented and intelligent than a human doctor because, as she puts it, "a vet can't just ask their patient were it hurts. They need to figure it out themselves".

My opinion? A vet is someone who can see the humor in having your arm buried up to the shoulder in a cow's butt.

Dr. Dean Adams, the vet surgeon, was checking Doofus's temperature when we entered the recovery ward. Doofus was stretched on his side, the length of his body shaved, wounds stitched in bright yellow medical string, his tongue lolling like a fat pink ribbon from his muzzle.

"102.5," Dr. Adams noted, tossing the rectal thermometer

into a kidney dish. He gave the veterinary nurse a smile. "I'm happy with that."

He turned to us, his smile widening. "He's not out of the woods yet, Caden, but he's heading in the right direction."

I crossed to the open cage in which Doofus lay, still and sedated. I couldn't help but give him the once-over. Hey, I'm one year away from being a vet myself, with more intern hours clocked in a clinic than anyone else in my class. Of course I was going to put my soon-to-be doctor's hat on.

"When can we take him home?"

Chase's question stroked my tightly wound nerves. Until that point I would have said it was impossible to be a nervous wreck and happy beyond belief all at once.

"Not for a few days, I'm afraid," Dr. Adams said.

I turned, aware Chase would have difficultly deciphering what seemed to be his natural mumbly intonation. I stopped myself repeating Adams when I found her chewing her lips, watching him. She was agitated, but doing her best to exude an air of calm. I needed to do the same. Giving Doofus's limp leg one last gentle pat, I moved to Chase's side and tapped Dr. Adams on his shoulder.

He lifted his head, eyebrows raised.

"Can we take him home soon?" Chase asked. I wondered if the slight change in wording was a subconscious defense mechanism: not repeating herself *per se*?

Those raised eyebrows dipped a bit and then realization dawned on his face. "Not for at least a week," he answered a little louder this time.

I wanted to let him know that as long as Chase could see his face, and his voice wasn't muffled by a hand or pen, or any number of things people seemed to stick near their mouth when talking, he didn't need to raise his volume. Not in this small area.

Instead, I stood by her side. One thing I'd learned about Chase Sinclair very early in our relationship, she didn't like people going all "knight in shining armor" on her when someone discovered she had a hearing impairment. I did it once very early on and wouldn't do it again. Not when there was chance of her catching me, at least.

I suspected I'd very much gone all "knight in shining armor" back on the freeway, with an added bonus off "incredulous anger" and a side-order of "misplaced panic" thrown in for good measure. I really owed her an apology.

"But you can come and visit him daily during his recovery, if you want?" Dr. Adams offered.

"We're from San Diego," I answered, gut clenching at the thought of Doofus not getting any affection during his recovery. "But I can check into a—"

"We'll be here," Chase said at the exact same time.

I stopped and gave her a frown. "How are *we* going to do that?"

Her answering smile was inscrutable. "*We* will work it out."

I continued to frown at her. She continued to smile at me. How's that for a role-reversal?

When I turned back to Dr. Adams, he was studying us both over the rim of his glasses. "That's good. It tears me apart when we've got an animal in our care with no one to show it some love during its recovery."

The feeling was entirely mutual. I'd spent many an hour in Briny Phillip's clinic back home making sure all the animals received comforting pats and words, but the ones that didn't have owners, who never saw a familiar face, I paid extra attention to.

"Thank you for saving the big guy today, Caden." Dr. Adams held out his hand.

I took it and gave it a firm shake. I liked this man. He was down to earth, and clearly as dedicated to animals as I was.

He chuckled. "I'm still not convinced putting your lives at risk was wise, but I am in awe of your compassion and commitment. You're going to make an amazing veterinarian when you finish your studies. In fact, you already are one now."

"Thanks," I said. I'll admit it, a goofy grin was all over my face.

"And if you ever feel like moving to the States for work," he continued, "come see me."

That goofy grin I mentioned? Even goofier now.

"Thanks," I repeated, a tad lost for words. Sure, I'd already been offered a full-time place at Briny's clinic, but whoa, talk about an ego rush. If I wasn't careful, my head would be too big to get through the door.

"You're welcome." Dr. Adams turned to Chase. "Get the temp – I've forgotten her name – to give you my card on the way out. And make sure she writes your contact numbers down, so I can call you and let you know how . . . what did you call him?"

"Doofus," said Chase.

"How Doofus is doing." With that, he excused himself and left us alone with Doofus.

I looked at Chase.

She looked at me.

We both licked our lips. I shuffled my feet. She chewed her bottom lip.

The memory of our kiss in the waiting room hung on the air between us, rivaling the pungent odor of the recovery room in potency.

Fuck it.

"So we kissed," I said. Or maybe blurted. "A full-on kiss."

Her cheeks filled with a delightful pink tinge I'd never seen there before. Chase Sinclair was blushing?

"We did," she finally agreed.

"Any chance we can do it again?" I grinned hopefully.

Chase rolled her eyes. "Let's just find a motel first."

I blinked. And because I'm a guy, a big fat tight spasm claimed my cock. "Err..."

Instead of responding to my obvious perplexity, she stepped past me to stand beside Doofus's cage. She ran her hand over his back leg, avoiding the bandaged wound. "Is he going to be okay?" she asked, without looking at me.

I let my gaze run over her profile for a moment, my chest tight, my groin tighter.

Motel? Really? Motel?

Finally, I pulled my hormones back under control, stuffed them in a dark box and let out a sigh. Reaching forward, I touched her arm.

"Stupid question, yeah?"

"The only stupid question is the one not asked," I said.

She let out a dry snort, turned back to Doofus and stroked his back leg again. "Unless you already know the *answer* to the unasked stupid question and it confuses the hell out of you."

"Can I help?" I asked, pulse pounding. "Clear up the confusion, I mean. If you're confused about how awesome I am at kissing..."

She let out a sharp sigh. "You know, O'Dae, sometimes your good-natured humor makes me want to punch you."

I didn't know what to say to that. So I said nothing.

Two ways of dealing with confrontation I'd learned from my parents' divorce: quiet ease or laid-back jokes. It was obviously time to go with the first option now, even if my gut told me to make another joke. My gut wasn't to be trusted sometimes, but I had to make amends for yelling at her earlier somehow.

A few minutes later, she dropped her hand from Doofus and gave me an ambiguous nod. "Let's go give Little Miss Regrowth our numbers."

"Who?"

She chuckled. "The temp behind the desk."

"Ahh. Sure, let's do that."

We were at the door when something suddenly struck me. "That explains the stilettoes," I said aloud to myself.

Chase arched an eyebrow at me, lips twitching. "But not the attitude."

Man, had I said it that loudly?

"C'mon." She wrapped her fingers around the door handle. "Let's get out of here."

After the most frustrating five minutes of my life – during which the temporary receptionist, aka Little Miss Regrowth, kept shouting at Chase and exaggerating her lip movements to the point it looked like she was having some kind of connip-tion, and to which Chase flung back snarky comment after snarky comment with enough bite a pit-bull would have been impressed – things reached boiling point.

I'm not lying when I say my muscles were taut with tension. I was half expecting Chase to lean across the counter and shake the girl every time she raised her voice higher and regarded Chase with open concern and pity.

I think it was the pity that did me in the most. Not able to take it any longer, I rapped my knuckles on the counter and fixed the temp with a level stare. "Given we're meant to be an advanced species," I said, "we really do know how to make those not considered *normal* by society's standards feel like crap, don't we?"

The temp blinked. "Huh?"

Chase took my hand and dragged me across the reception area. A second after that, we walked out of the animal hospital.

We were halfway across the car park, the warm sun beating down on us, the concrete under our feet doing its best to rival the rays in temperature, when Chase let out a ragged sigh. "You don't have to keep protecting me, Caden. Or defending me."

My chest tightened. "I'm not. I haven't—"

"Yeah, I *shouldn't* have let her get to me," she cut me off. "But I'm completely capable of dealing with shit like that by myself. I've been doing so for twenty-two years now."

"You were dealing with clueless receptionists when you were still in nappies?"

A blank look came over Chase's face, followed by a frown. She rubbed at her face. I didn't miss the exasperated groan muffled by her palms.

"I'm sorry," I said, catching her wrists and lowering her hands to her side. "I'm sorry. Didn't mean to . . . to . . . be me, I guess."

She studied me, silent for a moment. "You frustrate the hell out of me, O'Dae."

"I don't mean to," I answered honestly.

A frown pulled at her eyebrows and she shook her head. "C'mon," she said.

I cast her a look as we continued to walk toward the Speeding Dragon. "I think she'd get to anyone. I was waiting for her to start treating me like I was backward when she commented on my Australian accent. Maybe I should have thrown in a few more *crikeys* and *fair dinkums*?"

Chase snorted a laugh. The decided lack of frustration in it made me feel a little better. "Yeah. Of course, I didn't help things when I signed at you, did I?"

I grinned. "Not really. What did you sign, by the way? I missed it."

"That you should tell her your Chris Hemsworth's cousin."

I burst out laughing.

Chase flashed me a grin that was pure mischief.

When we reached the Volvo and got in, I buckled my seatbelt, doing my best to appear relaxed. My brain kept whispering a single word over and over: motel.

Finally, as Chase started the engine and pulled out onto the road, I couldn't hold it in any longer. Reaching over the center console, I touched her shoulder. "I don't expect you to stay at a motel with me," I said when she glanced my way.

"I know."

I had no idea what to make of that answer. My heart was thumping away in my chest, fast and crazy, and altogether too hung up on the fact that Chase had suggested we check into a motel together. I wanted to look at my crotch and mutter "Down boy", but suspected Chase would see me and know exactly where my thoughts were going.

"You should give Brendon a call," she said, lips curling in a smile as enigmatic as her previous answer, before she returned her focus to the busy street. "Let him know what's going on. Use my cell."

She waved her hand at my feet. A brilliant purple handbag sat on the passenger side floor. She was giving me permission to go searching in her handbag for her mobile phone.

Wow. This was a next-level moment.

I scooped up the bag and rested it on my lap, then opened the zipper to reveal its contents. I don't have a sister – I'm an only child, remember – but I do have female cousins and female friends. Permission to go looking through a handbag is a big deal.

"Nice bag," I said, trying to be cool.

She grunted. Keeping my big dude hands steady, I moved things around, searching for her mobile. There was a purse (also purple), about fifty packets of chewing gum (all in various stages of consumption), a hairbrush, two glasses cases and three pairs of sunglasses, what may or may not have been a crumpled parking fine, two granola bars, two tubes of lip balm, a small leatherbound sketch book, the edges of the paper frayed and well-worn, and so many loose pencils I didn't bother counting.

There was also a hard plastic container I recognized as her hearing-aid case.

Chase. In a bag. Her personality, her passion, her stubbornness, all right there in a purple bag.

"It's in the side pocket."

Her voice – and the slight humor in it – made me lift my head. I scowled at her with mock reproach. "Don't laugh at me."

She did exactly that.

I couldn't maintain the ruse any more and grinned, returning my attention to her bag. I found her mobile and withdrew it from a pocket inside that I hadn't noticed before. I tapped on the screen, and touched her arm.

"Four two four two," she said without looking at me.

My chest got tighter. I was not only being granted access to her bag, I was being granted access to her phone's security PIN.

I was halfway through keying in the number when the phone pinged in my hand – a very loud tone accompanied by a very powerful vibration.

"Shit," Chase blurted, with a harried look at her phone.

Before I could stop myself, I read the incoming message that appeared on the screen.

Don't forget your toothbrush, babe. D.

"Donald the Dude has sent you a message," I told her. I couldn't drag my eyes from that message. And my throat was so thick, my mouth so dry, the words came out a scratchy mess.

Pulling in a deep breath, I finally looked over at her.

"Ignore it," she instructed, her eyes fixed back on the road. Her hands gripped the steering wheel with knuckle-whitening force.

I nodded. I'm aware the action was ridiculous, given she wasn't looking at me, but if I tried to answer with words, what would have come out would have been something along the lines of "This guy, Chase? Really, this guy? *This* is my competition? This guy is a dick."

Re-keying her security code, I drew in another deep breath, dialed Brendon's number and waited for him to answer.

The whole time, however, Donald the Dude's message kept flashing in my head. It didn't stop during the entire time I spoke to Brendon. Not at all.

Don't forget your toothbrush, babe. D.
Don't forget your toothbrush, babe. D.
Don't forget your toothbrush, babe. D.

I really *really* didn't like that guy.

FOUR

"A dog is one of the few things in life that is as it seems."
~ Mark J Asher

Chase

I didn't listen to Caden talking to Brendon. Listen. Ha ha. I should say, I didn't focus on it. If I'd focused on it, I would have been able to make out the words. Instead, I let his voice be the fuzzy, muffled collection of sounds a voice is to me when I'm not trying to hear it.

Instead, I focused on the road. And my completely unexpected plan to check us both into a motel.

I'm not sure where that plan had come from. I'm equally unsure why I didn't retract it when Caden gave me the chance. I was meant to be seeing Donald tonight, after all, although I was already beginning to suspect even if I was in San Diego I wasn't going to Donald's. Being with Caden, even after what happened between us on the freeway, was making me realize very clearly the difference between a healthy relationship and a toxic one.

Although *relationship* wasn't exactly the correct word, when it came down to it. I wasn't really in a relationship with either of them. Not in that context, at least. But Caden, with his sometimes infuriating relaxed humor, was infinitely . . . more comfortable to be with.

Comfortable. Was that the kind of word a girl of twenty-two wanted to use to describe a relationship?

I would have thought no, but then, neither were the words *emotionally manipulative*, and that's what came to mind with Professor Douchebag.

Wherever the plan to stay in a motel had come from, I was following it through. It didn't matter that driving back and forth between LA and San Diego on a daily basis wasn't that big a deal. Southern Californians do it all the time.

It didn't matter Mom and Dad would freak out. We were going to check into a motel.

Sometimes I think my father might be right about me being emotionally cracked.

I'd have to let my boss at the pet shop know I was going AWOL for a few days. I'd definitely have to let Mom and Dad know the same, even with the inevitable freaking out. Caden was letting my sister know, via Brendon. To be honest, I was half expecting to hear Amanda squeal through the phone, bad hearing or not.

What was I doing?

I'd like to think I was doing it because of Doofus, and a part of me *was* doing it for that very reason: the thought of the dog having no one there during his recovery did not sit well with me at all.

When Tanner was diagnosed with leukemia I was still at college, spending my days being arty and clever, my afternoons screwing the cool Art History professor, and my nights doing the same whenever he called me. Pathetic, right?

Tanner's diagnosis made studying seem less important. What was important was being there for my nephew when my sister couldn't. What mattered was being there for my sister when our dad . . . well, that's a whole different story. Suffice to say, watching my nephew fight death put things in perspective for me, and I no longer wanted to spend my days in an art studio surrounded by people who thought weed would un-tap their muse so they could find the answers to life's great mysteries, or that eating olives and cold cuts made them the epitome of bohemian chic.

I know an injured stray is not at all in the same league as my nephew having leukemia, but it was having a similar effect on me. A living creature should never have to suffer alone. And Doofus was a *defective* living creature. He had a disability. As clichéd as it sounds, I couldn't help but feel like he'd been brought into my world because I knew how that felt: to not function the way God – or Mother Nature, or Buddha, or whoever the hell really was in charge – intended.

But being there for the dog, making certain he knew on some doggy level he was cared about, wasn't the only reason. Nor was it, I fear, the main reason.

The main reason for announcing Caden and I were going to check into a motel was because I wasn't ready yet not to be in his company. Which was problematic, given only a few hours ago I was adamant he could "bite me" in his attempt to make me fall in love with him.

Okay, I wasn't even *close* to that. But the bastard was firing things in me that hadn't fired for a long time. Not since Professor Douchebag did his number on me.

The kiss in the parking lot at LAX had shaken me a little.

The kiss in the animal hospital's waiting room had shaken me a lot. Like I mean, holy fuck, was-that-an-earthquake, a lot.

The interlude in the motel was more about . . . Maybe, just maybe, if Caden and I . . .

I swallowed, my head roaring. My blood pumped through my veins like a flooded river. I could damn near feel it coursing through them, the cannon-like pounding of my heart feeding its rapid force.

Was I really about to check us into a motel just so I could . . . just so *we* could . . .

And what would Donald do at nine o'clock when I was a no-show? The fact he'd texted me twice since our airport meeting, plus the call to invite me to his house . . .

In the time I'd been with him he'd never exhibited any signs of jealousy toward any of the other guys I interacted with. What did it mean that he seemed to now, after only a brief introduction to Caden?

Donald was one of my father's work colleagues. Was it possible he knew of Caden's role in saving Tanner? Did he see Caden more of a threat to whatever screwed-up claim he had on me?

I thought of Donald. Pictured him. Donald, to whom I'd given my heart. Donald, who'd stomped on said heart – and my dignity along with it – when he declared me too imperfect, too *defective*, to be in a serious relationship with. Donald, whom I'd caught whispering into the ear of another student – something he'd never done to me – in his office a few days later. Donald, who'd never taken me out to any public function, who'd told me when he was dumping me he couldn't have a partner who couldn't converse normally with people at art gallery openings or other cultural events.

Donald who'd started screwing the other student with perfect hearing a week later . . .

I gripped the wheel. What the fuck had I been thinking? I'd agreed to see *that* Donald at nine? Professor Douchebag? I called him Professor Douchebag for a reason. I had to remember that. I had to . . .

And yet, on some disturbed, unnerving level my stupid, stupid heart, *wanted* to see him. He'd been the first man to make me feel like I had worth . . . the first man to treat me like I wasn't a child needing to be protected, to be constantly reminded I wasn't living the way I should.

He'd listened to me. Encouraged me. And now he was calling me again. Calling me *babe* . . .

I stopped the train of thought before it could send me into a spiral I did not want to head down.

Yanking on the steering wheel, I flung the Speeding Dragon into a sharp right turn, hit the gas, and then a few seconds later, banked the Volvo into a sharp left before hitting the brake.

The sudden acceleration and abrupt halt sent both Caden and me jerking forward and backward in our seats. My teeth clicked. The seatbelt pressed between my breasts. The Speeding Dragon shuddered at my mistreatment of him. I'd apologize later with a sudsy bath and some Turtle Wax, but for now, my focus was on where we were.

In the parking lot of the Happy Traveller Motel.

Heart racing, I stared at the front of the motel – the first one we'd come across since leaving the animal hospital.

Caden said something beside me. I wasn't ready to look at him, to ask him to repeat himself so I could hear. I needed to digest what I was doing for a moment.

The Happy Traveller sat there in the bright sun, its signage like something from the 1950s, the illuminated Vacancy sign announcing there was a room waiting for us. It didn't look like a dive, it looked . . . dated. Tired.

Was this where I was . . . where we were . . .

Oh boy.

"Okay," I said, opening my door with a gusto that belied how nervous I was feeling. "Let's do this."

Caden's fingers wrapped around my wrist, halting my rather manic exit from my car. I fixed my gaze on his face, pulse beating in my throat like a butterfly that had overdosed on Ritalin.

"Why are we here, Chase?" he asked.

The question sent a tight finger of tension sinking into my tummy. It also seemed to steal any ability I had to form an answer.

A slow smile pulled at his lips. I watched it, my throat so tight I could barely breathe.

"Y'know," he said, his grip on my wrist loosening, "in all the times I've come over here to see Brendon and Amanda and Tanner, I've yet to go to Disneyland."

I frowned. And blinked. All at once.

Caden smiled wider. "I really think we should go to Disneyland. My treat? What do you reckon?"

"Now?" The word came out as a croak.

He nodded, releasing my wrist completely. "Let's do it. I've wanted to go on the "It's A Small World" ride since I was five and every time I mention it to Bren he shakes his head and walks away from me for some reason."

My tummy fluttered. I looked up at the Happy Traveller's facade, taking in the shadowy interior on the other side of the grimy glass, the dated décor, the receptionist who . . . yes, was wearing hair curlers.

I turned back to Caden. Disneyland. Or a motel room trapped in the 1950s.

Or dinner with Donald . . .

"You can laugh at me when I scream on the rollercoaster,"

Caden said, his smile growing playful. "And I will scream. It's probably a good thing you can't hear me that well."

I burst out laughing. I couldn't help it.

I make jokes about my hearing all the time. Why wouldn't I? If nothing else, it really ticks Dad off.

I've also been known to use it to my advantage when asked to do something I don't want to do. When I was a kid, I got out of so many arguments with my parents for not doing chores by pretending I'd never heard the initial request. It took Mom until I was thirteen before she caught on to what I was doing. I'm pretty certain Amanda might have tattled on me, as big sisters are wont to do.

Even now I can bluff Dad with a confused look if I don't feel like answering a question he's adamant on asking. Questions like, when was I going to do something with my life, when was I going back to college, why would I throw my life away working in a pet shop . . . ?

When it comes to my defective hearing, I'm okay with making fun of it, or making it work for me. But until right this very moment, no one in my life apart from my mother, my sister and my brother-in-law had ever made fun of it. People either tip-toed around it like it was a subject too fragile to mock, or were aghast when *I* joked about it. They did it out of some kind of misguided sense of compassion and tact, I'm sure, but they still did it. Having Caden make a joke out of it . . . yeah, it was incredible. I know that probably makes no sense, given how irritated I was with the way the temp back at the animal hospital treated me, but it made me feel . . .

Normal.

By poking fun at my bad hearing, Caden O'Dae had made me feel more normal than I had in I don't know how long. He'd put it out there, in the same way someone would tease a friend about a bad haircut, or a poor choice in clothes.

Tears filled my eyes. Holy crap, I was actually laughing so much I was crying. When was the last time that had happened? Had it ever?

Wiping at my cheeks with the back of one hand, I yanked the car door shut with the other. "Disneyland it is," I said, grinning at him.

"I am so getting a photo with Goofy," he said.

"You *are* goofy."

He preened.

I laughed again, rolling my eyes as I pulled away from the Happy Traveller.

It took us over an hour to get to Anaheim, and another twenty minutes to find a place to park. In that time, Caden sent a few texts to his family back in Australia using my cell. At some point I was going to have to take him somewhere he could get a US SIM, but he said he wanted to go to Disneyland first. He also took a selfie with me in the background and sent it to Brendon with the explicit instruction he show it to Tanner.

He wouldn't show it to me. I suspect he was pulling some kind of face in it. The one thing Caden had never been shy about teasing me over was my driving technique. Mom says I have two speeds: off and hypersonic. Hey, when I want to be somewhere, I want to be there. Is there anything wrong with that?

As we walked toward the main gate of Disneyland surrounded by swarms of people, the urge to take Caden's hand, to thread my fingers through his, flooded over me with such power my stomach clenched.

As if aware of my thoughts, and without looking at me even once, he took my hand in his. Just like that. Like it was the most natural thing in the world for him to do.

My stomach clenched again. So did other parts of me.

Swallowing, I adjusted my fingers until my palm pressed perfectly into his, and returned my attention to the entry gates ahead of us.

We were almost at the ticket booth when my cell vibrated into life in my pocket. The noise level was too loud for me to hear the accompanying tone so when I withdrew it with the assumption it was either Mom or Dad wanting to *talk* about my plans to stay in LA, I wasn't prepared to see the text from Donald.

Do you know what I'm thinking? We should go to Disneyland tomorrow. Together. What do you think?

I stumbled to a halt, staring at my cell. What the hell?

Jerking my head up, I scanned the crowd around us. I don't know why. Did I really think I'd see him here? But still, what were the chances of Donald suggesting we go to Disneyland together on the *very* day I was going with Caden?

Disneyland? How many times had I ached for him to take me somewhere public and he never would, and now he was suggesting Disneyland? Together?

What. The. Hell?

No, change that. What. The. *Fuck?*

"Everything okay?"

I turned to Caden, pulse faster than my liking. "Yeah," I said, my smile feeling brittle. It was just like Professor Douchebag to screw me up like this.

Reminding myself that I'd decided he was not going to do this to me anymore, I smiled at Caden again. This time, however, it felt more real. More relaxed. "It's all good."

He studied for a moment. His eyes flicked to my cell for a split second, a frown on his eyebrows, and then he returned his attention to me. He nodded. "Of course it is. You're with me."

I laughed. A genuine one. Caden's habit of making light

of everything often rubbed me the wrong way . . . but just as often it was exactly what I needed.

I tried to pay, but Caden wouldn't let me. "What don't you understand about *my treat?*" he asked, sliding his credit card under the security glass at the ticket booth.

The park was busy. And I mean busy. Warm and sunny day busy. Every ride had a line that stretched forever. Thank God I used the brains my father was so disappointed I was wasting, by setting up a Disney account and downloading an app that gave us the legal right to push in (AKA, the *FAST PASS!*) while we were waiting in line to buy our entry tickets.

As it was, even with that we still had a wait.

Standing in a line at a theme park is not something I'm good at. It has nothing to do with being impatient – well, not that much – and everything to do with the fact I'm standing in the middle of a group of people in a rowdy place where everyone is shouting over everyone else, which turns what little sound I *can* hear into a mess of jarring noise that scrapes against my nerves and makes me as irritable as all hell. The same goes for waiting in line at the movies, what few concerts I go to, at the cafeteria at college, in bars . . . Basically, me and waiting in line don't go well.

Waiting in line with Caden, however . . . We didn't talk, there really wasn't a point given the level of noise around us, and I didn't want to sign, but just standing beside him, just feeling his palm on mine . . . it was a whole different experience.

Sometimes we ate ice cream. In the line for Small World, I kept stealing licks of his while he was gawking at everything around us. It wasn't until I went in for the millionth surreptitious lick, that he surprised me by dabbing the tip of my nose in peppermint chocolate-chip ice cream, and I realized he'd been aware of what I was doing the whole time.

He laughed loud enough at my stunned reaction that not only did the people around us inch away a little, but I heard it clearly over the noise of the park.

Heard it. Felt it. All the way to my soul.

And in feeling it, a warm sense of contented happiness swelled through me.

Confession time: I know "It's A Small World" is one of Disneyland's most iconic and beloved rides. I know it's a symbol of what Walt wanted the people of the world to believe, I know it's got more nostalgic importance than anything else at Disneyland, but man, as we spent the eternity that ride lasted, sitting in that creaky little boat and jerking and jolting our way past singing animatronic display after display I'd never been more glad to be Hard of Hearing. If I'd been wearing my hearing aid, I would have taken it out and thrown it in the murky water.

I did my best to hide my grumpiness from Caden. He sat beside me, watching those creepy robot-children sing and dance, hardly blinking, both his hands holding one of mine. A rhythmic vibration flowed through his thigh, pressed against mine, and it took me a while to realize he was tapping his foot to the song I mercifully couldn't hear that well.

We were halfway round, the "children" of Chile chirping about just how damn small the world was, when he turned to me, released my hand and signed *Holy snapping duck shit, this world isn't small enough! Think if I jumped I could swim away from this madness?*

I laughed so much our boat rocked.

After that was finally over, we pretended we were Indiana Jones on the ride of the same name; followed that up with a crazy push-shove exploration – along with what felt like a thousand other park goers – of a massive artificial tree attraction based on the movie *Tarzan*. Caden told me there was Phil

Collins music being piped through hidden speakers all the way throughout the attraction. Not for the first time I found myself ticking off another perk of being defective.

When we were back on the ground, once again in the thick of the crowd, with the sinking sun painting us in golden heat and stretching shadows, I consulted the map of the park, working out if we had enough time to go on the Pirates of the Caribbean ride before we were due our turn on Space Mountain. I was chewing on my bottom lip, ignoring the people bumping into me, when I felt a warm hand slide over the back of my neck and warm lips press to my one working ear.

I stiffened at the unexpected contact. And then I heard him. Softly, almost inaudible but there all the same. Whispering.

Caden O'Dae was whispering in my ear. Whispering the lyrics to the Phil Collins song about always being in his heart.

I heard the words. I heard Caden's voice. I heard his whisper. His voice played with my senses. His fingers played with the hair at my nape. His breath played with my flesh. His beard tickled ear.

It was so nice. So perfect. So normal. He was whispering in my ear, just a normal kind of thing a guy would do with his girl . . .

I turned to that whisper, that breath, the back of my head moving in the gentle cup of his palm. I found his eyes, and gazed into them. And then cupped his bearded jaw in my hand and brushed my lips over his.

For a heart-stopping second I felt him stiffen, and then we were slammed into by a shouting, laughing teenager wearing a UCLA T-shirt and mirror sunglasses, and whatever was going to happen next didn't.

What did happen was that the teenager, who towered above me and was almost double Caden's size, grabbed at my shoulders with a laughing grin, said something that may or may not have been an apology, and then directed his mirrored sunglasses at Caden.

I watched Caden shake his head with a smile, waving his hand in an *it's okay* way. *No worries*, his lips formed, the rising noise of the crowd destroying any hope I had of hearing his voice. *It's all good.*

I felt his chest vibrate with the words though, my shoulder pressed as it was by the UCLA teenager, against his chest.

It wasn't *all good*. We were having a moment. An intense moment. And now we *weren't* having that moment. And while I should have been thrilled by that, I wasn't. I was disgruntled and confused and exasperated and . . . and . . . flummoxed.

Flummoxed, a word my father had thrown at me over and over when I'd dropped out of college.

I'm flummoxed, Chase, why you're doing this.

I'm flummoxed why you're quitting like this.

I'm more than flummoxed by your behavior, missy.

That last one had started a fight that had raged for weeks, ending only when I quoted Malcolm X at him, ("Just because you have colleges and universities, doesn't mean you have education.") and Amanda stepped in to stop him saying something we both would have regretted. Dad loves me. He really does. He's just a control freak who has high expectations. *And* issues with a daughter who doesn't function the way she's meant to. And who doesn't believe academia is the be-all-and-end-all.

I've probably spent a lot of my life flummoxing Dad, but here *I* was, *being* flummoxed.

It was a weird emotion. I didn't like it.

Huffing out a breath I suspected some might label petulant, I shrugged off the teenager's hands on my arms and began weaving my way through the throng. The noise – a messy soup of indistinct sounds – scraped at my nerves. I frowned, hugging my ribs. The deeper I moved into the thick of the crowd, the more the fuzzy rumble assaulted my one working ear. I pressed my palms to the sides of my head, over my ears. It's a ridiculous thing, I know, a person deaf in one ear and partially deaf in the other covering her ears, but the noise was driving me crazy.

It wasn't loud, it never is for me, not unless I'm wearing my hearing aid. It was just . . . there: a chaotic mishmash of sounds with no definition, no clarity, nothing. Just noise.

So much noise.

So much—

A firm hand curled around my wrist, bringing me to a gentle halt.

Caden. I didn't need to look to know. I was already more familiar with the feel of his skin on mine than anyone else I knew. Standing still, I closed my eyes and inhaled as deeply as my lungs would allow. I counted the thumps of my heart – a strong rhythm in my chest beating faster than it should – and then opened my eyes and looked up at Caden.

Worry filled his face. He'd removed his sunglasses so I could see his eyes. *I think we should leave the park* he signed, lips moving as he spoke the words as well. *This is not good for you.*

I tried not to bristle, but failed. "I'm fine," I said, letting him hear my irritation.

He studied me, expression unreadable.

"I'm fine," I repeated, signing it this time, moving my fingers a little snappier than needed.

He pulled in a slow breath, closed his eyes for a second and then looked at me. "I'm sorry," he said.

A lump filled my throat. "For what?"

"Being over protective," he answered.

I swallowed. "Don't do it again," I said, keeping my voice calm.

My head was whirling. He was making it harder and harder to stubbornly keep him from being a contender for "relationship" category. Having sex with him was one thing. Falling for him . . .

I'll do my best, he signed with a grin.

I snorted out a laugh and rolled my eyes. "Let's hit Space Mountain," I said, raising my voice so he could hear me over the crowd. "I want to feel your scream vibrate through my body."

I don't know if that was the equivalent of flirty-talk for a Hard of Hearing person, but it sent a little lick of excitement through me the second I said it.

Caden grinned, although concern still lingered in his eyes. "I'm going to make your whole body quiver," he countered.

Another lick of excitement snaked its way though me, and this time my nipples got in on the act, puckering into tight points in my bra. A fluttering tension bloomed in my belly, part nerves, part anticipation.

"Race you there," I blurted, now so totally flummoxed I think I'd moved into bamboozled cluelessness.

Before he could respond, I spun on my heel and bolted, ducking and weaving through the crowd like the star quarterback I wasn't, my whole body already quivering in ways I hadn't prepared myself for.

Oh boy.

Caden

I screamed. Loudly. And often.

I am a rollercoaster junkie. I've been on every roller-coaster Australia has to offer and screamed my way around them all. It's a very specific scream, my rollercoaster scream. If you took a scream of sheer terror and fed it into a universal translator set to *laughter*, that's what my scream sounds like.

Rollercoasters are adrenaline-charged fun. They are, I was discovering, even better when ridden with Chase. She laughed the whole way around Space Mountain. An open-mouth, head-thrown-back, completely and utterly uninhibited laugh. It was incredible. I loved it.

I loved her.

She was a prickly mess, a rollercoaster of emotions wilder and more unpredictable than any of the ones we'd ridden here at Disneyland, but I loved that about her as well. Maybe I was a glutton for punishment, or too romantic for my own good, but it was what it was. Riding Space Mountain with Chase was one of the best rushes of my life.

When it was over, when the ride came to a juddering halt, I gave her a wide grin, my heart crazy, my pulse the same and said " So? Was that good for you too?"

She laughed some more. "I felt you all the way to my core."

My groin thought that statement pretty fucking awesome.

Climbing from the carriage, we made our way from the ride, back into the fray of park goers. Day had quickly turned into evening, and my body and mind were doing three things.

One – telling me I hadn't slept since 2011.

Two – reminding me I hadn't eaten since roughly the same year.

Three – suggesting to me if Chase and I found a motel room now, the chances of us ending up naked and sweaty were very, very high.

Body thrumming, and not because of Space Mountain, I took her hand in mine and gave her fingers a squeeze.

"I think we should get something to eat," I said when she looked at me.

Not what you were expecting? Hey, I might be a guy, but I'm also a *nice* guy. Got it?

Chase nodded.

We decided on hot dogs. Followed by churros. And a bucketful of soda. And then more ice cream. One of the advantages of being young and fit: you can eat a shitload of crap and it won't come back and bite you on the arse 'til you're at least forty.

We were finishing our ice cream when Chase's mobile buzzed in her back pocket. She took it out, looked at the screen with a frown and then showed it to me. "This make any sense to you?"

The screen glowed with a text from an American number I didn't recognize. The message I understood without any problems.

BUN test results good. CNS undamaged. CFS analysis good. Hbg levels excellent. Dog recovery progressing well. Talk tomorrow. Dr. Adams

There were a lot of acronyms and abbreviations in the text, a lot of veterinarian jargon, but the long and short of it was, Doofus was doing well.

"What is it?"

I smiled at Chase. "I think he's going to be okay."

"Doofus?"

I nodded.

"Awesome," she cried, wrapping her arms around me to give me a tight hug that also incorporated a little dance. "That is awesome."

I still don't know how I avoided not wearing her ice cream.

What I *do* know is, when she pulled back to smile up at me, I leaned in to kiss her. As with every kiss I'd initiated with Chase – in fact, as with damn near everything I did regarding Chase – there was no conscious decision, there was only instinctual, gut action. I kissed her, tasting peanut butter chocolate-chip ice cream on her lips. I kissed her, holding her as close to me as I could, one hand flat to the small of her back, the other holding my ice cream, which was most likely melting down her back by now.

I kissed her, and she kissed me back, the nutty sweetness of her mouth nothing compared to the deliciousness of her tongue sliding over mine, or the feel of her body pressed to mine, her hips, her thighs, her sex, all aligned to mine with a perfection every molecule in my existence recognized and celebrated.

My head roared. My heart pounded. My dick did what dicks do when a guy is being kissed by the girl he's completely head over fucking heels about. For a split second I feared Chase was going to pull away from me – there was no way she could not have felt the fierce spasm that made it jerk in my jeans. Instead, I felt a low moan vibrate in her chest before she deepened the kiss.

The world erupted in fireworks: loud explosions that shuddered right through me. As much as I'd like to say I was being metaphorical, *literally* the night was suddenly filled with fireworks.

We pulled away from the kiss, still holding each other as we gaped up at the dark sky. Bright colors of pyro-technic mastery detonated above us in a display that left the Melbourne New Year's Eve fireworks for dead. Around us, our fellow park attendees oohed and aahed. Chase's arms snaked up around my neck and I lowered my gaze from the fireworks to her face, loving the way the colors exploding in the sky cast her face in the same hues.

Fuck me, I was completely lost to her.

My throat tight, I drew her closer to me, a pain in my chest I couldn't fathom. We stood that way for what felt like forever, and at the same time barely a heartbeat. When she turned her gaze to me, when I saw the happiness in her eyes, I could do nothing else but drag in a shaky breath and smile at her.

She held my stare. We didn't move. I thought I felt her phone vibrate in her hip pocket, but if it did, she didn't acknowledge it. Instead, very slowly, she rose up onto tiptoe and pressed her cheek to mine. "I think it's time we found ourselves a motel room."

Her statement sent thick ropes of tension through me. Her warm breath on my ear did the same. The feel of her breasts against my chest twisted those ropes into exquisite knots.

I swallowed. And then nodded.

Her phone vibrated again in her pocket, but again she ignored it.

Something itched at the back of my head, like an idea wanting to be heard, and then Chase took my fingers in hers and nothing else mattered to me but walking with her, hand in hand, out of Disneyland. We didn't speak until we were out of the park. There was no point. The noise was overwhelming even for my ears, and to be honest, there was nothing to be said. We knew what we were going to do. What did we need to talk about?

I let Chase take the lead as the crowd around us began to thin. Instead of turning right toward the car parking area where the Speeding Dragon sat waiting for us, she turned left.

Still holding hands, still wordless, we walked along the sidewalk of a strip of tourist shops and chain restaurants and motels. Chase pulled on my hand and turned up a footpath leading to a motel with a neon palm tree for a sign. The knotted ropes in my stomach twisted tighter. The Vacancy sign glowed green fluorescent at us as Chase pressed her palm to the door and pushed it open.

Ten minutes later, we were in our room. It was cozy, clean, and completely generic in every way. In the middle of it, was a queen size bed.

I stared at it. Took in its multi-colored, abstract-patterned spread, its matching pillows and cushions. The soft thud behind me of the door closing made me jump.

Jesus, I was a nervous wreck.

Swallowing again at the lump in my throat that didn't seem to want to bloody well bugger off, I turned to Chase. She stood with her back pressed to the door, watching me. My gut clenched. My groin throbbed.

Her phone rang in her pocket.

Without breaking eye contact with me, she withdrew the phone, silenced the ringing and shoved it back into her pocket. It hit me who was so desperately trying to reach her. Who was expecting her at his place at nine . . .

And then Chase was no longer leaning against the door. Chase was closing the distance between us. Chase was pressing her body to mine, her hands smoothing up my chest, over my shoulders, into the hair at the back of my head.

Chase was kissing me, and I was kissing her back. And Donald the Dude could go fuck his ear.

I know I've spent quite a bit of time telling you what a nice guy I am, and I stand by that claim, but at that point the nice guy had stepped aside for the horny, hungry, possessive guy who ached for Chase with every fucking fiber in his body.

I kissed her, my tongue lashing over hers, my teeth nipping at her lip, and tore at her clothes, desperate to have them gone. The only thing allowed on her body was my hands. No, not just my hands. My hands, my mouth, my tongue . . .

I think I tore Chase's shirt as I yanked it down over her shoulders, but given she was damn near ripping apart the zipper of my fly, I think we were even. The second her shirt was free of her body, I dragged my lips free of hers and moved them to her breast. I didn't wait to remove her bra. I captured the hard point of her nipple through the dark-purple satin and sucked.

"Oh God," she cried out, scoring her blunt nails over my scalp.

I moved to the other breast, this time allowing myself the torment of a few seconds to tug the satin aside, before claiming her tight nipple with my mouth.

"Holy crap," she burst out, clawing at the back of my shoulders.

Pain and pleasure laced through me, sinking into my balls. I drew on her flesh again, concentrated pleasure flowing through me at the feel of it in my mouth, between my teeth, against my tongue.

I don't know when I dropped to my knees, nor do I know when I peeled Chase's shorts and underpants from her. I was enveloped in a cloud of desire, an inferno of need. I'd been reduced to a creature of base function: to make her mine. To taste her, make her erupt in pleasure, to make her cry out my name as I made her come over and over.

The second my tongue swiped over the warm flesh between her thighs I lost any other reason for existing. Parting her with my thumbs, I found what I sought, and laved it with the tip of my tongue, my head spinning with the intoxicating taste and smell of her arousal.

Her fingers combed and fisted at my hair. My name fell from her over and over in rasping pants.

"Holy crap, Caden," she moaned.

I can't tell you how hard I got, how fucking stiff and excited, at the sound of my name uttered with such pleasure. I continued to worship her sex, greedy for the taste of her on my tongue and the sound of her in my ears. She rolled her hips into my swipes, her breath growing faster, shallower. Her thighs trembled against either side of my head.

"Caden," she panted. "Caden, I'm going to . . ."

I stopped, scooped her up in my arms and turned to the bed. She laughed with wicked joy as I tossed her onto it.

"Beat your chest, caveman," she ordered, grinning up at me.

I did so, hard enough to make myself cough. Chase laughed, the wonderful sound turning to fresh groans as I joined her on the bed, kneeling between her ankles to shove her thighs wide and resume my exploration of her sweet sex.

She moaned my name again, her heels digging into the duvet, her hips thrusting upward. I took advantage of the change in her position to cup her arse, squeezing each cheek as I delved into her wet heat with my tongue.

"Goddamn you, Caden," she growled. "I didn't expect you to be this . . . this . . ."

I nipped at her flesh with my teeth. She bucked, hips ramming upward, her cry raw with pleasure. And then she was coming. Her release flowed from her and I reveled in it, licking its warmth from her flesh, feasting on it.

It was her shaky, weak laughter that made me stop. With one last gentle stroke of my tongue over her sex, I lifted my head from between her thighs to watch the aftermath of her orgasm linger on her face.

Beautiful. It was beautiful. She was beautiful.

Wow, she signed, eyes closed, breath nothing more than ragged pants. I wriggled onto the bed beside her, my heart wild. My cock throbbed and pulsed, its engorged length jutting free of my open fly. I gave it a quick glance.

"Proud of yourself?"

Cheek resting on my bicep, I grinned up at her. "Hell yeah."

She laughed. I loved the sound of it.

From the floor, her mobile rang its extra-loud ring. I couldn't help myself. I rolled my eyes. "He's determined. I'll give him that."

Chase pulled a face. I waited for her to say something else. She didn't, she just let out a wobbly breath.

My cock throbbed and pulsed, impatient for attention. I ignored the damn thing. As horny as I was, I was enjoying the moment of being with Chase in her post-climax languor more. And also, to be bluntly honest, feeling very smug with myself about the fact that while Donald the Dude was trying to call her *I* was making her come.

Yes, I'm very much a twenty-three-year-old guy. We are essentially walking, talking, testosterone-fuelled egos eighty percent of the time.

When her phone fell silent, she let out another breath. I wriggled my way up beside her, making sure my cock didn't nudge or whack into her thigh as I did.

She rolled her head to the side when I was eye-level with her, her smile small but warm. "That was the most incredible orgasm I've ever had," she said.

I grinned. "Imagine what I can do when I'm not jetlagged."

She sniggered, a very naughty, very devilish snarky sound. "Imagine."

The urge to lean toward her and kiss her swept through me. Her lips were right there, so close to mine. Her eyes shone with a question and a promise that made my already hard dick harder. Her fingers were tracing a slow path up the outside of my thigh, getting dangerously close to said dick.

I pulled back and shuffled off the bed. The fact my open jeans were hanging low on my hips and my erection kept whacking about, slapping my stomach and hitching on the zip of my fly made the whole move far from elegant and graceful. I must have looked like an un-co idiot. The thing is, I wanted to kiss Chase so much it hurt, but my lips and tongue and mouth had been between her legs. I wouldn't want the taste of my release fed to me, so why would Chase?

Finally on my feet, I grabbed the waistband of my jeans and pulled them up so they weren't falling off me. "I'll be right back. Just going to freshen up before I rock your world with more of my amazing skills."

She burst out laughing. "Okay. I'm not going anywhere."

Do you have any idea how good those words were to hear? It took me exactly eight seconds to rinse my mouth and splash water over my lips and chin. I scratched my fingers into my beard and then splashed more water on my face. On the ninth second – yes, I counted them – I emerged from the bathroom.

And froze.

Chase was completely naked on the bed, stretched on her side, waiting for me. My breath caught in my throat. She was beautiful. So beautiful.

"Cat got your tongue?" she asked, lips curling.

I shook my head.

"Get over here."

I took two steps, and then froze again. "Shit." The

profanity burst from me in a sharp breath. "Shit shit shit," I repeated, scrunching up my face this time.

"Errr . . . what's going on?"

I opened my eyes and met her confused stare with a sheepish grin. "My condoms are in the Speeding Dragon."

She studied me, her expression impossible to decipher. "You think we're at the condom stage of the relationship, Caden O'Dae?"

I blinked. A hot ball of something horrible roiled in my stomach.

"Well?"

I didn't move. The ball in my stomach grew to a boulder.

And then she grinned. "Gotcha."

The air gushed from me in a whoosh. I think my ramrod stiff cock even wilted for half a second. "Bloody hell, Chase," I protested, rubbing at my stomach. "Don't do that to a guy."

She laughed. And then scrambled from the bed. "Poor Cadey," she soothed with snarky delight as she stalked toward me.

"Poor Cadey is correct." I dropped a look to my groin and then back up to her face. "We almost had a heart attack."

She rolled her eyes, slid her arms around my waist and did that incredibly sexy rise-up-onto-her-tiptoes thing where her body slides against mine, before capturing my bottom lip with her teeth and giving it a little nip.

I couldn't help but groan.

She eluded my attempt to snag her into a tight hug, however, skipping backward, her eyes dancing. "Take a load off, O'Dae," she said before spinning around to show me her back and butt. It was equally as exquisite as her front, I have to say, especially with the sexy little tattoo of a pizza-eating Buddha above her right cheek. "I'll go buy some."

The ball in my stomach turned to liquid, impatient steel in my groin.

She scooped up her shorts and slipped them on – sans undies, oh man – and then pulled her shirt over her head – sans bra, double oh man. "I'll be back," she said, raking her nails through her spikey aqua-blue hair. "Don't go anywhere."

"I'm not going anywhere," I answered, grinning at her as I made a big show of stripping off my jeans.

She rolled her eyes and grinned back.

"Course you aren't." She adjusted her shirt and slipped her feet into her sneakers. "Your passport is in the Speeding Dragon."

And with that she left, a spring in her step and a grin on her face.

I studied the closed door for a moment, and then lowered my attention to my groin again. "Stay."

My cock pulsed.

With a grunt, I finished removing my jeans, kicked them across the room and then crossed to the bed. I dropped onto it and let out a shaky sigh, slumping backward and threading my fingers behind my head.

My heart was racing. My head whirled. I stared at the ceiling, my eyes darting around the white expanse like excited insects.

Chase and I . . . Chase and I were finally going to . . . finally going to . . .

Her phone rang.

I jolted upright, looking around the room.

There. Still on the floor. She hadn't taken it with her.

For a moment, I stayed motionless, listening to Pink sing 'Walk of Shame'. A heavy pressure squeezed my chest. Was it Donald the Dude? Likely, given the time he'd expected Chase to be at his place had long gone. Should I answer it? And if I did, what would I say? What would *he* say?

The phone fell silent before I made a decision.

I studied it, the pressure on my chest growing heavier. I imagined the man sitting at a dining table with burned-down candle stumps, glaring at his phone and tapping his feet.

I grinned. And then startled when Chase's phone began ringing again. Same song.

Heart wild, gut knotting, I scrambled off the bed and hurriedly picked it up, swiping my thumb over its screen to connect the call.

"G'day," I said into the phone with as much Australian larrikin charm as I could. "Chase Sinclair's phone."

Silence answered my greeting.

My gut knotted some more. I could go two ways here: I could tell Donald the Dude to back the fuck up, that Chase wasn't his any more, or I could be the better man and play it cool.

"Is Chase there?" Donald asked. His tone screamed I-am-trying-to-be-suave-about-this.

"No, sorry," I answered. "She's out. I'll let her know you called – it's Douglas, right? – but we're going to be pretty busy when she gets back."

The click in my ear told me the conversation was over.

Shit, I really shouldn't have done that. Said that. That definitely wasn't playing it cool. And it was completely out of line. I'd have to tell Chase when she got back.

Fuck. I was an idiot.

Crossing back to the bed, I slumped onto the edge. Admitting I'd over-stepped my boundaries to Chase was going to be a serious mood killer. But I'd have to do it. I wasn't going to lie to her.

And let's face it, Donald the Dude *was* a tosser. I'd seen

how uncomfortable Chase had been at LAX when he'd touched her. He needed to get a clue and I was happy to help him do so. The guy wasn't good for her. I could see it in the tension that fell over her every time he called or sent her a text. Sure, I probably shouldn't have answered her phone, but it was the right thing to do.

As long as he left her alone now . . .

I drew a slow, deep breath and closed my eyes. I needed to refocus myself. Get my thoughts off Donald the Dude and back onto Chase. Back onto the reason she'd left the hotel room so quickly.

I needed to reclaim that buzz.

I was determined to make what was about to happen between her and I incredible. Profound. Unbelievable. I was going to move her, not just physically, but emotionally, mentally, hell, philosophically. I was going to give her so much pleasure her whole outlook on life was going to change.

I was going to . . . going to . . .

I'm pretty certain you can guess what I did, right?

I have no clue when I fell asleep, nor for how long I was in the land of Nod, but when I finally opened my eyes the bright sunshine streaming through the gauzy curtains told me it was well into morning.

I squinted at the light, completely disorientated. Shifting on the bed a little, I peered around. It seemed someone had replaced my brain with fuzzy wool while I slept. Where the hell was I?

A soft moan – no, not even a moan, a soft noise behind me stripped out the wool, replacing it with the vivid memory of the last twenty-four hours. My heart smashed up into my throat. My groin – already in its usual morning-wood state of erectness – throbbed.

Chase. Chase and me. Chase and me and the dog.

Chase and me and Disneyland.

Chase and me and orgasms.

Chase and me and the lack of condoms.

A warm arm smoothed over my hip, that soft noise – the kind a person makes when sound asleep – caressed my senses again. I couldn't help but smile. The woman I loved was in bed with me.

It was going to be a good day.

FIVE

"Money can buy you a fine dog, but only love can make him wag his tail."
~ Kinky Friedman

Chase

Confession: I've never slept with a guy. I've never fallen asleep in the same bed with a guy.

My first sexual experience was when I was seventeen. My high school's quarterback. We did it in the back of his car, or rather, his mom's car. I thought we were the classic jock-and-geek love story. Turns out, we were the bet-you-can-bang-her cliché. Also turns out he did it for twenty bucks.

How's that for ego shattering?

My next sexual experience was with Donald. In his office. Donald and I never did it in his bed. Like, ever. We did it in a motel once, near San Diego State University, but we didn't stay the night. Donald had an early lecture the next day and papers to mark. I snuck back into my room at two in the morning. Thankfully Mom and Dad didn't hear me.

Interesting enough, we *did* do it in the back of his car once as well, in the SDSU parking lot one night after I'd stayed back from class to talk to him about an assignment. It was an ostentatious black Porsche convertible. I love convertibles. Well, I used to. Now, not so much; they make me think of Donald. The roof was down and the moon was high and the air smelled of summer jasmine and a late afternoon storm. I'd come staring up at the stars, Donald's groans in my ear, his hand under my shirt, squeezing my breast. I remember thinking at the time it was the most romantic moment of my life.

God, I was deluded back then.

I wasn't sure if *this* moment was the most romantic – waking up in bed with Caden after falling asleep beside him the night before, wearing just my underpants and T-shirt and with the worst case of morning breath ever – but it sure felt . . . special.

It took me a while to comprehend where I was when I first opened my eyes, to process the strange bed, strange light, and even stranger sensation of a body beside me. But when my brain finally caught up, a goofy smile stretched my lips and my tummy fluttered with a warm yumminess I don't recall experiencing ever before.

"Morning."

I lifted my gaze from his bare chest, past his trim beard, his mouth, to his mesmerizing blue eyes.

My tummy fluttered again. So much fluttering. This time, my girly bits joined in.

"Morning," I answered. Even to my ears, my voice sounded husky and scratchy. "Have you been awake for long?"

"Not to sound like some creepy dude, but I've been watching you sleep for a while now."

I rolled my eyes, snuggling a little more onto my side and tucking my hands under my cheek. "That must have been exciting."

"It was." He grinned. "You make this sexy little snoring sound. Like this . . ."

He made the loudest, buzzing, nasal noise I've ever heard (and I've heard my dad snore – whoa). The whole bed vibrated with the force of it.

I burst out laughing, whacked him in the chest, flattened him to the bed and straddled his hips, pinning him to the mattress. "I do not snore," I protested, even as the hard pole of his erection rubbed against me. It felt good. Really good. Really *really* good. Another whoa. My whole body reacted to it.

"You do," he insisted, eyes dancing with laughter. "Like this." The earth-quaking snoring sound tore from his nose again. "It's the sexiest thing I've ever heard."

I whacked his chest again, pouting, as I wriggled on his lap. The feel of his rigid length grinding against me was delicious and exciting and damn near made me pass out with nervous anticipation. "You're not nice, O'Dae."

"I'm bloody awesome," he countered, wrapping his hands around my back to draw me down. "And apparently I have this weird snoring fetish because listening to you just now turned me on big time."

I laughed out an *ewww*, just as he flipped me onto my back and covered my body with his.

His erection nestled with perfection between my thighs, nudging at my entry with hard intention. If it weren't for my panties he would have been buried deep inside me. Of that I had no doubt.

"Sorry I fell asleep last night," he said, the laughter fading from his voice as his gaze held mine.

We'd arrived at *that* stage of flirting. The stage where it's no longer flirting and had progressed to foreplay.

Oh wow. Why did I feel like I was about to explode already?

I lifted my shoulder in a nonchalant shrug. "It's okay. It's not like I went running about buying condoms for us." I raised my eyebrows. "Oh wait, yes I did."

He chuckled – which made his cock twitch against me – and then he lowered his face until his lips were wickedly close to mine. "Let me make it up to you?"

I turned my head before he could kiss me. Instead, he kissed my cheek.

"My breath will be yucky," I said, my cheeks growing hot. Who wants to kiss a girl when she's just woken, right? We might be flirting, we might have done things with each other that were beyond flirting, and yes, he had already given me the best oral sex orgasm of my life the night before . . . but morning breath is still morning breath.

He cupped my cheek with a steady hand and returned my gaze to his. "I don't give a rat's arse," he answered, before capturing my lips with his.

His kiss was gentle. Exploratory. Not tentative, there was nothing hesitant or shy about it, but more considered and thorough.

Then his tongue found mine, his strokes modulated and intense. There were no words, no unnecessary noises or groans, just his mouth moving over mine, his tongue touching mine, sliding against it, mating with it.

I did groan then. A low vibration deep in my chest. It tingled through me, fed the desire I'd felt for this guy – this annoying, persistent, tenacious Australian – for so long I could barely remember a time when I hadn't. I raked my fingers through his beard, up the back of his neck and tangled them into his hair.

He responded by taking our kiss to the next level. His cock pulsed at the junction of my thighs. I gladly and willingly surrendered to the intoxicating mastery of his kiss, wrapping my leg around his hip and drawing him closer to my body with my calf and heel.

I didn't hear his moan of approval but I felt its tremor in his chest, pressed against my breast, so close to my heart. And then it was his hand on my breast, his fingers gentle but urgent. I arched beneath him, wanting him inside me. I wanted that so much: Caden O'Dae sinking into me, his thrusts long and slow and deep and perfect.

No, I didn't just *want* it. I needed it. I ached for it. I ached for him.

I balled my fists tighter in his hair, desperate for more. Hoping he could feel my feverish hunger in the way I rolled my hips and ground the button of my clit to his trapped erection.

He tore his mouth from mine and replaced his hand on my breast with his mouth.

I let out a cry, arching in pleasure as he drew on my nipple through my shirt. "Holy fuck, Caden," I blurted, eyes squeezed shut, fists tight in his hair.

He lifted his head, long enough for me to whimper in protest, and then he was lifting my shirt up my torso to expose my breast to his gaze. To his mouth. He drew on my nipple, nipped it, sucked it, his tongue and teeth instruments of sensations I couldn't even begin to define or explain. As insane as it sounds I orgasmed at the concentrated pleasure.

The climax shuddered through me, an intense contraction of muscles around a cock that wasn't there. I whimpered again, actually rolling my head side to side, moaning his name, clawing at his back.

He returned his attention to my mouth. For long, wonderful minutes he kissed me and worshipped my breasts. Occasionally something would tug at my soul and I'd open my eyes just as he'd lift his head and gaze down into my face, as if we were attuned with each other so much we knew when the other needed eye contact.

Those minutes would pass silently, our stares locked, our breaths mingling, a small half-smile on Caden's lips, a throbbing beat in my throat and sex, and then he would take possession of my lips or my nipple again, or I would pull him down to me and capture his mouth with my own.

I don't know how long it took before I was aching for him to penetrate me. Caden might have already given me the most amazing orgasm of my life, but my body was not sated. Not even close. I balled my fist in his hair, tearing his lips from mine. "Fuck me, Caden," I pleaded. Whoa, when had I ever pleaded for anything in my life? "Now."

He shook his head. "Nothing as base as that, Chase."

The declaration sheared through me. My heart, hell, my soul, throbbed with a warmth and joy beyond my comprehension.

I didn't stop him when he moved off the bed. I knew what he was going to get. I also knew I didn't want him to. The thought of something as impersonal and clinical as a condom separating our bodies ripped at me. I almost told him to stop, that we didn't need them, but I didn't. Sure, I was on the pill, but I was also rational enough to know so was my sister when she got pregnant with Tanner. He walked over to the table and picked up the box of Trojans I'd bought the night before.

He flicked me a quick smile. "Extra large? Is this you being hopeful?"

I laughed. "Hell yeah. Now get that shirt off and get your ass over here, O'Dae," I ordered.

He'd pulled his shirt up over his head and tossed it aside by the time he made it back to the bed. I ran my gaze over his upper body, enjoying the sight even as a part of me realized how nervous I was about looking at the rest of him. A fine smattering of honey-blond hair dusted his broad chest, trailing a path down the middle of an impressive six pack to the shallow dip of his navel and lower.

Lower.

I finally moved my gaze lower and my heart thumped faster.

I swallowed. Holy fuck, I was glad I bought extra large condoms.

Licking at my dry lips, I shifted on the bed, every part of me impatient for every part of him. He was lean and muscular and had that sexy-as-all-hell V kind of muscle thing happening near his hips that made a girl want to trace its sculpted form with her tongue.

I would do that. Later. After we'd—

Caden opened the box and withdrew a whole row of condoms. "This should get us through the next hour," he said.

I laughed, the sound becoming a whoop of surprised delight when he threw himself into the air and onto the bed. He kissed me again, but this time our bare bellies slid against each other. This time the soft hairs on his chest tickled my breasts, my nipples. Have you ever experienced that? A hairy chest rubbing against your body? It's singularly one of the most erotic and wonderful sensations I can imagine. The velvety rasp of Caden's hair against my nipples sent shock after delicious shock of pleasure and lust and hunger through me. I groaned into his mouth and wrapped my thighs around his hips. I was impatient for him to slam into me, but I was loving the hell out of our playful foreplay as well.

Finally, he broke the kiss , his eyes seeking out mine. "Are you sure?" he repeated, his murmur low enough I had difficulty hearing him.

I traced my fingers up and down his back and pulled his groin harder to mine with my legs. "I've never been surer."

With a shaky breath, he drew away from me, settling himself into a kneeling position between my spread thighs. He tore one of the square condom packets off the end of the row and opened it. As I watched him align the lubricated sheath to the tip of his erection, I noticed his hands were shaking.

He was nervous. Or overwhelmed. Or both.

Whatever it was, it detonated a fresh wave of desire for him I had no defense against.

Without a word, I sat up, plucked the condom from his fingers and smiled up at him. "Let me," I mouthed.

I had no doubt he could read my lips. His Adam's apple jerked up and down his throat and he nodded. "Okay."

Once again, I had difficulty hearing him, but I didn't need to hear him to be connected to him, to be experiencing this completely with him. I just needed him. Just Caden. Everything else was inconsequential.

Bending forward, I cupped his scrotum in one gentle hand, and then took his entire length in my mouth.

"Chase," he groaned, body trembling. "Fuck me, that's good."

I repeated the motion, reveling in the way his body reacted to my mouth, my hand.

When I sensed the quivering in his body had reached fever pitch, when his hands scored rough lines over my scalp, I

knew it was time. After all this time, we were finally going to
. . .

I withdrew my mouth from his length and then slowly
covered it with the condom.

His eyes rolled back in his head, his chest heaving, as I
reached his balls.

"I apologize in advance," he said, "for not lasting as long as
I want to."

Tight wet heat bloomed between my thighs. I affected
him so much he doubted his staying power. How many guys
did I know who would confess to something like that? It was
perfect and wonderful and it made me love him even more.

Did I say love? I mean want. Yeah. Want. It made me
want him more. So much more than I thought I ever could.

Rising up onto my knees, I brushed my lips against his. "I
consider your impending premature ejaculation the ultimate
compliment."

A shaky laugh fell from him as he smoothed his hands
over my hips and squeezed my butt. "In that case . . ."

He hooked his thumbs between the elastic of my panties and
my butt and inched them down. Over my hips, over my ass, down
my thighs, easing me down until I was flat on my back on the bed,
panties off, his condom-covered cock nudging at my entry.

His gaze found mine. His hand did the same. Our fingers
threaded together, palm to palm, and then his cock was
parting my folds.

"Harder, Caden," I moaned, the exquisite sensation of his
flesh sinking into me too much to contain. "Harder. Faster. I
want you inside me now. I want—"

He rolled his hips and slammed into me in a fluid,
powerful thrust.

Oh wow. Oh wow. Oh wow. The ability to process

thought failed me. The amazing sensation of Caden's length stretching me, filling me, blocked any intelligent response I had.

Oh wow. Oh wow. That was it. Oh wow. Over and over.

Oh my fucking God *wow*.

Staring up at him, as connected to him with our eyes as we were elsewhere, I gasped and smiled at once. "Wow," I laughed.

He grinned, his heart thumping fast in his chest against my breast, his length embedded deep inside me. "Wow is good. Wow is an understatement."

"Wow is all I've got right now," I answered, although I think the words were more a breathy moan. I squeezed my inner muscles around him, loving the way his breath hitched at the contraction, the incredible feel of his body in mine.

"Let's see if I can help out with that," he said, before slowly withdrawing and then plunging back in.

"Oh boy," I groaned, head spinning at the wave of pleasure the new invasion sent crashing through me. "Oh wow . . ."

Caden chuckled, and then took possession of my mouth as his hands explored my breasts, my waist, my hips, the backs of my thighs. I gave myself totally to the moment, undone by the sensations he awoke in me. I'd fought every feeling, every attraction I had to him since the second he'd entered my life, I'd denied what he made me feel, how he made me feel, and in doing so, I'd denied myself.

And now here I was, overwhelmed by the sheer perfection of being with him.

Clawing at his back, I arched beneath him, wanting to take him deeper. I felt his groan, felt his body react to the slight shift. His breath blasted the side of my throat, hot and wonderful and wild. His beard tickled my shoulder. His fingers teased my nipple.

We moved as one, in exquisite harmony, his thrusts driving me closer and closer to a detonation I had no freaking hope of holding at bay. He'd been the one scared of coming too soon, and yet here I was on the precipice of total eruption.

"Caden . . ." I panted against his lips, my body trembling and thrumming. "Caden . . . I'm going to . . ."

He dragged his lips up to my ear, nipped my lobe and groaned, "Oh God, gorgeous, me too."

I burst out laughing, the happy sound quickly dissolving into moans and whimpers as my orgasm shattered my world and nothing existed except the concentrated pleasure shearing through me, and Caden's breath on my neck, his hands on my body and his flesh in mine.

I laughed and came, and Caden did the same. I've never felt a more wonderful quaking of a body than I experienced then. We came together, we existed together.

And as he continued to thrust into me, as a second orgasm began to build and then erupt through me, not even the thought *oh wow* formed in my head. All there was was pleasure. Pleasure and a sense of everything being the way it was meant to be.

Caden

"Okay," I murmured, incapable of finding the energy to lift my head or raise my weight from Chase's body. "*Oh wow* definitely doesn't cut it."

She didn't respond, and I realized she hadn't heard me. I lifted my head, needing to see her face, her eyes.

"I think you destroyed any advanced vocabulary in me as well," I said when her gaze found mine.

Her chest was heaving with shallow, rapid breaths. Her lips were parted and slightly swollen from my kisses. I touched her bottom lip with my thumb, wanting nothing more than to kiss her again. So I did. My cock – still embedded inside her – pulsed against the tight heat of her sex. I'd need to move soon, to withdraw and deal with the condom, but I didn't have the strength.

Not just because I was physically drained, but because I was exactly where I wanted to be, where I'd longed to be for so many months now.

Studying my face, she smiled, at once shy and playful. "I *am* that awesome, y'know."

To prove it, she squeezed her inner muscles, sending a wave of fresh pleasure through my spent cock. I laughed, and then – as much as I didn't want to – moved off her. My body reacted to the sensation of leaving hers, giving up one last throb that was both pleasurable and torture. When a guy has reached maximum pleasure any sensory experience is insanely hyper intense.

I got up and crossed to the bathroom, where I made quick work of dispensing with the condom, and then flicked on the shower. "Join me?" I called over my shoulder.

It took a second for my post-coitus fuddled brain to realize Chase would not likely have heard me. Christ, I really was discombobulated by pleasure. Drawing a deep breath, I walked back out to the bed. Chase was lying on it, flat on her back, staring at the ceiling, drawing slow circles on her belly with her fingertips.

As I approached her, she rolled her head and smiled at me. "Did I mention I'm quite impressed with your overall package?" she said, waving a hand in the vague direction of my lower body.

"I aim to please," I said with a smile. "I also aim to shower. Want to join me?"

She shook her head. "I'm going to quickly go out and buy some clothes. I can handle not wearing underwear for the day, but I think I'd like a new shirt and jeans or something."

I let my smile turn to a dirty grin. "You realize I'm going to be horny all day knowing you won't have any undies on, right?"

She flashed her teeth at me in a grin as filthy as mine. "Hell yeah."

Laughing, I headed back for the shower.

I was dry, dressed and combing my damp hair with my fingers the bloke's way, when Chase returned. She strutted into the bathroom naked, wriggled her butt at me and squealed when I lunged for her. It was only the fact her phone started ringing that prevented me hauling her up onto the bathroom vanity and doing wicked things to her body.

"Someone's calling you," I told her, releasing her from my arms.

"Damn," she pouted, eyes twinkling. "Can you get it for me, please?"

I snatched a quick kiss, slapped her butt just below her Buddha tat and hurried out of the bathroom before she could retaliate. This was Chase after all. She would retaliate.

By the time I got to where her phone sat on the bedside table, the caller had given up. For a second the memory of my conversation with Donald the Dude the previous night haunted me, dampening my elated mood, and then Chase's phone dinged and vibrated with a message and I put thought of the professor aside. Dropping onto the edge of the bed, I picked up her mobile. It was a text from Dr. Adams, the kind of text I wanted to read. A smile spread over my face and a happy warmth flowed through me.

Doofus was doing well. We could come in and see him whenever we wanted.

I was just pondering over the fact that awesome sex with Chase had made me bloody hungry, when Chase emerged from the bathroom. I took one look at her and burst out laughing.

"What?" she asked, eyebrows high, melodramatic confusion on her beautiful face as she executed a half-pirouette.

I grinned. "Love the duds, gorgeous."

She looked down at what she was wearing. "Don't I look incredible?"

A tie-dyed purple and blue tank-style dress covered her from boobs to mid thigh, sinfully snug and sporting a gaudy image of Mickey Mouse and Pluto. Whoever the artist was, they mustn't have been exactly . . . lucid when creating the image. Mickey looked stoned and Pluto looked like an orange demon dog with a possible case of rabies.

"Something tells me," I said, "that's not official Disney merchandise."

Chase gave me another one of those naughty smiles I loved so much. "I suspect you're right. But I couldn't resist."

I ran my gaze over her. What with her wild pixie-cut hair, dyed the color of the ocean, pierced eyebrow, incredible body and long legs, she looked like a sexual deviant's ultimate Disney fantasy.

Christ, she was hot. And mine.

"Ready to go see Doofus?" she asked.

"You really not wearing any undies?" I asked in return.

For an answer, she turned, stuck her butt out at me and hitched up the hem of her new dress.

"Chase," I said, shaking my head when she turned back to

face me, "if I wasn't so damn hungry I'd do things to that hot arse of yours right now."

She strutted past me, lips twitching. "C'mon, Aussie boy. We've got a dog to see."

WE GRABBED breakfast at the International House of Pancakes next to the motel. I'd never been into an IHOP before but fuck a bloody duck, was it an experience. Who knew there were so many different ways to serve up a gallon of sugar and salt on a plate of pancakes?

Because I am a five-year-old boy at heart, I ordered a plate of chocolate choc-chip pancakes with ice cream and hot chocolate fudge sauce. With a side order of bacon and a chocolate shake.

Chase sat opposite me, watching me eat the whole thing with disbelief on her face. On the table in front of her sat a bowl of fruit salad and yogurt and a black coffee.

"I can't believe you're eating that," she said, her eyes tracking my fully loaded fork as it moved from my plate to my mouth.

I stuffed my mouth full of the sugar overload, chewed on it a few times and swallowed, grinning the whole time. "Hey, when in Rome," I said, reaching for my shake.

"What do you normally eat for breakfast?"

"Vegemite on toast," I answered, before taking a massive slurp of chocolate milk.

"What is it with you Australians and that disgusting stuff?"

I plonked my shake back down on the table. "Them's fighting words, missy."

She shook her head and chuckled. "Yeah, yeah. Just don't

ever try to make me eat it. I still can't believe Tanner, my own flesh and blood, likes it."

I scooped up another mound of chocolate choc-chip pancakes with my fork and smiled. "He's half Aussie. Of course he's going to like it. Maybe even two-thirds Aussie, if you count my brilliant bone marrow."

"Eat your sugar, weirdo," Chase ordered, lifting her coffee to her lips. "We've got a dog to get to."

As much as I enjoyed my somewhat indulgent breakfast, I must admit I was regretting it a few hours later. Standing in the Laguna Niguel Animal Hospital, with its distinct smells, my stomach was making it very clear it wasn't happy with me.

Doofus, however, was.

We stood beside his cage, Chase crooning about how awesome he was as I checked his chart. His readings were good, although his temperature wasn't behaving the way it was meant to. His core temp was still high, and according to Dr. Adams, he was refusing water and food. Not what I wanted to hear, but not overly worrying. Not yet, at least. If he continued to do so tomorrow, he'd need a drip.

A part of my mind added up the costs incurred so far. Dr. Adams hadn't mentioned payment, but I doubted he'd be treating Doofus for free. Which meant this trip to the States was costing me a fortune. Ouch.

At the slight brush of Chase's shoulder against mine, I turned, watching her rub her forehead against Doofus's through the bars, her eyes closed, her smile wide and genuine and totally beautiful. A fortune, but completely worth it.

I'd just double my paid intern hours with Briny when I got home. While I was completing my doctorate. And prepping for my mid-year exams.

Oh man.

Maybe I could work off some of the bill via unpaid work

at the clinic? I was about to tell Chase I was going to go have a chat with Dr. Adams when her mobile phone started vibrating in her bag followed by the familiar loud ring.

It had taken a few incoming calls on Chase's mobile for it to dawn on me that when Donald the Dude called, her phone played Pink's 'Walk of Shame', most recently last night while she was out buying condoms.

A thick lump filled my throat. Guilt and anger threaded through me.

Doofus's ears dropped close to his head, a low whine coming from him.

A strange stillness fell over Chase and she chewed on her lip, scratching his neck. I wanted to ask her if she was going to pick up the phone, but at the same time couldn't bring myself to utter a word.

I'd yet to tell her about my chat with the professor last night. I should have by now. The fact I hadn't was slack. Possibly even deceptive.

I should have told her before we had sex this morning, but I'd allowed myself to get caught up in the moment. Or maybe I was just letting myself think it was the moment that had prevented me from telling her. Maybe it was really the fact I knew she wasn't going to be happy.

Maybe it was the fact I was protecting her from confusion and she hated being protected.

Maybe I was being selfish . . .

Fuck.

As we stood there, Doofus's tail thumping gently and his ears flat to his head, the song filled the silence. I waited for Chase to get it. She didn't.

Finally, silence resumed, as much as an animal hospital can be silent. Dogs whined, barked, cats meowed, birds chirped and squawked. I'm positive I heard the distinct screech of a sulphur-crested cockatoo coming from one of the other areas in Recovery.

Sliding Chase a sideways look, I returned Doofus's chart to its hook on the front of his cage.

Christ, I had to tell her.

"Chase . . ." I said, my voice a husky scratch.

Her chest rose and fell with a shaky breath, and then she was talking to Doofus again. "We'll bring you back something yummy to eat," she told him, scratching at his ears, which were once again in a happier position. "Grilled cheese, maybe?"

"Reckon we could find some Vegemite around here?" I asked, needing to break the tension trying to replace our earlier ease. I'd tell her later. I would. Along with the fact giving a dog bread wasn't a good idea, especially a sick dog. I think showing off my vet knowledge now was probably not good timing.

Timing. Huh. It seemed me and timing weren't on the best of terms at the moment.

She shot me a mock glare. "We're wanting him to live, not die of poisoning."

I laughed. She smiled. And then frowned when her phone vibrated and pinged with an incoming message.

"You should get it," I suggested, even as the words scraped at me like razorblades.

An unreadable expression fell over her face. She studied me, as if looking for something in my eyes, and then withdrew her phone from her bag.

You have no freaking clue how much I wanted to read the message. I mean, if you had to rate it on a scale of one to ten, one being a curious itch, and ten being an imperative so vital the very fabric of existence was at risk, it was a fifty.

I stubbornly fixed my stare on Doofus.

The tones of her typing out a reply drilled into me, each key-strike a blow against my confidence and ego. It was stupid. For all I knew, she might have been telling Donald the Dude she'd just had the best sex of her life and it wasn't with him so would he mind pissing off and leaving her alone. My fragile male ego, however, was concocting other messages. Messages that created a heavy lump in my throat and a churning knot in my gut.

If anyone tells you love makes you invincible, tell them they're full of shit. Love makes you paranoid and insecure and nervous you're going to fuck it all up and lose the best thing that's ever happened to you.

From the corner of my eye I saw Chase return her phone to her bag. Pink started singing almost straightaway. Doofus whined, his ears drooping again.

Chase didn't answer it. Instead, she turned and offered me a wry smile. "Let's see if there's anything we can do here to work off Doofus's bill."

My chest tightened. We were so perfect for each other. We thought the same way, approached problems the same way . . . The difference between us was I didn't have another interested party circling me like a shark.

There was little I could do about that, except stay true to who I was and stick to the course I'd mapped out, which was basically being myself. If I couldn't convince Chase we were meant for each other by being me, then why should she be with me when I wasn't?

For the next three hours, Chase cleaned out all the animal cages and environs, and I performed basic medical check-ups on recovering animals, and did an inventory of the small animal vaccinations.

Before we left, Chase snuggled into Doofus one last time. She murmured things to him I didn't hear. Chase doesn't murmur often. It took me a few months of knowing her to realize it was a hearing thing. I've seen her murmur to Tanner, and once she murmured something to Amanda that made her roll her eyes and shake her head, but that was about it.

No under-the-breath mutterings, no secretive whispers. When Chase wants to say something, she does. Whatever she was saying to Doofus, it was accompanied by a gentle stroke of his shoulder, her eyes closed. The sight filled my throat with a thick lump.

Animals and Chase. My emotional downfall? Or my emotional strength?

We spent the rest of the afternoon sightseeing. Chase took me to all the tourist traps. I posed in front of the Chinese Theatre on Hollywood Boulevard, I planted my hands in Hugh Jackman's handprints and grinned cheesily. We ate what was either a really late lunch or a really early dinner at the Nickel Diner, which was just as fantastic as Yelp claimed. We found Robert Downey Jnr's star on the Walk of Fame and I realized just how big a geek Chase was when she actually laid down on the footpath beside it and had me take her photo. Of course, she got to see my geeky side in full force when we found Patrick Stewart's star and I spent the next hour dropping quotes from both Star Trek and the X-Men movies.

When she responded to one of mine with the appropriate quote, I had no choice but to haul her to my body and kiss her. It was the first real contact we'd shared since her text conversation with Donald the Dude. I want to say she didn't stiffen a little when I did it, I really do. I want to say that more than anything.

Unfortunately, I can't. Something had happened; a dark cloud had fallen over her heart, her mind, and I didn't know what to do about it.

I sure as hell knew, no matter how much I wanted to, I couldn't tell her about taking the guy's call the night before. Not while she was unsettled.

Was I being a coward? Probably. Putting off the inevitable? Definitely.

Making it worse for myself? Yeah. I was making it worse for myself.

But I hated the thought of upsetting her. I can't stress that enough. Hated it. I didn't just want to protect Chase from any physical harm or mental harm that came her way, I wanted to shield her from emotional pain as well.

So I stayed mum on the subject, doing my best to ignore the lump of guilt building in my gut.

It didn't help when I made the mistake of leaning over to her while we were watching a street performer at Santa Monica Pier, and whispering in her ear how talented the guy was. She jerked away from me, eyes wide, confusion on her face. It was then I realized what I'd done. I'd whispered in the ear that was completely deaf. Shit. What was wrong with me? How could I be so stupid?

"Sorry," I blurted, my chest tight. "Sorry, I—" I bit back the word *forgot* before it could leave my lips.

She studied me, her expression unreadable, and then turned back to the street performer. "It's okay," she said, a small smile curling at the corner of her lips.

I let out a ragged breath. I rarely forgot about Chase's hearing impairment. It wasn't necessarily in my thoughts constantly – she was Chase Sinclair, Amazing Girl to me, not Chase Sinclair, Deaf Girl – but it was like a distant notion in the back of my head most of the time. Forgetting now, whispering into the ear that was completely deaf . . . I couldn't help but feel like I'd somehow been insensitive.

The slip niggled at me, an itch that wouldn't go away, for the drive back to the hotel.

I chatted the entire trip, making inane observations about LA, the traffic, and any animal I happened to see. I know an embarrassing amount of trivia about animals and have a habit of sharing with whoever happens to be near me when I see one. We passed a Labrador (Did you know Labradors have webbed toes to help them swim faster?); a Poodle (The Poodle actually originated in Germany, not France. The French love the dog so much, however, they made it their national dog); a Clark's Grebe (The collective noun of the grebe genus of birds is a "water dance"); and of all things, a giraffe traveling in a trailer marked *L.A. Zoo* (Did you know that in Atlanta, Georgia, it's illegal to tie a giraffe to a telephone pole or street lamp?). I babbled the whole time. There really was no other word for it. Babbled. Like the idiot I was.

Chase hadn't stopped me babbling, but she hadn't really engaged in it either. Her responses had been distant, almost disconnected, like she was lost in thought.

You have no idea how hard that was. As a guy, I want to fix things, it's what guys do. As a guy madly in love with her, I knew if I pushed her I'd lose any chance of being with her completely.

So I continued to babble. Like an idiot. The one consolation I took was that Chase didn't pull up to the curb at any stage and tell me to get out. That was something.

The sun was well and truly below the horizon when we arrived back at the motel. We climbed out of the Speeding Dragon in silence. It had been a long trip back. We'd planned to change motels so we could be closer to Doofus but hadn't gotten around to it yet.

A cool night breeze blew at us as we approached our room, a chilly reminder it was late fall in Southern California.

I was trying to suppress my shiver when Chase paused opening the door. Still gripping the handle, she gave me a look over her shoulder. "Kiss me? Please?"

"Okay," I said, before closing the distance between us and brushing my lips over hers. As much as I wanted to take her into my arms and show her how much I desired her, loved her, I kept the kiss as tender and sweet and gentle as I could.

I stepped back. The lights from the motel danced in the depths of her eyes, hiding whatever she was thinking from me.

Her lips curled in a slow smile I had no hope of deciphering, and then she let out a ragged sigh. "Let's go in."

She headed straight for the bathroom. I sank into the room's only armchair, a turbulent, unsettled mess.

It had definitely been a day I wouldn't forget. A day that had started with a bang and looked to be ending with a strained whimper. There were moments in it that would rank up there with my favorites, and I wasn't just thinking of the incredible sex we'd shared that morning. Moments when we were at the hospital, where our eyes would connect through the bars of an animal's cage, and we would both smile.

Moments of connections more than just sexual. Moments that seemed tainted by the unavoidable, invisible presence of Donald the Dude.

What should I do about that? Clearly my little chat with him hadn't warned him off. Every fiber in my body wanted to take Chase's phone, call him up and tell him to fuck off. But then every fiber in my body clearly wanted me to get a black eye from Chase for doing so.

Still, that didn't stop my fantasizing about coming face-to-face with the guy again. About introducing my fist to his jaw. Hey, I'm a guy. A nice guy, to be sure, but I've still got testosterone to spare and the girl I loved to protect, and everything about Donald the Dude screamed *jerk*. But there was more to their relationship than Chase had let on. I don't think there was a malicious reason behind her lack of sharing about their past, but he definitely had a tapped line to her emotions, if not her heart.

Fuck.

I was mid ponder – eyes closed, hands hanging loosely over the arms of the chair, legs splayed – when Chase straddled my lap. Warm and naked Chase.

I gazed up at her, my hands automatically moving to her hips, up her back.

Her skin had that velvety softness that comes with having a warm shower. She smelled like soap, and Chase, and heaven. Her hair was damp, her eyelashes spikey with water. Her lips were parted. She watched me. Neither of us spoke.

Neither of us made a sound as I drew upright and took her nipple in my mouth. I worshipped her breasts, her throat, her chin, her lips, with my mouth and hands and lips.

She held me, hands in my hair, thighs hugging my hips, sex pressed to my groin. At some point, I removed my jeans. Or maybe Chase did. Or we both did. My jeans ended up off, a condom ended up on my dick, and we were making love.

I used to cringe when I'd hear that term: making love. But that's what this was. There was no other way to describe it.

It was beautiful. Powerful.

We didn't speak, just held each other's gaze as she rode my body, and I thrust up inside her. We both came, her a microsecond before me, and even that was quiet. Profound and potent, unlike any sex I'd had before. More than sex. More than a physical act. So much more.

Finally, as the contractions of her sex around my dick grew as erratic as my upward thrusts, she arched on my lap and let out a hitching moan.

I flattened my palms to her back, drove harder, faster up

into her, my release a fierce river flooding from me, and pressed my lips to her ear. "I love you, Chase," I whispered, lost to the raw pleasure, the pure sensation, the words barely more than ragged pants. "I love you, I love you so fucking much."

She didn't reply. Instead, she clung to me, her heat constricting around my length, and then slumped against me, burying her face into the side of my neck.

It wasn't until I awoke hours later, when the morning sun was streaming through the window, that I realized what I'd done: whispered in her deaf ear. Poured out my heart, confessed how I really felt for her on a breath she would have felt but not heard.

Fuck, way to mess up the moment, dickhead.

I looked around the motel room, eyes scratchy, and realized Chase wasn't there.

I was alone.

SIX

"Dogs never bite me. Just humans."
~ Marilyn Monroe

Chase

Waiting in the reception area of the animal hospital for Dr. Adams, I stared at the message I'd just typed on my cell. The words blurred. It's surprising how difficult it is to read small black letters on a white screen when your eyes are full of hot, stinging tears.

I read the words I'd written again. My chest felt like it was being crushed by an invisible weight.

It's over. I can't do this anymore.

The sentence danced into black smudges as I blinked, and then cleared into sharp focus again. I stared at the words, branded them into my brain, my heart, and then hit Send. My cell vibrated in the way it does to let me know my message was on its way to its recipient. What would he do when he got it?

I shoved my cell into my pocket and rubbed the back of

my hand over my eyes. Behind the counter, the same temp watched me with open curiosity, her gaze constantly flicking to my ears. What did she think I was going to do? Grow new ones?

Turning my back on her, I stared out the window at the parking lot and attempted to regain some control of my emotions. Would Caden be awake yet? Had he got my message? How was he going to react when he did? What was he going to do?

I swallowed, feeling like I was about to explode. I hadn't really thought through what I was doing this morning when my cell had pinged with an incoming message. Caden had been so deeply asleep he hadn't moved, hadn't stirred when it pinged again.

I'd been lying beside him, trying to work out what the hell I was doing. Not just with Caden, but with me. With everything...

Two nights in a row spent with him in a motel room. Two nights of not going home. Two nights of ignoring Dad's texts, and replying to Mom's with *I'm okay. Mom. Don't worry about me.*

Two nights in Caden's arms, singularly the most wonderful place I've ever fallen asleep.

And then, yesterday, I'd foolishly let myself read one of Donald's texts. It was an eloquent one. Long for him.

I miss you, babe. I've been thinking a lot of how badly I treated you. I know you were too good for me, and I'm not surprised there are other men wanting you. But do those other men give you what you really want? I can. If you give me another chance. Please, give me another chance. I miss you. D.

Other men. I didn't need to be a genius to know he was referring to Caden.

My stomach had knotted, a moment of guilt so potent it

physically sickened me. Standing in the animal hospital beside Doofus's cage, with Caden right next to me, I'd wanted nothing more than to throw my cell across the small room and have it smash against the wall. How dare he do this to me again? How dare he.

Heart wild, I'd tapped back a simple response.

Donald, I can't keep playing this game. It's destroying me. Please stop.

I ignored everything he'd sent after that. In fact, I'd shut my cell off. I didn't need it. I was confused enough without his contributions. I'd been hell bent on keeping Caden at arm's length and yet, here I was, doing the exact opposite.

Yeah, me and confusion were on really close terms.

Those close terms got even closer when I'd asked Caden to kiss me. When I climbed onto his lap . . .

Goddamn it, I was falling in love with him. What the hell was I doing?

I didn't sleep much after that. My head was a turbulent mess of confusion and uncertainty when my cell pinged in the morning.

Trying not to disturb him, I'd grabbed it up and read the message from Dr. Adams. And then scrambled to my feet as quickly as I could, chest tight.

Doofus was deteriorating.

I'd located my discarded clothes and pulled them on. Caden had continued to sleep. Chewing on my bottom lip, I'd touched his knee. He didn't wake. I'd squeezed his thumb and given his hand a bit of a shake. He still didn't wake. Clearly he was exhausted.

I knew the feeling. I was emotionally drained from the last forty-eight hours. Caden was probably physically drained as well. Jetlagged. Exhausted. And dealing with my shit without a word.

He knew Donald was messing with my head. He knew I was confused. He knew all that, and yet he continued to be Caden – the guy I'd tried to convince myself I didn't want anything to do with.

Huh. We'd so moved beyond that. We'd so moved beyond "Caden O'Dae could bite me." He had. More than once, exquisite nips of my lips, my nipples, my shoulder, my hip . . . He'd made me feel incredible. Special. Beautiful.

And he'd whispered something in my completely deaf ear. Twice.

It hadn't worried me at all the first time. Not at all. In fact, it had filled my tummy with a lovely warmth. He would have only slipped up like that if my hearing issues meant nothing to him. With a lifetime of being defined by my poor hearing by those around me, someone forgetting it was pretty close to wonderful.

But that wonderful feeling only confused me more when it came to what my end goal with Caden had originally been: to not fall for him.

When he'd whispered in my deaf ear while we were making love however . . . that messed me up. Not because *he* forgot, but because *I* couldn't hear him.

I couldn't hear him. I couldn't hear the words he was sharing with me.

Words I'm sure, in my heart and soul, were words more important and profound than any ever uttered to me before. And I *couldn't hear them*.

I couldn't hear them because I was defective. Faulty.

How could I expect Caden to deal with that, when I couldn't deal with it?

I know it's wrong to let something like that fuck me up, but it did. It made me even more confused about who I was.

He'd whispered to me last night, as we came together.

Whispered words I didn't hear. Words I wanted to hear so badly, even as I argued with myself that I didn't.

He'd moved from the chair to the bed, while I'd cleaned my teeth, staring at my reflection in the mirror, trying to fathom what was going on in my head. I'd come out of the bathroom and found him asleep on "his" side, snoring softly. The fact we already had sides filled me with a happiness I didn't want to think about.

My lips had curled into a smile before I realized it. So much for not succumbing to Caden's charms. I'd smiled more since he arrived, laughed more, *felt* more than I had in months. Since the moment Donald told me it was over, in fact.

Did this mean I was acknowledging Caden was more to me than just an acquaintance? Could I maintain that simple concept any longer, when I'd been the one who practically dragged him into a motel room? When I'd lost myself to the pleasure of his touch? When I'd bolted from the room in search of condoms to take our relationship to a level I had previously sworn had no hope of occurring?

Without any answers presenting themselves, only more questions I wasn't ready to deal with (like, did I *really* want to be in a relationship with a guy who lived on the other side of the world?), I'd curled up on my side of the bed, facing him, and fallen asleep.

My dreams had been . . . disconcerting. In them, Caden and Donald played what I think was chess, although every move resulted in them inflicted with wounds from invisible blows, until they were both bloody, bruised and whining. And during the whole game the sound of blaring car horns wailed constantly.

I don't remember who won the game, only that I wished the car horns would stop and the whining would cease.

The need to pee had woken me before the victor claimed his prize – which I think was me. My heart a thumping hammer in my ears, I'd climbed from the bed, padded to the bathroom and peed, and then returned to the bed.

I didn't go back to sleep. Instead, I watched Caden, tracing his face with my eyes. I knew it so well by now, and yet, lying there watching him sleep, I noticed things I hadn't noticed before. Like the occasional strands of ginger-gold in his trim beard, like the dark-honey straightness of his eyebrows. Like the way the lashes at the very edges of his eyes curled so much more than the rest.

I think I could have lain there forever just looking at him, my mind disconnected from reality, drifting instead on an intangible mist of what could be a wonderful thing . . .

And then the message from Dr. Adams had arrived:

Need you here ASAP. Your dog's vitals are critical.

I'd spun into some kind of panic mode. I can't really explain it. I'd attached a ridiculous amount of emotion to that dog in a short space of time. The fact he wasn't doing well . . .

Before truly considering the consequences of my actions, and not wanting to disturb Caden from the sleep he so obviously needed, I'd scribbled the word *vet* on the motel-supplied note pad and then left, driving straight to the animal hospital. Doofus needed to see someone who loved him, and I know it makes fuck-all sense, but I was in love with that dog already.

Along the way I'd received three messages from Donald – all wondering where I was and asking when he could see me again – and ignored four incoming calls from him. I wish I could tell you the sight of his name on my cell's screen didn't bother me but unfortunately, I'd be lying if I did. Despite everything that had happened between me and Caden, the second Donald's name appeared on my screen my tummy twisted into a granny knot that would give a knot expert a migraine.

Something had to be done about it. Standing in the reception area, waiting for Dr. Adams to arrive, I'd typed out the last text I ever intended to send to Professor Douchebag – *It's over. I can't do this anymore.*

So there I was, expecting Donald's response, my stare fixed outside, my pulse crazy, when a hand touched the back of my right shoulder with gentle pressure.

I spun around in a wild semi-pirouette, chest tight.

Dr. Adams smiled, and then gave me a confused frown. "Where's Caden?"

"Asleep."

His eyebrows rose.

"He's jetlagged," I said quickly. "He only landed in LA two mornings ago."

Dr. Adams held up a hand, as if sensing the agitation in my voice. "It's okay, Chase. Unfortunately, there's nothing he can do here anyway."

The knot in my stomach turned into a seismic ache. "Is Doofus . . . is he still alive?"

Dr. Adams nodded, but I saw no hope in his eyes.

"Can I see him?"

"He's not good, Chase," he cautioned.

"I watched my baby nephew almost die from leukemia," I shot back, frustration slicing at me like hot razor blades. "I can handle seeing a dying dog."

Dr. Adams frowned, and then nodded. He held out his arm toward the door behind the counter. My feet didn't want to move. My eyes burned, the tears I'd only just reigned in once more threatening to undo me.

In my pocket, my cell pinged and vibrated into life.

Dr. Adams looked at me. "When you're ready, Chase," he murmured.

Giving him a jerky nod, I pulled out my phone and looked at the screen. Donald had sent me a text.

Seeing you at the airport made me realize how much I miss you, babe. Please believe me when I say I will make amends for hurting you. I want you back. I will fight for you if I have to. I will chase you. I need you. I will look after you. Protect you. D.

I read those eight sentences three times, my head roaring. The biting taint of disinfectant filled my every breath. I was about to shove my cell back into my pocket when it vibrated in my hand.

I know you were with the Australian. I understand. And forgive you. D.

Angry flooded through me. Both at Donald *and* myself.

Forgive me? He was going to *forgive* me? For being with Caden? Professor Douchebag was going to forgive *me*? Where the freaking fuck did he get off telling me he *forgave* me?

I was very much *with* the Australian. There was no denying it. Not after the last two nights. Very much with him and very much contemplating being with him even more, so why the hell was my heart thumping so hard at the words *I miss you*? From Donald? Why the hell was my tummy clenching at *I will make amends*? And what the fuck was my body doing reacting to *I will look after you. Protect you*?

What the fuck was wrong with me? Why did he make me feel this . . . this stupid, messed-up, pathetic, ridiculous desire for him?

No, desire was wrong. Desire is too strong a word, too positive. It wasn't desire, it was a craving. The kind a junkie experienced when desperate for a hit of the very thing they know is going to kill them. I hated that sensation. It tainted everything else.

Fuck.

I'd deal with Donald later. After this. Right now, all I knew was that a dog I barely knew, a dog that had been rejected, was dying and alone.

Alone and in pain.

Jesus.

Ramming my cell into my pocket, I smiled a wavery smile at Dr. Adams. He touched my shoulder, his answering smile sad, and walked us out the back. Little Miss Regrowth tracked my path the whole way, curiosity on her face.

The stench of animal faces assaulted me the second we passed through the door to the back section. I tried not to gag but failed. The smell in an animal hospital is seriously worse than the smell in a pet shop, trust me. Maybe it has something to do with all the drugs and medication the animals are on.

As I crossed to Doofus's open cage, he rolled his dark liquid-brown eyes at me and thumped his tail.

"Hey boy," I whispered. "I'm here."

Doofus thumped his tail again. That was his only movement.

"What happened?" I asked, feathering my palm over his side as I looked at Dr. Adams. "I thought he was recovering? Yesterday he was so good."

"Doofus became dehydrated and seemed weak and uninterested in food or water. Not a good sign," he said. "Unfortunately, we think he's suffering from a post-op infection. The vet on duty last night, Dr. Simmons, administered intravenous antibiotics, but so far Doofus is not responding the way he should. Sometimes this happens to big dogs when they try to move. Unfortunately, because Doofus doesn't have a properly formed back leg his weight redistribution has caused uneven movement."

"So he's dying because he's defective?" The question coated my mouth in bile.

Of course, that wasn't the case. Doofus was dying because he sustained massive injuries from being hit by a car. But my brain didn't want to let me see that. My brain wanted me to see a dog who was getting kicked by life over and over because he was like me – not functioning properly.

Dr. Adams's chest rose and fell with a sigh I didn't hear. Pity filled his eyes as his focus flicked to my ears, just for a second. "No, Chase," he said. "He's not dying because he's defective. And as long as he can start responding to the antibiotics, there's a very good chance he's not dying, period. We have to wait and see. And pray."

I scrunched up my face and turned back to Doofus. Pray. Huh. Praying had done sweet F A for me when I was a little girl, begging God to make my ears work so my daddy wouldn't be so disappointed with me. Praying had done even less when I'd tried once again to beg Him to take Tanner's leukemia away.

Yeah, praying wasn't an option.

Stroking Doofus's side, I bit at the inside of my lip and blinked at my tears. Life is a fucking big pile of poo sometimes.

In my back pocket, my cell pinged again. Doofus pricked his ears. Not a lot, but a little. His eyes rolled toward me again, and once more his tail moved slightly.

Until that point in time I didn't think it possible to miss someone like I missed Caden. I wanted him there so much. I needed him there. To comfort the dog he'd saved, to say goodbye to him. To hold me and tell me it was going to be okay. I needed more than anything to press my cheek to his chest and feel the words vibrating against my ear.

Why hadn't I woken him? Why was I doing this alone?

My phone pinged again. Doofus's ears pricked as before, and then he closed his eyes.

My heart stopped. "Doofus?" I whispered.

He opened his eyes. I wasn't an animal expert like Caden, but I could tell they weren't working properly.

"What are his chances if he doesn't start responding?" I asked, without looking at Dr. Adams.

If he answered, I didn't hear him. At times being Hard of Hearing is a blessing. Instead, I felt his answer in a warm hand on my arm. And then I felt it in the way he walked away and left me alone.

Life is fucking horrible. I pressed my forehead to Doofus's and closed my eyes. I'm not sure how long I stayed there for. Long enough for the tears leaking from my eyes to dry to taut tracks of salt on my cheeks. Long enough for me to decide I hated the world. It sucked. The world laughed at any attempts we made to exist in it without pain. Just when we thought we had the world figured out, what our job was in it, it ripped that misguided knowledge away from us.

When I finally lifted my head, Doofus licked my fingers and wagged his tail slightly. I wished he hadn't. It only made my heart hurt more.

"We could have been so awesome together," I whispered.

He licked my fingers again. I couldn't help but notice how dry his tongue was. I wished Caden was here to tell me what that meant.

I turned and walked away from Doofus. I had to. I couldn't stay there any longer. Back in the waiting room my cell vibrated in my pocket. I ignored it. There was no one I wanted to talk to at the moment.

Okay, that was bullshit. I wanted to talk to Caden. I fixed my burning eyes on the brunette strip of hair belonging to

Little Miss Regrowth and tapped my fingers on the smooth surface of the counter.

She jerked her head up, discomfort and trepidation on her face. "Yes?" she shouted.

The urge to shake her crashed through me. Thankfully, I ignored that as effectively as I ignored my buzzing phone. "Can you please let Dr. Adams know I've left?"

"Sure," she continued to shout. "Is the dog dead?"

I studied her, then leaned a little closer toward her. "What do you want to do with your life?"

She blinked. "What?"

"Because whatever it is," I continued, "make sure you don't have to interact with people. Because you suck at it."

Not waiting for her response, I turned and left.

The morning sun lashed at me as I crossed the parking lot, bouncing off the Speeding Dragon's windshield in blinding shards. I winced and squinted. Great. There went another one of my working senses.

I shoved my hand into my bag to retrieve my sunglasses when my cell started vibrating in my pocket once more. Pulling my hand out of my bag, I dug out my phone and rammed it to my ear. "Stop calling me," I snarled.

"It's tricky for me to make you forgive me," Donald's smoke-and-whiskey voice rumbled in my ear, "if you don't come to see me when you promise."

I froze, my heart pounding in my chest like a goddamn cannon. And then I let out a hitching whimper when a taxi drew to a halt directly in front of me and Caden climbed from the back seat.

Caden

I hadn't gotten a US SIM card for my phone yet. I'd intended to get one at LAX but when I'd found Chase with Donald the Dude that plan had gotten lost in my head. Then I'd planned to get one soon as we arrived in San Diego, but Doofus had entered our life and once again, I'd forgotten all about it.

Fortunately I've got an iPhone, which means as long as I've got a Wi-Fi connection I can text and FaceTime for free to other iPhone users. Thank you, Steve Jobs. That meant Mum and Dad back in Australia could chat to me as often as they liked while I was over here.

On the assumption my phone was charged, of course. Which it wasn't. It had been over forty-eight hours since I touched down and the thought of charging my phone hadn't crossed my mind. Thank God I'd asked Brendon to let Mum and Dad know I'd arrived and was A-OK.

So when I woke up to find Chase AWOL I did more than kick myself that I'd yet to plug my phone into a power point. I'm not going to tell you what I said. Probably better you hang onto the idea I'm a civilized person in crisis for a while longer. Nor do you want to hear what I said as I upended my bag, searching for the universal adaptor I'd brought with me from Australia.

I set my phone to charge and then stomped around the motel room for a bit, frowning at everything. Discovering I had no way of contacting Chase directly was frustrating. Especially after yesterday. It didn't occur to me to use the landline in the motel room. I'm going to blame being half asleep and flustered beyond all logical thought.

It took me longer than it should have to find the message from her on the notepad. The penny dropped a second after my brain processed the bad news about Doofus: Chase must have gone to the animal hospital.

How do I know this?

A little backstory about my past experience with Chase, if I may.

The day after my bone marrow had been transplanted into Tanner, I had a reaction to the general anesthesia. Classified as severe hypothermia, I had chills and was shivering so badly my body began to shut down. Scared the crap out of me.

Suffice to say, when I began to lose feeling in my extremities and couldn't breathe properly, I was rushed to the ER. By the time I arrived, I was convulsing violently. When all this happened, Chase was at work at the pet shop. I'm not sure why, but Amanda sent her a text telling her I was on the way to hospital. At this point in our relationship, Chase had rarely acknowledged my existence with anything other than the odd grunt, rolled eyes and sarcastic snipes about my beard.

Apparently the second she got the text, she bolted from the pet shop – mid interaction with a customer who was, according to Brendon, buying a sulphur-crested cockatoo for $450 dollars, a bird so common in Australia it's considered a pest.

I regained consciousness in the hospital with a burning throat and a gnawing hunger, to find a scowling Chase sitting beside my bed. She denies it, but Amanda tells me she sat there the entire time I was out of it, complaining about how goddamn inconsiderate I was and how she'd lost a sweet commission on a sale.

When I came to, she grunted at me, told me I needed a haircut and left. I didn't see her for the rest of the time I was in hospital.

That's Chase. She's impulsive. She springs into action the second her gut tells her to. Her heart is massive no matter how much she tries to convince people otherwise.

The second I read the word *vet* written on the notepad, I knew exactly where Chase was. I'm not going to lie, relief rushed through me for a selfish moment. She hadn't taken off because of us, she'd taken off because Doofus was in trouble.

I dressed quickly, and checked my phone. 12% charge. That would have to do.

Thanking God for free motel Wi-Fi, I tapped out a text to Brendon telling him Doofus had taken a turn for the worst and I wasn't sure when I'd get to San Diego. I stuffed my phone, charger and adaptor into my duffle bag and then hailed a taxi. I told the driver I was in a hurry and then sat in the back for the entire trip, fidgeting with worry. Freaking LA traffic meant it took me longer than I hoped to get there. Seriously, LA traffic is insane. How do people not go crazy? Peak-hour traffic in Melbourne is like a trickling stream compared to LA.

Chase was out the front of the Laguna Niguel Animal Hospital when my taxi pulled up in the parking area. I knew before opening the door she was not in a good place, emotionally. What I didn't know was why, but I hoped to hell it was something I could fix. Or at least, something I could help her through. I've been the emotional support for more than one pet owner who's had to say goodbye to their beloved animal, and while I wanted nothing more than to walk into Dr. Adams' clinic and see Doofus alive and well, I was bracing myself for the fact that wasn't the case, and that Chase had been there to see him pass. Or worse still, when he was euthanized.

I didn't want her experiencing that kind of emotional hell. It sucks. It hurts. It tears you apart and leaves you feeling raw. And given Chase had ridden the emotional rollercoaster of Tanner's battle with leukemia right along side her sister, being with the dog she'd helped save when it was put to sleep – a dog with a disability that I suspected Chase felt a powerful affinity for – would be enough to break her heart all over again.

I paid the driver and closed the cab door, my eyes locked on her face. I crossed to where she stood, watching me, her mobile clamped to the side of her head. My gut clenched into a cold ball when she turned her back to me.

"I wanted to be here, Donald," I heard her say into the phone.

Great. Donald the Dude was in her ear. Great. Fucking great.

"I know," she said, still with her back to me. Discomfort radiated from her. She gripped her upper arm with fingers that were white. "Yes, I know. But I—"

He said something to make her fall quiet. To make her shoulders slump. I had no idea what it was, but I wanted to punch him for it. I'm not a violent person, hell, even on the rugby field I'm more about speed and fancy footwork than brute force and crunching bones, but right at that moment the need to smash my fist into Donald the Dude's perfect jaw almost crippled me.

I stopped a few feet from Chase, chest tight, and watched her. She shuffled her feet and shook her head. It was a weird habit she had – shaking her head while on the phone when the person on the other end had no hope of seeing it. I found it completely endearing.

"Why?" she said suddenly. An uneasy prickling heat crept up the back of my neck and over my scalp at the harrowed conflict in her voice. "I don't understand, Donald. After all this time, why are you so determined to—"

She stopped, nodding her head.

"Okay," she said finally.

Holy fuck, I didn't like the sound of that word passing her lips – lips I'd tasted only the night before.

"No, I don't think I will. I've told you we're done. I can't keep doing . . . Okay, I'll *call* you when I get—"

For whatever reason, she didn't say the word *back*. What she did do was hang up and shove the phone into her pocket.

I waited until she turned to face me. When her eyes found mine, I offered a gentle smile. "You weren't there when I woke. Is everything okay?"

She shook her head. "No. Doofus has an infection."

I wanted to tell her I was asking about her, about *us*, but I didn't.

"An infection?" I echoed. "I'm assuming he's now on antibiotics?"

She nodded this time. Agitation radiated from her, thick and disquieting.

"It's going to be okay," I said, smoothing my palms up her arms as I smiled again. "Trust me."

A shaky sigh fell from her. "Caden . . ." she began.

Pink started singing 'Walk of Shame' from her pocket.

Before I could stop it, I rolled my eyes and let out an exasperated growl. "The guy doesn't take a hint, does he?"

Chase frowned. "What do you mean?"

I swallowed. "Do you want to get it? Answer it? If you don't, I guarantee he'll ring again in a few seconds. I've noticed he does that."

I was starting to get angry, which was worrisome. I didn't do anger. I did jokes. The trouble was, I didn't seem to be doing *them* right now either.

"No." Chase shook her head. "I don't want to answer it."

My gut clenched at the tension in her answer. It was my turn to sigh. "Chase," I said, "I have to tell you something. I should have told you before now, but I keep putting if off."

Her frown deepened. She pulled away from me. A little. "What?"

Pink suddenly topped singing, Donald's call no doubt now going to Chase's voicemail.

"Ah fuck," I muttered, rubbing at the back of my neck. "The other night when you went out to get condoms, Donald the Dude called."

Chase's expression grew still.

"And I answered," I finished.

She didn't blink. She stared up at me, unmoving. "What did you say?"

My stomach clenched again. A hot ball filled my throat. I could have spun some bullshit about not really saying anything, but I wasn't a liar. And I sure as hell wasn't going to lie to Chase. "I told him you were going to be too busy to call him back."

Her eyes widened, her lips parted and she gasped, recoiling a little from me. "You what?"

"I told him you weren't available to talk and that you'd be too busy when you got back," I said. Holy crap, my chest felt like it was being crushed in an invisible vise.

"Why did you do that?"

"Why?" I raised my eyebrows. "Because the guy is a dick, Chase. Because when I first saw you with him at the airport, you looked uncomfortable. Because when he touched you back there, you visibly flinched. Because he won't leave you the fuck alone no matter how many times you ignore his calls or texts, or tell him not to. That's why."

"And you think that's your job? To guard me from men like Donald Perry?"

I should have caught the warning in her voice. I should have clamped down on my rising anger. I didn't. I should have tried for a witty comeback to defuse the situation. That was my normal *modus operandi*. But then, I *also* shouldn't have waited this long to tell her what I'd done. For a guy who's pretty switched on, I was being rather idiotic. "If you're not going to protect yourself, Chase, then someone has to."

She sucked in a sharp breath. And then pivoted on her heel and hurried away from me.

Shit. Shit shit shit.

"Chase," I yelled, running after her. I grabbed at her elbow but she shrugged me off and kept walking. "Chase, wait."

She didn't. Instead, she raised her hands so I could see them above her head and signed *fuck off*.

I quickened my pace, running past her. She didn't look at me.

"Chase." I stopped directly in her path, holding out my palms toward her. "Wait."

She came to a halt, her glare hot. "Do you have *any* idea how it feels to discover people think you are incapable of looking after yourself?"

"That's not what I meant," I protested.

She arched an eyebrow at me. "Try again, O'Dae. This time with the truth."

I opened my mouth. And then closed it again. The truth was exactly what she'd suggested: I was worried she couldn't make the right decision when it came to the Art History professor. But for fuck's sake, I loved her. I was allowed to be worried. Especially when this dick wouldn't leave her alone.

"Chase," I said for the fourth time. What I was going to say after that had yet to enter my head.

"Yep." She crossed her arms over her chest, stare fixed on my face. "That's me. The girl everyone seems to think needs to be treated like a toddler."

"Bet you'd look cute in pigtails," I said, even as I knew the flippant line really wasn't going to help. But as I said, it was my normal way of dealing with confrontation. Laugh it off. Joke about it. Ignore the anger. Smother it with witty comebacks.

She threw up her hands. "So, treat me like I'm a baby and then make jokes? You know what, O'Dae? I need to go. Away." She stabbed her finger toward the ground at her feet. "From here. Now."

That invisible vise around my chest clamped tighter. "Chase . . ." I began.

She turned before I could say anything else. "Don't follow me," she threw over her shoulder as she hurried toward the Speeding Dragon.

I stood stock-still, unsure what to do or say. "Please let me fix this," I called, watching her pull her car keys from her bag.

She stopped, shoulders slumping. "Don't, Caden," she called back without looking at me.

My heart tore at the wretched contempt in her voice.

The sound of Pink sheared through the air. I ground my teeth.

Chase dug her phone out of her pocket, looked at the screen and then turned to me, phone extended. "Want to talk to him?"

"For God's sake," I said, incapable of holding back my frustration. Why wasn't she seeing what Donald the Dude was doing was wrong? How could she *not* be worried about him? "The guy's practically stalking you with how often he calls."

"He does it because he thinks I may not have heard my phone the first time," she shot back.

I threw up my hands. "So, not a stalker. Just a condescending dickhead, then. I feel infinitely better for you now."

"Go to hell, Caden," she snarled. She swung back to the car and yanked the door open, Pink still singing.

The situation slammed into me: what I'd said, how I'd hurt her. "Chase," I said, raising my voice to almost a shout.

She paused, but didn't look at me. Pink fell silent. I've been a Pink fan for as long as I can remember, but honestly, right then, if I never heard that song again it would be too soon.

"He's not good enough for you," I said, watching her back. "No one is. But if you let me, I'll spend the rest of my life trying to be." A wry laugh I knew she wouldn't hear rattled in my chest. "No joke."

Looking over her shoulder, she scowled. "I don't need to be protected."

"Have you ever thought," I took one step – just one – closer to her, "that those trying to protect you do so because they love you?"

Her scowl slipped. She closed her eyes and turned back to her car. "I'm going. I'll call you later."

And without another word, another look at me, she lowered herself into the driver's seat, closed the door and started the car.

Not a single funny, witty or sarcastic came to me. Not one. All I had was my churning gut, my thick throat, and a rising feeling everything I'd hoped for was slipping through my fingers.

Everything.

"Drive safely," I said, the words barely a murmur as she pulled out of the parking area onto the street and drove away from me.

Crap.

SEVEN

"Once you have had a wonderful dog, a life without one is a life diminished."
~ Dean Koontz

Chase

Mom and Dad. Everyone has them at some point in their lives. What their relationship is like with their mom and dad is dependent on all matter of things. My relationship with my mom is wonderful. Mom is the mediator of our family. Mom is the peacekeeper. Mom should work for the United Nations, given she's managed to keep Dad and I from killing each other.

I love my mom, and I'm not ashamed to admit it. She understands me, accepts me, and encourages me to be who I am.

More than once I've wondered why she and Dad are still together. I know the answer: because they love each other. I've seen them play footsies under the dining table when they're eating dinner. I've seen them finish each other's sentences more than once. I've seen Dad watch her walk through the living room, when he thinks no one is watching him, the love and admiration in his eyes . . .

I think it's moments like those that make me hate him less. Actually, hate is a strong word. Do I hate my father? No. I just wish he'd be as understanding about who I am as Mom is. But, as Dad is fond of saying, if wishes were horses . . .

Thank God Dad was at work when I let myself into my home. The front door makes this squeaky whine that I can feel all the way up my arm, and it no doubt alerted Mom to the fact I'd arrived. She met me in the middle of the living room, as I was trying to hurry to my bedroom, the reading glasses she wears when in work-mode perched on her nose.

"Hey Mom," I said, trying to walk past her.

She didn't let me. Without a word, she snagged my arm and pulled me in for a hug I had no defense against.

I also had no defense against the hot tears that welled up in my eyes. They stung, and no matter how many times I tried to blink them away, they persisted.

Suffice to say, when Mom finally released me from the hug – her hands anchoring me to her still, via a gentle grip on my wrists – my cheeks were wet.

"Hey, baby girl," she said, her smile warm and gentle. "You need to talk?"

I shook my head and sniffed. "Not yet," I answered. "Think I need a shower first."

She smoothed her palms up my arms and brought our foreheads together with a gentle touch, like she's done ever since I was a little girl and upset about something. Most of those times I was upset over my crappy hearing, or Dad.

"Love you, Mom," I said, as she pulled away.

She smiled. "Take a shower. I'm grading papers, but when

you get out I'll stop and we can fix lunch together. What do you think?"

"I think it sounds good." I kissed her cheek and then made my way to my bedroom.

It had been two nights since I was here, and while that wasn't long, it felt like a lifetime. So much had changed since then. So much had happened.

I crossed to my bed and dropped onto its edge, letting my gaze roam around the room. It didn't surprise me at all to find it coming to rest on one of Caden's previous sock-puppet creations, currently sitting on my bookshelf.

A hot lump filled my throat as I studied it. It was Tooth-less, the black dragon from the *How to Train Your Dragon* movies. Tanner loved those movies. So did I. How could I not? They were about a young person not living up to their parents' expectations and learning that was completely okay.

Had Caden known that's how the film spoke to me? I'd never questioned him on why he made the puppets he made for me, but maybe I should have?

Pushing myself to my feet, I walked over and picked up Toothless from the shelf. Its wool was soft beneath my fingers. Its felt green eyes looked up at me. I couldn't help but feel like the goddamn thing was judging me.

The lump in my throat grew thicker.

"I don't need to be protected," I muttered at it.

Huffing, I tossed the puppet back onto the shelf and stomped back to my bed. I had a right to be angry, damn it. Caden had way overstepped his bounds answering Donald's call. And let's not talk about him telling Donald I was going to be too busy to call him back.

Who the hell did he think he was? Who did he think I was?

I threw myself onto my bed, tummy first, and fisted my

hand beneath my chin. Of course, the position meant I was looking at the Thor sock puppet Caden had made me.

I glared at it. It looked back at me, hand-made Fosters can in its "hand".

A soft tap on my calf saved Thor from being flung across the room.

Twisting, I looked up to find Mom standing beside the bed. *Can I sit?* she signed.

Mom does not sign at me often. That she was now meant one of two things – she was going to tell me something she suspected I didn't want to hear, or Dad was home. Which I guess, in this incident, could be essentially the same thing.

Repositioning myself onto my side, I nodded.

She lowered herself to the side of the bed, watching me with concerned eyes. "I was going to let you decompress for a while," she said with a small frown, "but changed my mind."

"Why?"

Her frown disappeared. "Because I'm the mom. It's my job to take away my baby's pain."

I snorted, and then rolled my eyes. "Can you get someone deported?"

"Ahh." Understanding filled her face. "What's Caden done this time?"

Before I go on, I should point out, Mom thinks Caden is the Best Boy In The World (caps intentional). Ever since he arrived in our lives with his matching bone marrow and saved Tanner, Mom idolizes him. She's allowed to, I guess. He saved her grandson, after all. If she were religious, she'd fully expect him capable of walking on water.

Thankfully, she isn't. Religious, that is.

What she is, was grateful. We all were. We just had different ways of showing it. Dad showed it by rarely acknowledging Caden existed (although I suspect that was because Caden was Brendon's cousin, and Brendon completely messed up Dad's plans of Amanda dating his teacher's aid, so by default, Caden was the enemy). Amanda showed it by letting Caden sleep on their couch whenever he wanted and for as long as he wanted. Mom showed it by baking.

Baking.

One time when Caden was visiting, she baked him cookies. To the best of my knowledge Mom has never baked cookies in her life. But she baked them for Caden. They were a crumbly mess of chocolate chips, and I think she used self-raising flour instead of plain flour, but she baked them. From scratch.

For Caden.

Another time, she paid a small fortune for an imported packet of Tim Tams – an Australian chocolate cookie that are completely delicious – and baked him a Tim Tam cheesecake.

Caden thinks Mom is awesome. I know this because he tells her every time she places some newly baked delicacy in front of him.

"Caden," I said, already feeling on the defensive, "answered my cell and . . ."

I petered off. Mom knew nothing about Professor Douchebag. God, I can't even imagine what she'd say if she did. I didn't *want* to imagine.

She raised her eyebrows. "And? That's it?"

My stomach lurched a little. "And he thinks I need to be protected. And I don't."

"Protected from what?" A puzzled smile played with her lips. "Life?"

I let out a sigh. "Kind of."

"You know it's his nature, right?" She brushed a non-existent strand of hair away from my cheek, her eyes softening.

"Think about what he did for Amanda and Brendon. He protects those that he feels need to be protected even if he's not aware of it. And his career choice? A veterinarian? A protector of animals? You're going to have to accept he wants to keep those he cares for safe."

My heart did a stupid little flutter at the word *cares for*. I was doing my best to convince myself I didn't want Caden O'Dae to care for me.

My best, I have to admit, wasn't very good.

I searched for my earlier anger. "I don't need to be protected," I declared, returning my chin to my fist. I glared at the sock-puppet Thor regarding me with blue-button eyes from my pillow. "He's not my boyfriend."

"And yet," Mom said, loud enough for me to understand her without turning to watch her lips, " you just spent two nights in a motel with him. I'm not judging, sweetheart, but that kind of behavior suggests him being *something* along those lines. And lets face it, he doesn't come to the States over and over just to see Tanner and Brendon, does he?"

Heat spread through my cheeks. I pushed myself up into a sitting position and fixed my focus on Mom. "I'm not sure I know what you're saying."

She laughed. "Yes, you do. And you're being stubborn about it. Stubborn like your father, I might add. But, it's not my place to tell you who you should fall in love with."

My mouth fell open. "Mom!"

She shrugged. If ever there was a teacher shrug, that was it. The kind that said, if you're not listening to the lessons I'm giving you it's not my fault you're floundering. Mom has written more than one bestseller about education. When I was eight I told her I was going to be a teacher too. Dad told me not to be stupid.

"Nor is it my place," she went on, "to tell you that

spending two nights in a motel with a boy could be considered leading that boy on if you've got no intentions of venturing into boyfriend and/or love territory."

"You're not helping me," I grumbled. She wasn't. What she was doing was making me feel guilty. Damn it.

She lifted an eyebrow at me. "Aren't I?"

I huffed out a sigh.

Mom straightened from the bed, bent and kissed my forehead, and then walked to the door. She stopped on the threshold and turned back to face me. "Shower, baby girl," she said, her smile warm. "Take the time to think about what you're really angry about, or who you're really angry with."

I nodded, that lump back in my throat. Love. God, why did she have to go and use the L word?

"Mom?" I called. I don't know why, but I wasn't ready for her to go yet.

She gave me a smile. "Baby girl?"

I opened my mouth. And closed it again when Dad appeared behind her, his glower directed firmly at me.

Great.

"You finally came home, I see?" he said, loud enough I wanted to tell him not to shout.

"Charles," Mom warned, pressing her palm to his chest.

I looked at him, my tummy knotting.

He was in his usual Professor Sinclair, PhD attire: tweed jacket, button-down shirt, tie and chinos. His glasses – as always – were spotless.

"Two nights, young lady," he said, wrapping his fingers around Mom's wrist and removing her restraining hand, his stare locked on me. "Two nights. I don't know why I'm surprised. Or disappointed."

"Me either," I shot back, his words cutting more than they

should. It's not like I was five. Or not used to this. We'd been at this game for a long time, after all.

"Can I assume you didn't have your hearing aid with you?" It wasn't a question. More an accusation.

Mom shook her hand free of his grip and pressed her palm to his chest again. "Out, Charles. Until you remember you've been worried sick about our daughter, you're not allowed to talk to her."

A fresh lump joined the one already in my throat. And then I sneered. Of course he'd be worried. He didn't think I could function in the real world without running the risk of dying or being run over or . . . or . . .

"I'm hungry," Dad said, turning. "And I've got work to do."

I watched his back as he walked away from my room.

Mom let out a sigh. "I know you're thinking horrible thoughts about your father right now," she said. There was no missing the sadness in her voice. Even my woeful hearing could detect it. "But he has been worried."

"Y'know," I said, curling my knees up to my chest to rest my chin on them, "one of these days I'd like Dad to show me he's worried by hugging me and telling me he's glad to see me. Not by pointing out my failings."

Pain flickered over Mom face. Guilt sliced through me. Dad pushed so many of my buttons, but the one I hated the most was the one that made me say things to Mom that hurt her.

She was caught in the middle. Stuck between the man and the daughter she loved. If only we could love each other the same way she did us.

But wishes and horses . . . wishes and horses.

"I'm going to have a shower," I said, climbing off the bed.

She nodded, chewing on her bottom lip (the typical

Sinclair woman's response to confusion. I did it, Amanda did it, and Mom did it), and then left. I suspect to give Dad a lecture.

I stood in the shower until the water ran cold. It was a good way to pretend I wasn't crying.

It took me longer to dress than normal. I wasn't in any hurry to see Dad again, and yet at the same time I wanted to pick up our argument right where we'd left off: me being a disappointment to him, him being a constant reminder to me I was defective.

Oh, the joys of family life.

I knew Dad was going to be less than approving of my chosen attire. That was probably why I selected it: short denim cut-off shorts with the smiling emoji embroidered onto each back pocket, a crop-top tank complete with torn hem and a large, bejeweled Rolling Stones lips/tongue logo on the chest, and the highest flip-flop wedges I owned. Just for kicks, I spiked my hair into a faux Mohawk.

Yeah, I was being a brat.

I walked out of my bedroom, ready for the battle. I was disappointed when Dad wasn't to be found.

"Where is he?" I asked when I joined Mom in the kitchen.

She was making bacon and cheddar sandwiches. My favorite. For a while I was a vegan, but only because it irritated Dad. Do you know why we have canine teeth? I do. Dad told me every meal I sat down to in his company that was *sans* meat.

Mom flicked a sideways glance at me and shook her head. "Chase," she admonished, "do you have to antagonize him?"

I shrugged, plucking a slice of cheese from the pile. "Does he have to treat me like I'm a baby?"

"Maybe when you behave like one, he does," she shot back.

I rolled up the cheese into a cigar shape and stuck it in my mouth.

She rolled her eyes. "He's in his office. He mumbled something about another professor from school popping by."

Swallowing, I reached for another slice of cheese, and then let out a laughing yelp when Mom whacked the back of my hand with the flat of the butter knife she was holding.

I laughed. And then hugged her. "Thank you, Mom."

She nudged my forehead with hers. "After lunch, we'll fix this Caden situation, okay? You and me."

Hugging her tighter, I nodded. "Okay."

I didn't know how fixable the situation was between Caden and me. I knew how he felt about me, and I was beginning to suspect that how I felt about him was *so* what I didn't want to feel about him . . . but Mom was right – it was Caden's nature to protect. And it was my nature to hate being protected. How did we align those two personalities to function without it turning into resentment and anger?

And what about Donald? I needed to deal with the unhealthy hold he had on my heart before I could truly move on, and it was clear he wasn't ready to let that hold go.

"Set the table for lunch, baby girl," Mom instructed. As always, I loved the way her voice vibrated through me when she spoke while I hugged her. It was one of the safest sensations I had ever experienced.

Dad came into the dining room as I was placing glasses of iced tea on the table. I didn't look at him.

He moved to his chair – at the head of the table, of course – and lowered himself into it. "Fall term is open for enrolment," he said loudly. "You can still get classes."

Biting back a sigh, I turned to face him. "Can I, now?"

He adjusted where I'd put his glass and then met my stare. "Of course. I could pull a few strings and get you into the English Lit. program, rather than you continue art."

"Of course," I said, arching my pierced eyebrow. (Dad did not like my pierced eyebrow. Not one little bit.) "I'd go into the upper level English classes, correct? The ones you're in charge of?"

"Of course," he said. "My daughter wouldn't be slumming it in the other classes."

"And you'd be there," I went on, keeping my voice neutral. If Dad sensed my mood, he didn't show it. "To make sure I was okay? That I was finally living up to my true potential?"

His eyes narrowed. "And why *wouldn't* I be wanting you to live up to your true potential? I'm your father. I want what's best for you. Christ knows you've thrown every offer of help and advice I've ever given you in my face. Maybe it's time to realize you need help? Maybe it's time you stop this ridiculous charade of being capable of—"

"I *am* capable," I snapped back. Hot tears stung my eyes. Hotter anger coated my throat. It was just then, right then, that I realized how little Dad looked at me for who I was. How much of a burden was it to have a broken little girl? He'd never been able to accept it. He'd spent my lifetime trying to fix it.

Fuck it. I was unfixable.

My anger grew. My skin prickled with it. My scalp crawled with it. I took all of it, all the anger, all the pain, and shoved it into my gut where it roiled and built inside me like a volcano. I had to leave now before he said something else. Because if I didn't . . .

The front doorbell chimed – louder than the average doorbell, thanks to Dad installing one specially designed for the Hard of Hearing. I flinched. I couldn't help but notice Dad did as well. Good. I shouldn't be the only one on the verge of eruption.

"That'll be Perry," he said, rising to his feet.

An icy finger trailed up my spine. I blinked. "What did you say?"

He frowned at me. "That will be Professor Perry," he said, enunciating each word like I was from another planet.

That icy finger buried itself into my chest, a drilling pressure. My head throbbed.

Professor Perry. Donald. Here. Professor Douchebag was here.

My stomach rolled. I felt nauseous. And angry. Seriously angry. Not at Dad. Not at Donald. But at the world. The world was fucking with me and there was nothing I could do to fuck with it back.

I turned, although spun is probably a better word, ready to flee. I had no idea why Donald was at my home, but I didn't want to see him. I *definitely* didn't want to see him in the company of my parents.

Mom stood behind me, carrying two loaded plates. Beside her, his smile relaxed, his gaze skimming over me as if I was of no consequence, was Donald.

"Perry." Dad walked past me, hand extended to Donald. They shook hands. "Your timing is perfect. My daughter and I were discussing her return to college."

Donald raised curious eyebrows in my direction. "It's Chase, isn't it?"

I didn't move. Didn't respond. If I did, I feared I might throw up. Mom frowned at me, but I couldn't respond to that either.

What the fuck was going on?

"Chastity," Dad supplied. "She was in your Art History class last year. But no, I'm suggesting she study English Lit."

Donald chuckled. The sound of it sank into the pit of my tummy like a hot weight. "Taking after her old man, eh?"

I pressed my palm to my mouth. I was going to be sick. I really was.

"I've got to go," I said, looking at Mom. "I forgot I told Amanda I'd help her with Tanner today."

Mom's frown deepened. She slid Donald a look. My stomach rolled again. Oh God, I did not want her wondering about Donald.

I looked at Donald, fighting to keep myself composed. "It was nice to meet you again, Professor Perry," I said, forcing a smile to my lips. "Don't look for me on campus, however. Dad's delusional."

Dad's scowl blackened. I hurried from the dining room before he could respond. I did not look at Donald. Snatching up my keys and cell from the console table, I yanked open the front door.

And stopped at a gentle hand on my arm. Mom.

I shot her a look over my shoulder, my smile wobbly. "I'm okay. Dad and I were having a fight before you and the professor came into the room, is all."

She didn't look convinced.

"I'm going to go see Amanda," I said. "It's probably better I'm not here while Dad plans out the rest of my life for me."

Sorrow flickered across Mom's face. "Okay."

I risked another second of being in the same breathing space as Donald, and gave her a kiss. "I'll call you later."

Love you, she signed.

Love you back, I signed in return.

I'd just wrapped my fingers around the Speeding Dragon's door handle, when someone touched my elbow.

I didn't need to turn to know who it was. "Leave me the fuck alone, Donald," I growled.

"I miss you, babe," he said, his lips near my ear, his chest brushing my back. I could barely discern the words. God knows what he would say if my parents saw him this close to me. "Please let me help you forgive me?"

Babe. Forgive. Miss . . .

I ground my teeth. I didn't need this. I didn't. I wasn't . . . I wasn't . . .

Capable?

I could hear Dad's voice demeaning my abilities. And now he'd brought the one man who'd ruined my chances at completing the college education I'd wanted. Dad's ability to find the thing that hurts you the most and use it against you was devastating. He'd done it to Amanda with Tanner, and he'd done it to me over and over with my hearing. Mom said he didn't do it on purpose, and I guess I knew he didn't. But . . .

Without looking at Donald, I shook off his hand and opened my car door. "Enjoy your time with my father. I'm sure whatever reason you came up with for coming here will make your failure to talk to me bearable."

He murmured something in protest.

I ignored him until I was buckled into my seat. Then, and only then, did I look up at him with a wide, cold grin. "What? I can't hear you, remember?"

He opened his mouth, but I closed the door on his response, started the car and reversed out of the driveway.

I didn't look at him.

What I did do was drive to Amanda and Brendon's. Sometimes only a sister can understand the frustrations of family.

AMANDA HUGGED me when I walked into their apartment, her expression worried. Had Mom called her? Warned her? Sent her a text telling her I was on the way and angry with Dad?

If only it were that simple.

"Tanner awake?" I asked, searching over her shoulder for my nephew. If I focused on the hug, I'd be in tears. I didn't want to be in tears. Tears were for those incapable of dealing with the insanity of life.

I was dealing. I was.

Amanda let me go and shook her head. "He's taking a nap."

Despite the fact Tanner is three and has been cleared of cancer, he still has a long battle ahead of him. He tires easily. He gets sick easily. His immune system took a battering and it's taking his little body a long time to catch up with his whole *I'm-three-and-indestructible* attitude.

I let out a sigh and wandered into the living room. I'm not so selfish and self-absorbed that I'd wake him up from something as important as sleep. So I dumped myself onto Amanda and Brendon's sofa, parked my ankles on their coffee table, snatched up the remote and turned on the television.

What the fuck was I doing?

The cushion beside me shifted as someone joined me on the sofa. "Everything okay?"

I turned and looked at Brendon.

Brendon is an eternal optimist. That attitude sometimes drives me mental, but it has its perks. Like giving the guy a perpetual smile. It was hard to be grumpy in Brendon's company. Of course, part of my grumpiness was the result of his cousin, so I wasn't finding it so hard at that point in time.

It didn't help that Caden and Brendon could be brothers, they were that similar in looks. If Brendon grew a beard . . .

"Well?" he prompted with raised eyebrows.

"Your cousin pisses me off," I said.

No point in beating around the bush with Brendon.

"What's he done?"

I shook my head and rubbed at my face with my hands. "Nothing," I grumbled into my palms. I wasn't there to bitch and moan. I was there to decompress. To get my head around things I should already have my head around.

"Want me to beat him up for you?"

The question took me by surprise. I couldn't help but laugh. "No," I said, smiling even as I shook my head. "Not yet, at least."

Brendon studied me for a heartbeat, and then dipped his head in a single nod. "Let me know when. He's due a nipple cripple or two."

"Eww." I shoved at him. Shoving at Brendon is like shoving at a brick wall. "Go away, weirdo."

He grinned at my laughing protest and got to his feet. "Consider me gone."

Amanda didn't waste any time replacing him on the sofa. When she dropped onto the my right side – the side with the partially working ear – I knew what was coming.

"So?"

I stubbornly refused to react. Or look at her. Instead, I changed channels. When the hell had Ellen become so skinny?

"Chase."

"Oh look," I said. "It's the *Robocop* remake. Or is it a reboot?"

"Chase."

I continued to channel-surf. "Think I need one of those," I

said, watching a woman with a body forged by countless years of working out and food deprivation, doing her best to convince me how easy it was to lose weight and look good by buying one of the torture devices she was currently swiveling around on. I changed channels.

"Chase."

A really, really young George Clooney was looking very sexy in hospital scrubs while barking instructions to a really, *really* frazzled nurse.

"Chase."

Before my thumb could press the remote again, Amanda plucked it from my hand.

I huffed out a breath that was part growl, part groan, and slumped back into the sofa, folding my arms over my chest.

"Mom called," she said.

I snorted out a chuckle. "Did she tell you Dad and I were at it again?"

"She did. She also said you were acting weird around one of Dad's work colleagues who was there to see Dad."

My tummy turned into a twisting knot. Yeah, Mom never missed anything.

"What gives?" Amanda asked. "Who was it?"

I didn't answer. If I said Donald's name, everything would come spilling out, and I didn't think I was ready for that kind of confession.

When I insisted on remaining silent, Amanda did what she always used to do when we were younger and I was ignoring her: she dropped herself firmly onto my lap, straddling my thighs and trapping me.

"Hey!" I protested, trying to squirm out from under her.

Amanda is not a big girl at all, and when Tanner was diagnosed with leukemia, she lost a lot of weight. A scary amount, to be honest. Now that's she's married to a personal trainer, she's become this super fit, super strong woman. Once upon a time I would have been able to get her off me, but not any more. I love Brendon to death for how happy he's made my sister, but right at that moment I wanted to smack him. This was an unfair advantage.

"Hey," she said back, holding my head still between her hands. "Talk to me."

"You're not going to like what I'm going to say." As far as excuses go, it was a lame one. I knew it, and by the way Amanda laughed, so did she.

"I mean," she said, not relaxing the pressure on my thighs or my cheeks, "if you want to sit here and sulk like a baby I'll let you, just say the word. But I can't promise Bren will follow suit. You know what he's like. So I figure it's better for you to tell me what's got you so snippy – and while we're at it, where Caden is. Brendon's first line of attack will be to pick you up and swing you around above his head, making helicopter noises until that scowl's gone."

"I'm not Tanner," I grumped.

"True," Amanda agreed with a contemplative nod, "but you're behaving like him when he wants a cookie and I give him an apple."

I reached up and tried to remove her hands from my face. She still didn't budge. When had she got so strong?

"So," she said again, wriggling her butt against the tops of my thighs. "Is this about an apple or a cookie?"

"Ow," I muttered, squirming on the sofa. "You've got a bony tailbone."

"Caden is the apple, isn't he?"

My tummy tightened at his name. Goddamn it.

"Talk to me, sis," she said, her expression growing softer. "Tell me what's taken your happy."

It wasn't my tummy that tightened this time, it was my

heart. I love my sister more than I can possibly articulate, bony tailbone and all. When I still didn't say anything, she slipped off my legs and curled onto the sofa beside me, taking my hand in hers and tucking a non-existent strand of hair behind my ear.

No matter how much I tried, I couldn't stop myself turning to give her a wobbly smile.

"Where's Caden, Chase? What's going on?"

"He's still in LA," I said. Christ, why did my whole body ache at that statement?

Her eyebrows rose. "And you're here? Why?"

A sigh tore at my chest. "Because he won't stop trying to protect me. Because he thinks he knows what's best for me, and what isn't."

"And you don't like that."

It wasn't a question. She knew me well, my sister.

"I don't. But I like . . ." I stopped. Tears were burning my cheeks. Annoying, stupid, ridiculous tears.

Amanda tucked that imaginary strand of my hair behind my ear again. When we were younger, when I had hair long enough to sit on, she used to twirl a strand around her finger while we watched television together. Then, when I turned all that hair into dreadlocks, she'd tug on one whenever she wanted attention. The tucking action was her new thing, her response to the new pixie-cut, I guess. She studied my face, my eyes. "This isn't just about a dog, is it?"

Before I could answer, Brendon appeared in the living room and my heart swelled with happiness. On his hip, still rubbing the sleep from his eyes, his hair a spiky blond mess poking up in all directions, was Tanner.

"Someone wants a hug from Aunty Chase," Brendon said, crossing the room to deposit Tanner on my lap.

"Aunny Chase!" He snuggled into me in the way only

three year olds can – with absolutely unabashed delight. "Where you been?"

"Caden and I got held up in LA," I said. For some reason, my cheeks filled with heat.

Tanner's eyebrows shot up in an expression so like Amanda's I laughed. "Did they have guns?"

"Oh champ, I don't mean that kind of held up," I said, giving him a comforting hug and tickle. He giggled and squeezed me back.

He pulled away and gave me a curious look. "Where's Cade?"

"He's still in LA."

Tanner pouted. "Why?"

Tanner had a serious case of hero worship for Caden. It had nothing to do with the fact it was Caden's bone marrow that saved his life, and everything to do with the fact that Caden makes the best sock puppets and draws the best pictures and carries Tanner around on his back singing songs about Batman and Superman and Iron Man, and wears T-shirts and socks with superheroes all over them, and is fun and crazy and . . .

I closed my eyes. If I didn't, tears were going to spill, and Amanda and Brendon were watching me too damn closely for me to let that happen.

"S'okay, Aunny Chase," Tanner said, patting my shoulder. "Cade will come soon."

I opened my eyes and gave my nephew a wet smile. "He will," I mumbled.

Tanner frowned, and then a wide grin split his face "Is he bringing the doggy here?"

I burst into tears. Brendon scooped Tanner from my lap, and Amanda drew me close and nestled me under her chin, her hand smoothing up and down my back. She murmured words I didn't hear but felt. Soothing words that vibrated like a low hum in her breast. I burrowed into the sensation, trying to stop my tears and failing.

Fuck. I was a mess.

When I finally got control of myself I wiped at my eyes and nose with the back of my hand and levered away from her body.

She looked at me, worry all over her face. "Okay, Chastity, time to cough up and explain what's going on."

I let out a shaky sigh and sniffed. There was nothing refined or ladylike about the way I'd been crying. It gave "ugly tears" a new definition. There are few people in the world whom I would allow to see me like this. Amanda is one of those few.

"Talk," she said now, watching me swipe at my nose. "We need to fix this."

Such is Amanda's approach to life. Problem? Fix it. When it came to her own problems . . . well, that's a different story. I'm sure if you ask her, she'll tell you.

Caden and I had sex, I signed. *A lot of sex.*

"On that note," Brendon said, "I think Tanner and I will go buy what we need for dinner."

"Ice cream!" Tanner cried with delight.

"Boiled chicken and brown rice," Brendon countered, his face a mask of mock seriousness.

"Ice cream," Tanner repeated with a wild shake of his father's shoulders.

"Egg-white omelet and buckwheat pancakes!" Brendon replied with equal enthusiasm.

"Ice cream!" Tanner insisted, wriggling on Brendon's hip and grinning widely.

Brendon turned to us both. "We're going to go buy some ice cream."

"Ice cream!" Tanner cried victorious.

I smiled. I couldn't help it. In the face of such joy, the woes of my stupid, conflicted heart were no match. "Make sure you get peanut butter chocolate chip," I told Tanner.

Of course, *that* reminded me of the last time I'd eaten that particular flavor of ice cream, and who I'd been with, and what we'd done shortly after, and my smile crumbled. Amanda slipped her arm around my shoulders.

Sympathy and understanding filled Brendon's smile. He knew what it felt like. Although I don't think he ever got dumped by one of his professors. To the best of my knowledge, the only person to ever dump him was my sister. And now look at them: married and trying their hardest to get pregnant again.

Hitching Tanner farther up his hip, Brendon stepped closer and bent to drop a kiss on my forehead. "It's going to work out," he said when he straightened. "Trust me."

I blinked at the tears threatening to overwhelm me, and rolled my eyes. "You're a born optimist. Of course you would say that."

His smile turned to a grin. "Yes. Yes, I am. Isn't it wonderful?"

I couldn't help but laugh. It was a wobbly laugh, to be sure, but a laugh.

"We're outta here," he declared, turning to Tanner, who was watching us all with the kind of contemplative frown little children wear when exposed to the pathetic-ness of the adults in their life. "Let's go get a wheatgrass and kale smoothie!"

"Ice cream, Daddy," Tanner corrected.

"Wheatgrass and kale ice cream?" Brendon suggested.

Tanner's giggle was answer enough.

"We'll be back in fifteen, twenty minutes," Brendon said to Amanda.

She smiled up at him, a smile Brendon bent down and kissed.

"Love you, both," my sister said.

"Love you back, Mommy," Tanner declared. "C'mon, Daddy. Ice cream!"

"Ice cream," Brendon laughed.

I watched them go, my heart clenching. In case you haven't picked up on the clues yet, I love my family. They are amazing and supportive and real. I don't know what I would do without them.

At the feel of a gentle finger tucking behind my ear, I returned my attention to Amanda.

"Okay," she said, taking my hand, her smile soft. "Talk to me for real. What's going on?"

My throat grew thick. She was right. It was time for *real* talk. It was time for me to tell her everything. She was my sister, after all. She'd had my back from the day I was born.

Letting my gaze jump around the room, I settled on one of Tanner's Transformer toys lying on the floor. "I was in a relationship with my art history professor early last year."

Silence greeted my confession.

I looked back at her, flinching in advance at the censure I knew was going to be on her face.

Yep. There it was. Ouch.

"Professor Perry?" Amanda asked.

I nodded.

"The one who wears suits made out of hemp, has all those books published, and walks around the place like he's the proverbial Second Coming?"

Okay, so Amanda didn't like Donald. I didn't either. One problem down, a gazillion to go . . .

"Yes. That art history professor," I confirmed in a wry tone. "Donald Perry."

Amanda studied me like I'd suddenly grown an extra head. "He's like, a hundred and fifty-seven years old."

"He's forty-seven," I corrected.

"Oh, hell, what was I *thinking*?" she said, smacking her palm to her forehead.

"Amanda," I growled.

She let out a sigh. "Sorry. Sorry. You just . . . Professor Perry? Really, Chase? Professor Perry?"

I shrugged. "He gave me some of the best sex of my life."

"Holy fuck, sis." Confusion filled Amanda's face. "Why?"

"Why was I in a relationship with him? Because . . . because I was in awe of him, of his intelligence. His knowledge about art. His charisma. He's very charismatic."

Amanda didn't look convinced. "He's being investigated by SDSU. Did you know that?"

I frowned, the information unsettling me. "I didn't. Do you know why?"

"I don't. Dad mentioned it in passing to Mom the other day. Apparently he's on extended leave at the moment." She shook her head, studying me like I'd grown an extra head. "He might be charismatic, Chase, but still . . . Professor Perry? You're so much better than that. I don't understand why you'd be with him. I just don't."

I sighed, slumping deeper into the sofa. "He paid attention to me," I said finally. "He treated me like I was a grownup. Like I wasn't . . . wasn't defective. One lesson, he asked me to stay back, complimented me on my essay on Dali, and the next thing I know, we're swapping saliva and his hand is up my shirt."

Amanda stared at me. "Was it just that one time? You used the word *relationship*."

"It lasted a whole semester."

She pressed her palm to her mouth. I waited for her to digest my revelation.

It took her a while.

"Okay," she said eventually. "So it's over. So explain to me why you're—"

Before she could finish, Pink started singing from my cell.

Without making eye contact with Amanda, I dug my phone out of my pocket and held it to my working ear. "Can I assume you're not at my parents' house any more?" I said.

"No," he answered. "I'm not. I'm at my place. The question I have is, when are *you* going to be at my place?"

Two firm fingers pinched my thigh, hard enough to hurt. Mouthing a silent *oww*, I glared at Amanda.

She glared back at me. *Tell him you don't want to talk to him*, she signed.

I frowned at her.

"I can't stop thinking about you, Chase," Donald continued. I had to give it to him, he was determined. And adamant we were meant to be together. Where was that determination when he was with the grad student in his office?

"Every breath I take, I'm convinced I'm breathing in your scent," he went on. "Every woman's voice I hear, I think it's yours."

Tell him you're not interested, Amanda signed, her sharp motions the equivalent of shouting. *Tell him you're seeing someone else.*

"So every woman sounds like me?" I asked into the phone.

Amanda pulled a face and made a gagging action with her finger and mouth.

"Complete with missing consonants and slurring?" I added before Donald could respond.

"That's not what I mean, babe," he reproached, like I was

a petulant child. "And you know it."

Amanda's fingers and hands moved, an evil grin curling her lips. *Tell him you just had the best sex of your life with another guy. In fact, tell him you're in the middle of it now and you need to get back to it.*

I waved a shushing hand at her.

"What I know," I said, my heart racing, "is that you told me that I was defective and you couldn't be in a serious relationship with someone with a disability."

Amanda's mouth fell open. She gaped at me. And then pure, concentrated rage flooded her face. *He did what?* she signed.

"He did what?" she said aloud, fury turning the words to a snarl. Obviously she was too angry for just one form of communication.

"Is someone there with you?" Donald asked.

"I'm with my sister," I answered, dropping my forehead into my hand.

"And the hottest guy on the planet," Amanda said loudly.

"What?" Confusion and alarm filled Donald's voice.

"Donald," I said, eyes closed, head in my hand, "why are you so adamant you want us to be a thing again? Why? Is it because you saw me at LAX? Or is it because you saw me with another man?"

He didn't answer that. Instead, he said, "Be at my place in fifteen minutes, babe. I know you want to see me. I need to *show* you how sorry I am."

There was no missing the emphasis on the word *show*. Nor the implication behind it.

My stomach tightened. The trouble was, I really didn't know if it was from disgust, rage or, God help me, an idiotic, pitiful need for his approval.

And if it was the latter, what the hell did I do to stop it?

EIGHT

"The average dog is a nicer person than the average person."
~ Andy Rooney

Caden

Walking into the hospital as Chase drove away was an exercise in mental torture. It took all my willpower not to look back to see if she'd stopped. To see if she'd changed her mind. By the time I got into the reception area I felt like I was about to splinter into a million pieces. So much for not being ruffled. What I needed right there and then was some good news about Doofus. And maybe an excuse to make a joke about something.

The temp – whose real name was Timpani but who I could only think of as Little Miss Regrowth – smiled at me when I entered.

"Is your girlfriend okay?" she asked.

Girlfriend. Huh. It would take forever to explain the

complexities of our relationship, so instead I nodded. "She's tough."

An unconvinced frown pulled at her forehead. "I guess she has to be, being disabled and all."

Thankfully an elderly woman with pale pink hair and a pinker Shih Tzu under her arm hurried into the hospital and approached the counter, saving me from responding. It's probably not a good move to call someone an insensitive, ignorant twat when you're a visitor in their country, right?

"Caden?" Dr. Adams poked his head through the door behind the counter as Timpani turned to the stressed pet owner. "Come through."

"Thanks, Dr. Adams," I said.

He waved a hand at me with a smile. "Dean will do."

I followed him to the recovery room where Doofus had been the day before. When I saw the dog, my heart dropped.

It's an odd term of phrase *heart dropped*, but it's so accurate. Physically, my heart didn't shift its position in my chest cavity at all, but at the sight of Doofus, the place in my chest where my heart sat suddenly felt empty, a pounding weight taking up residence in my gut in its place.

Doofus, for his part, wagged his tail weakly at my presence.

"Chase tells me he's got a post-op infection," I said, concern eating at me.

"He's a fighter," Dean said at my side, "but for some reason he's not responding to the antibiotics."

I crossed to Doofus's cage, opened it, and placed my hand on his side. My throat wasn't letting me breathe. I ran an inspection over the dog, trying to engage my vet's eyes and brain.

"And you don't know why?" I asked. Dean had done an

amazing job on the dog's dislocated back knee, and the sutures on his wounds were impressive.

"Not at this stage. Randolf – the vet on duty last night – suspects complication from his perforated bowel," Dean answered. "It was a mess in there when you brought him in. Randolf put him onto antibiotics straight away, but they should be having an effect by now. I'm going to run some blood tests and do a CT scan, see if there's something we've missed. Would you like to watch?"

I nodded.

He clamped a firm hand on my shoulder. "This is not how you saw your third day in California going, is it?"

A dry laugh scratched at my tight throat. "Not really. I'm not really being a great guest for Chase and her family."

"Is she in the waiting room? Doofus's condition shook her up pretty bad."

"She's gone back to San Diego," I said, stroking my hand over Doofus's head. His tail thumped faster, but nowhere near as fast as it should. "She's got things to take care of."

Holy crap, did those words tear at my heart.

How exactly was she going to take care of Donald the Dude? And how was I going to convince her that she was meant to be with me, when I was staying put here in LA? I couldn't leave Doofus. He wasn't mine, but he wasn't anyone else's either, and the thought of abandoning him to whatever fate lay ahead of him just didn't sit right with me.

Dean let out a grunt before giving my shoulder another squeeze. "Go dump your bag in the staffroom, Caden, and then come to Consult Room 2. It'll be good to have another pair of eyes in there."

He turned and left, leaving me with Doofus. Lowering my head, I gently rubbed my forehead against his. "We're going to fix this," I murmured.

He twisted his head a little, his movement shaky and frag-ile, and then a dry warm tongue flicked at my chin, rasping against my beard.

It was at that point I accepted I might not be returning to Australia with Chase as my girlfriend, but I would do every-thing legally possible to make sure I could return with Doofus. If he lived, I wanted him to come back home with me. It meant a likely six-month stint in quarantine for him, and a hefty bloody bill for me, but I didn't care.

This dog was now mine.

This dog, which, as it turned out, had a delayed response to antibiotics.

It took Dean almost twenty minutes to get into Consult Room 2, thanks to an emergency involving a cat, a plastic slinky and a little girl who thought the slinky would make a perfect collar for the cat.

By the time Dean arrived, with a few scratch marks on his wrists and forearms he hadn't sported before, Doofus's tongue color had began to return to a normal, healthy pink.

"Hey," he said, closing the door, "he's looking a bit better."

He was correct. Doofus *was* looking a little better. If nothing else, he was wagging his tail with more gusto and was holding his head up for longer stretches of time. Both good signs.

"Hand me the thermometer," Dean instructed, watching Doofus try to get me to pat his head.

I did so, my heart quick. I don't think I can fully articulate how deeply I wanted Doofus to improve on his own, without the need for further surgery.

Observing Dr. Adams take Doofus's temp, run blood tests on him, and perform more than one scan of his bowel area was an unusual way to decompress after the last forty-eight hours, I'll give you that, but I forgot about the shattered state of my heart. I was a twenty-three-year-old guy with a crush on a girl so powerful I didn't know what I was going to do if she rejected me. So I functioned as a veterinarian, doing everything he could to save the life of an animal.

Although to be honest, it seemed to me Doofus was pretty much saving his own life by this stage. "It's like we have a different dog on our hands," Dean commented, as Doofus tried to lick his face during the last scan of his bowel.

"Maybe he's just got a flair for the dramatics?" I said, trying not to get my hopes up. There was still a long way to go, but if Doofus was finally responding to the antibiotics, that *long way* had become a little shorter. And less traumatic for him. The last thing I wanted to see was him opened up again on the operating table.

Dean chuckled as he took Doofus's temperature again. "Maybe. Definitely a drop in temperature." He scratched at the back of Doofus's ear. "Let's get you back in your cage, boy. Don't want to tire you out." He gave me a quick look. "Think we might increase his dose by a quarter, just to give it an extra kick."

I nodded. It was a sound plan. One I would have suggested myself if I was in his shoes.

I took Doofus back to his cage, my heart – so recently heavy with grief and dismay – feeling far more buoyant.

It was ridiculous to think of Doofus's condition as symbolic of my relationship with Chase, but a part of me was doing so. I walked out of the recovering area strangely calm. I washed up, asked Paul if he minded if I charged my phone in the lunchroom, and then spent the rest of the morning helping out in the clinic.

I met the other vets who worked with Dr. Adams. We talked shop, comparing Australian practices with American. I talked to pet owners dropping off their beloved animals for treatment. I held the hand of the elderly woman as she said goodbye to her Shih Tzu that, I discovered, had inoperable brain cancer and was being euthanized that afternoon.

I ate lunch with Little Miss Regrowth, who asked me to say things like *crikey*, and *fair dinkum* and *struth* over and over, and told me how much she'd loved watching Bindi Irwin on *Dancing with the Stars*.

I went back into the clinic after lunch, doing all the things a volunteer at an animal hospital does. I was Caden O'Dae, vet-in-training. I didn't look at my mobile phone once, and refused to let myself think about Chase.

I was standing beside Doofus's cage, absently giving his ear a scratch through the bars as I read through his chart for the twentieth time, when Little Miss Regrowth – Timpani – tapped on my shoulder.

"Someone's been texting you, Cade."

I'm not sure when she decided she could call me Cade. Probably after the fifth time she asked me to say *g'day, mate*.

She handed me my mobile. I wasn't sure how I felt about the fact she'd taken it upon herself to retrieve it from the lunch room where I'd left it charging next to my bag.

"Thanks," I said with a tired smile.

She slipped her fingers down my arm. "Dr. Adams says you're staying at a motel while the dog is recovering. That your deaf *friend* went back to San Diego."

I nodded, my gut churning. There was no way I could miss the emphasis she'd put on the word "friend". "Yeah. I'll find one closer after I leave today. It took me longer to get here in a taxi this morning from the motel than it did to get from Australia."

She giggled at my very lame attempt at humor. Man, I really wished she'd go. I wanted to see who'd been texting me, but my mum had done a pretty good job of raising me not to be rude. I also had a fair idea of where this conversation was heading and I wasn't looking forward to it.

"You can stay with me if you like."

And there it was.

"Thanks," I said, doing my best to keep my voice warm and friendly, "but I'm good. It's part of the American experience, crashing at a motel, yeah? I'm hoping to find a Howard Johnson. I see them all the time on the movies and figured I'd check one out for a lark. We don't have those back home."

For all I know, we did. But it was the first American motel chain name that popped into my tired, frazzled, tormented brain.

Timpani pursed her lips, and then circled my wrist with her fingers, and wrote a string of numbers along my inner forearm with a pen. She actually wrote on my arm with a pen.

"That's my number," she said, smiling up at me. "Call me when you get tired of being alone."

My phone vibrated into life in my hand with a received text message, and there wasn't a hope in hell I could stop my *Oh thank God*, before it burst from me.

Timpani pursed her lips again and tottered out of the recovery room. I swear if she swung her hips any more she would have dislocated her lower spine.

I let out a sigh, feeling more relieved than I probably should have, and looked down at the new message on my phone.

It was from Brendon, and it was short and to the point: *Get your arse outside.*

I hadn't expected the sun to be so low in the western sky when I followed his instructions and got my arse outside. Where had the day gone?

I also hadn't expected to find Brendon sitting behind the

wheel of his car in the parking lot. My eyebrows shot up my head. I gaped at him. What the hell?

Grinning, he got out of the car.

I reversed the direction of my eyebrows, greeting him with a frown. "What the hell are you doing here?"

He laughed. And accepted my fist bump before giving me a rough hug. "My cousin is in trouble. Where else would I be?"

I knew the words weren't random. Nothing Brendon ever did was random. The greeting mimicked my own, delivered to him last year when I arrived unexpected from Australia when Tanner was in hospital.

"Are you alone?" I asked, casting his car a quick look. In Australia, Brendon had driven a very clapped-out hatchback. Since moving to the States and setting up his personal training business, he drove a SUV. The SUV sat gleaming in the sinking sun's rays, looking like a sports car disguised as a family car, complete with an Ironman booster-seat in the back.

"Yeah. Tanner is at home with Mandy." He paused. "And Chase."

My heart jumped into my throat. She was at Brendon and Amanda's place? I let out a ragged breath. I think I may have even slumped a little. Relief rushed through me.

"Where did you think she'd be?" Brendon studied me, clearly surprised at my reaction.

I scratched at my beard and shook my head. "I don't know. I was really hoping she'd still be here with me until I fucked up."

Brendon narrowed his eyes and tilted his head toward the car. "C'mon. Let's get out of here so you can tell me how you fucked up."

Hitching my duffle bag farther up my shoulder, I snorted. "When you put it that way."

We walked to his SUV and climbed in. "When did you decide to come to LA?" I asked as I buckled up.

Brendon started the ignition and grinned at me. "When Tanner and I were eating ice cream."

"Okay." I didn't believe it. I don't remember the last time my cousin ate junk food. Actually, that's a lie. I do. Tanner's second birthday party. Brendon had two slices of cake, a cup cake, three lollies – what you guys in the US call candy – and a whole can of lemonade. "Now when did you *really* decide?"

He laughed, and then didn't answer for a while, focusing instead on joining the busy traffic streaming past the animal hospital. "Where's your hotel?"

I told him, not in the least surprised when he laughed again. "Let's get you somewhere closer," he said.

I grunted. "Absolutely. Maybe then you'll tell me why you're here. And how Chase is going? And if she ever wants to talk to me again."

"Whoa." He shot me a surprised look. "The last thing I heard her say about you was that the pair of you had lots of sex. Are you really that bad at it she'd never want to talk to you again?"

"She what?" I stared at him, gut clenching. "She said what?"

Of course, he did another one of those annoying stretches where he focused on the road rather than my question. I'm eighty-two percent certain he did it on purpose.

It wasn't until we were coasting along with the rest of the northbound traffic that he finally answered me. "I decided to get my arse up here ninety-minutes ago, when Tanner and I came back from getting ice cream to find Chase pacing our living room, chewing on her bottom lip and looking more stressed than I've ever seen Chase look, while Amanda lectured her about some guy called Professor Perry. It seemed to me, given that Mandy was appalled every time she even *said* this Perry guy's name, that whatever was going on, you needed help. Figured you'd stuffed up somehow and needed family to smack some sense into you."

"Thanks." I let out a shaky sigh. "I think."

My gut continued to clench, a churning mess of uncertainty and guilt. Shit. Had I driven Chase back into Donald the Dude's arms by being an overprotective moron?

Brendon gave me a quick smile. I didn't miss the concern in his face. "I would have brought Tanner with me," he said, "but I'm not sure how well this dog that you rescued is, and I didn't want him getting upset if the news wasn't good."

My heart swelled at the sound of Tanner's name. Damn, I was impatient to see that little guy. He put everything into perspective, made you realize how free of problems your life really was.

So I'd been out of line with the girl I was in love. So I'd been overprotective with her. So she was conflicted about me. So I'd pissed her off so much that after we'd finally moved to the next level of our relationship she'd bolted home. So there was another dude doing his best to muscle me out of the picture. Compared to surviving leukemia by the age of two, those things were inconsequential. Still, my bloody heart and soul ached over them. Stupid heart and soul.

"How's he going?" I asked. "I can't wait to see him. I made him an Ant-Man puppet. It fits on my pinkie finger."

Brendon snorted out a laugh. "You really are *special*, you know that?"

I didn't miss his sardonic emphasis on the word "special". "You wish you could be as special as me."

He laughed again, shaking his head. "God help me. Now talk. What's the deal?"

"What do you know?" I asked.

"You and Chase did the deed, quite a few times apparently, she turned up at our place angry with someone, and I don't think it's just Charles, and Mandy is horrified by – I'm assuming, based on what I heard before I left – some kind of relationship Chase is having or had with this Professor Perry guy. That's it."

Fixing a blank stare on the tailgate of the car in front of us, I rubbed at the back of my neck. "Donald the Dude was her Art History professor at uni."

"Donald the Dude?"

"Perry," I said, the knot in my gut twisting tighter. "He was with Chase at LAX."

"*With* with? Or just with?"

I gave a wry chuckle. "At the time, I would have said just with. She didn't look overly happy when he touched her, that's for sure. But the bastard hasn't stopped calling and texting her since. She told me they had a thing while she was still his student, but it was over. The way he's constantly trying to contact her, I don't think he wants it to be." I laughed again, the sound devoid of humor. "Or maybe it's just because he realized he had competition when he met me."

Brendon shot me a quick glance. "Did you know this before or after all the sex?"

"Before."

"And he's the reason why Chase is at our place? Angry and upset and allowing Mandy to lecture her? By the way, I should point out, they're both signing. That should tell you something, right?"

"Fuck."

"You could say that." With a gun of the engine, he

changed lanes before giving me another glance. "It's more than this Donald guy though, isn't it? You wouldn't be here, looking the way you do, if it was just competition for Chase's attention you were facing. You've done something stupid."

I wanted to be insulted that Brendon would think that. I couldn't be.

"Yeah," I muttered. "I did. A few things actually."

"Okay." Brendon nodded. "Let's deal with them one at a time. First dumb thing. What was it?"

In case you're not familiar with Brendon, this is how he approaches life: with an unwavering determination to succeed. Add to the mix his optimism and firm belief he can achieve anything he sets his mind to and you've got a guy who doesn't waste time getting stuff done. It's one of the ways he and I are different. I joke about almost everything in life, he focuses on making everything in life exactly the way he wants it to be.

"First dumb thing," I said. "I yelled at her about her hearing when we were rescuing Doofus from the road."

"Doofus is the dog?"

"Doofus is the dog." I swallowed. "She ran out onto the road to help me, and almost got hit by a car. When we got back to the side of the road, I yelled at her. A lot."

"Why?" Brendon asked without taking his attention from the traffic. I was beginning to recognize the area, which meant we were getting closer to Anaheim.

"Because I'm thinking of ditching the whole vet thing and becoming an auctioneer and I was trying out my shouting voice."

Before I realized what he was doing, Brendon pulled the car to the side of the road and killed the engine.

I frowned at him. He twisted in his seat, resting an elbow on the steering wheel as he studied me.

"What?" I asked.

"Y'know, it's okay to get angry, cousin," he said. "It's okay to show you're pissed off at a situation. I know you don't think it is, that you have to smother your anger with lame jokes – normally ones at your own expense – but you don't."

I stared at him, not sure what to say.

"I remember when your parents got their divorce," he went on, his voice calm. "I remember watching them – and you – hide what you were really feeling. Hell, I heard Mum and Dad talking about your parents' split more than once, and they were of the opinion Aunt Rachel and Uncle Steven weren't doing you any favors not letting you see how angry, how upset they were about their marriage breaking up. I remember you bottling up your anger until you looked like you were about to burst. I think that's when you really started to throw out the witty jokes whenever you felt agitated or stressed. I get it. I do. But there are times when not looking like you're taking things seriously can fuck things up even more. Talking with me, now?" He shook his head, his smile warm. "You don't have to make jokes about yourself with me. You know that, right?"

I drew in a slow breath.

"Now," he said. "Why did you yell at Chase on the side of the road?"

Chest heavy, I puffed out a sigh. "Because she scared the shit out of me," I answered truthfully. "Because I thought she was going to get hit by a car because she couldn't hear it and it would have been my fault because I'd put her in danger and couldn't protect her when she needed me to."

"So, was the shouting about how you fucked up, or was it the fact you shouted about her hearing?"

I shook my head. "I thought it was about her hearing until she accused me of being over protective."

"Ahhh." Brendon grinned. "And there's problem number one. Chase does not *want* to be protected, Caden. Not ever."

A dry chuckle fell from me. "I figured that out eventually. Unfortunately, not until after Second Dumb Thing and Third Dumb Thing."

Brendon closed his eyes, pinching at the bridge of his nose. "Caden," he muttered, shaking his head. He looked at me again, lips curling. "Okay, hit me with them. Dumb thing number two."

"I forgot she couldn't hear in her left ear and tried to apologize."

He burst out laughing. I hadn't expected that. "You forgot she was hearing impaired and then tried to protect her feelings by apologizing?"

"Yeah."

"You forgot one of the defining aspects of the woman you love?"

"Way to make a guy feel good about himself, cousin," I grumbled.

"And that's it?" he asked, ignoring my feeble attempt at self-pity.

"I also whispered in her ear," I said, "while we were . . . err . . ."

"Ahh," he responded, saving me from actually saying *what* Chase and I were doing at the time. "I see. And you think you've offended her?"

"I don't think it helped my case."

"Your *case* is you're an awesome guy with an awesome heart who loves her for her heart, not her hearing."

The words sent something warm and fuzzy through me. Who said guys can't emotionally react to statements like that? Showing it, however . . .

"Dude," I said as a smile stretched my lips, "did you just say I have an awesome heart?"

Brendon laughed. "I did. I'm not so tough I can't say what's in my own heart. Have you thought that might be a good thing?"

"That I forgot?" I raised my eyebrows.

"That you're not hung up on her hearing. That you don't think of her as Chase who has a hearing impairment, but rather Chase who's the only girl you've ever loved?"

"Who says she's the only girl I've ever loved?"

He laughed. "Caden, I've known you since you were in nappies and I've never seen you so enamored. From the second you laid eyes on Chase you were gone."

"Enamored?" I snorted. "You been reading a thesaurus lately, cousin?"

"Blow me," he answered with a chuckle.

"No, thanks," I shot back. "I'm watching my calorie intake."

He shook his head, smile wide. "I think you're the only one who's holding onto Dumb Thing Number Two. Want me to sing that song at you? Let it go, mate. Let it go."

For a moment, an image of Brendon dressed in a sheer and gauzy blue dress, prancing about in an ice castle filled my head. Thank God it was just for a moment.

He was right though. Chase Sinclair *was* the only girl I've ever loved.

He was also right about the fact I didn't define her by her hearing. She was just Chase to me. When I was with her, I felt more content than ever. When I was with her, the world sang. When I was with her, everything was right and the way it was meant to be. I wanted to share my moments with her, my thoughts. I wanted to hear her thoughts on everything. I wanted to sit with her and watch movies. I wanted to exist in comfortable silence with her. She challenged me and completed me and made me like who I was when I was with her.

That had nothing to do with the fact she could sign, or that she had hearing difficulties, and everything to do with the fact she was Chase: snarky, witty, creative, intelligent, beautiful Chase.

God, what would I do if she never loved me back? If I'd destroy any chance of us being an "us" for real?

"So, Dumb Thing Number Three," Brendon said, starting the car again. "What is it?"

I waited until he was back in the flow of traffic before answering. If we were still parked, Dumb Thing Number Three was likely to earn me a punch to the arm.

"Well?" he prodded, a few yards down the road.

Fuck. Here we go.

"While Chase was out buying . . . buying condoms I answered her mobile when Donald the Dude called and told him she was too busy to get back to him."

"Ahh," Brendon said. "Now I understand."

Guilt lashed at me. I slumped in my seat, staring glumly at the road. The sun was almost behind the horizon now, bathing everything around us in a garish blood-orange light.

"It gets better," I said, watching as streetlights and business signs flickered to life around us. "I didn't tell her what I'd done for two days and then when I finally did, I told her if she wasn't going to protect herself from dicks like Perry, it meant someone else would need to."

"Fuck a duck, Cade."

My throat thickened at Brendon's groaned response.

"Yeah," I grunted. "Told you it got better."

He flicked me a glance. "First things first. You need to apologize for being a dick."

"What if I'm too late? What if Perry has swooped in and taken her from me?"

I wasn't expecting his chuckle, nor his smile. "Caden, Chase *likes* you. Neither Amanda nor I ask her to get you from LAX or take you back. She does it off her own bat. And every one of those sock puppets you've made her are on full display in her bedroom. Amanda told me. Chase isn't the kind of person who'd keep something given to her by someone she doesn't like. That Thor one you made her is on her bed. Her bed. So while this Perry guy might be trying like hell to get back into her life, *you're* in her bed every night."

The invisible pressure that had wrapped around my chest since I woke in the motel room to find Chase not there, seemed to fall away. "So what? Do I swoop in and prove to her I'm the one she wants?"

"Swoop in and show her you're the one she *needs*."

I laughed. Life was not, nor ever had been about doing things half-arsed for Brendon. Go hard or go home was his motto.

"Bit tricky to do," I said, "when I'm here in Laguna Niguel and she's back in San Diego."

"You have a phone, don't you? Call her. Text her. Apologize for being an overprotective idiot. Don't let her forget you. Be in her head. Be in it so much there's no room for this Donald dude. And as soon as you can get to San Diego, get there."

Squirming on my seat, I dug my mobile out of my pocket. It was fully charged now, care of the animal hospital's power, but I was still incapable of calling or texting her. I let out a ragged sigh.

"Let me guess?" Brendon said. "No US SIM yet?"

"Nope."

He chuckled. "I don't know why I'm surprised."

It was my turn to say "Blow me".

"With my strict calorie intake?" He laughed. "Hell no. Okay, let's see if we can find an Apple store to get your phone working. That'll also save Aunt Rachel calling me daily to find out if you're still alive. Don't get me wrong, I love your mum, but she's got a lousy grip on international time zones. I had a conversation with her about Russell Crowe, of all things, at quarter to two this morning."

I laughed, even as I itched to call Chase. "Mum would marry Russell Crowe if she could." I was kicking myself for not having a working phone. Of course, it hadn't mattered when the only person I wanted more than anything to talk to was right beside me, but now Chase was gone . . .

"Here." Brendon's mobile suddenly dropped into my lap. "Call her."

I looked at the iPhone, my heart fast. "What if she—" I stopped myself. No, I wasn't going to think about "What ifs". What ifs weren't going to achieve a thing.

Dialing her number from memory, I raised Brendon's phone to my ear and waited. It connected after five rings.

I opened my mouth to say I was sorry before Chase could speak, and snapped it shut again when her voicemail recorded message filled my ear. "This is Chase Sinclair. Do what you've got to do. And do it fast."

A heavy pressure wrapped my chest again. Fuck. My mouth didn't want to work. Neither, it seemed, did my brain.

"Chase . . ." I finally said into the silence. "This is Caden. I'm—"

The loud beep told me I'd run out of time.

Fuck. Again.

"She didn't answer," I said, handing Brendon back his phone. "Try again?"

I shook my head. "I'll get mine working. Besides, I don't know how comfortable I am having you sit beside me as I pour out my soul to your sister-in-law. I love you, dude, but seriously, boundaries."

Brendon laughed. "Fair enough."

"Find me an Apple store, good man," I said, pointing through the windshield. "Find me an Apple store."

We didn't find an Apple store. None opened, at least. We did, however, check out of the motel in Anaheim. I'd left nothing in the room, but the dress Chase had bought on our second day together still hung neatly over the back of one of the chairs. I collected it, finalized the bill and climbed back into Brendon's SUV. For some reason my heart was thumping fast.

"Sure you don't want to come back to San Diego with me?" he asked, as we drove toward Laguna Niguel. "If there's an emergency with the dog I can drive you back."

I shook my head. "No. I'll stay here. If there is an emergency, I'd rather be able to get to him straight away."

That also gave me time to plan my attack. And by attack, I meant apology to Chase. And when I was done with that, I was laying out a plan to prove to her that I knew she didn't need my protection, or my flippancy. A plan to show her my love was enough.

I loved her, and be fucking damned if I was going to let Donald the Dude destroy any chance we had together. And yes, I can see the irony in the fact I said I wasn't going to be overprotective of her while also silently declaring war on Perry's intentions for her, but that's the way it was.

By the time Brendon pulled up out the front of the motel nearest to the animal hospital, the sun was fully set and I was a thrumming mess of nerves and determination.

"One last chance," he said, as I climbed out of his SUV. "I'll bring you back if I need to. Amanda won't mind."

I grabbed my duffle bag, closed the door, and shook my head at him through the open window. "Go be with your family, dude. I'm good. I'm not going to fuck this up or let her slip away from me."

He nodded and gave me a wide smile. "Good."

Flipping him a wave, I turned and began to walk toward the motel's reception.

"Caden?" Brendon shouted behind me.

"What?" I called, turning back to him.

"The dog?" he asked, looking at me through the open passenger window. "Is it going to live?"

I drew in a slow breath and shook my head. "Honestly? I don't know. I hope so."

"It will," Brendon replied, one hundred percent conviction in his voice. "You've got a knack for swooping in and saving the day when all hope seems lost. This dog is going to be okay."

He drove away before I could respond.

And so endeth my conversation with Brendon.

I still had a lump in my throat when I entered Reception and checked in. The only room available was a Superior Suite that cost more than I made a week on my intern income. Ouch. The upside of such indulgence was the suite overlooked the tropically landscaped pool, had a bed bigger than my dorm room, and free Wi-Fi.

I'll say that again. Free Wi-Fi. What every poor traveling student needs when their planned three-week trip of seduction turns into a volunteer stint at a vet clinic doing recovery watch on a stray mutt.

Much to my chagrin, Chase didn't have an iPhone, which

meant I couldn't text her anyway, until I got a US SIM. Instead, I found a Denny's and ordered dinner.

Eating alone at a Denny's *is* as pathetic and miserable as it sounds. After finishing a massive plate of Bourbon Chicken Skillet, my stomach resumed its earlier grumbles over what I'd put in it for breakfast, now also obviously pissed at me for what I'd subjected it to for the last meal of the day. I ignored it, making as much use of the restaurant's free Wi-Fi as I could by texting Mum and Dad back home to let them know I was alive. Once finished, I wandered out of the restaurant into the cold night.

I stood on the footpath, staring up at the sky and the stars that weren't the ones I knew. My phone buzzed in my back pocket. I pulled it out, my heart fast, and read the message on the screen. I tried not to feel bummed it was from Brendon.

Amanda just called. Chase left for this Perry guy's place a while ago.

An invisible punch colder than the night and harder than a sledgehammer hit me fair in the chest. I stared at the message. She wasn't at Brendon and Amanda's. She'd gone to Donald the Dude's place.

She was with Donald the Dude.

Well, fuck a bloody duck.

NINE

"Dogs are not our whole life, but they make our lives whole."
~ Roger Caras

Chase

What was I doing here?

Closure?

The need to face him and know – really know in my heart, in my soul – I was done with him? He'd been under my skin for so long, I'd craved his attention, his desire for so long, that I needed to know beyond doubt I was done with him.

I had to. For my own sanity. For my own future.

I sat behind the Speeding Dragon's wheel, staring at Donald's place. If I wasn't already Hard of Hearing, I'd be deaf with the force of my heart thumping in my ears. It was a wonder the Volvo didn't shudder to pieces around me.

Thankfully neither Mom nor Dad had been home when I snuck into the house. I hadn't done that since I was a teenager. There was a note on the kitchen counter from Mom telling me if I was hungry there were leftovers in the refrigerator, and asking me to please send her a text because she was worried.

I read the note, tapped out a quick text on my cell (*I'm okay, Mom. Stop worrying. xoxoxo C*) and then ran upstairs to my room.

The snug white jeans, flip-flops, Star Wars T-shirt and beat-up leather bomber jacket weren't overtly sexy, but it was the outfit I'd been wearing the first time Donald let me know he was interested in me as more than a student.

Let him make of that what he would.

I sat in the Speeding Dragon, in the dark, in the cold, and stared at his house. I could see him moving around inside, the muted light of his living room casting his shadow against the curtains.

My heart continued to do its best wrecking ball impersonation in my chest. My stomach decided to join in by pretending it was a washing machine, churning away . . .

Fuck. Closure was a scary.

Dragging my eyes from his fuzzy silhouette behind the curtains, I looked at my cell, gripped like a life preserver in my right hand.

I doubted there would be a text from Caden, but that didn't stop me hoping. I'd sent him one over an hour ago. It had been a simple one. A lame one, to be honest.

I miss Doofus.

What I'd really wanted to say was *I miss you. I'm sorry. I don't mean to be a prickly pain in the ass.* Instead I'd sent a text about the dog.

I'd sat with Amanda beside me, staring at the screen, waiting for Caden to answer. I don't know what I wanted him to say, I just wanted him to make contact with me. I missed . . . contact with him. It had only been a few hours since I'd left him at the animal hospital, since I'd lost my temper with him in the parking lot, but I ached like a vital part of what made it possible to live had been torn from me.

"Maybe his phone isn't working? Brendon mentioned he still hadn't got a US SIM yet," Amanda had suggested. "Want me to call Bren? He might already be in LA by now? Maybe he's with Caden?"

I'd looked up at her, ready to say yes when my cell had vibrated into life in my lap.

Pink. Fucking Pink.

Please forgive me, babe. You know how good we are together. D.

I'd read Donald's message five times. Five. Then, without hesitation, I got to my feet.

"What are you doing?" Amanda asked, jumping to hers just as quickly as I hurried away from her.

"Going."

"Where?" she shouted, loud enough for me to hear.

I scooped up my keys and handbag, and strode to the door without looking at her. "To get some fucking closure."

She didn't come after me. She knows me. It would have been a waste of her time and breath.

Now here I was at Donald's place, watching him move about in his living room, preparing for my arrival. And waiting on a text from Caden that wasn't coming.

"And so it begins," I said to the empty interior of the Speeding Dragon.

I shoved my phone into my bag, opened the door and climbed out of the car. It took me fifteen steps to get to Donald's front door.

He opened it seconds after I rang the doorbell. "Chase," he said, his smile knowing.

A wave of cologne hit me. It's true your other senses become heightened when you lose one. My sense of smell was good. Sensitive. Donald's cologne wafted from him, reaching for me, slipping into my breath. It was the same cologne he'd worn when we were together, although I was beginning to question if the word *together* was an accurate descriptor. It stirred memories of hurried sessions in his office, of frantic making out in his car. I stood on the top step, waiting for those memories to affect me, to tighten my belly and my core.

Before they did, he said, "Come in."

Mouth dry, I crossed the threshold into Donald's home. The last time I was here we'd screwed like rabbits on the dining table, and then he'd told me I wasn't invited to the art gallery opening.

His hand moved to the small of my back, his fingertips resting on the upper most curve of my ass, as though it was his to grab. A ripple of something I couldn't identify crept up my spine and I squirmed.

This was not how I expected to feel . . . And yet, it was exactly what I needed to feel.

Three steps into his living room, Donald grabbed my upper arm, yanked me around to face him and then drove me against the back of the sofa, his hands pawing at my clothes, his lips crushing mine, his tongue—

Oh God, oh God, this was . . . this was . . .

"I knew the *chase* wouldn't last long," he groaned against my mouth, one hand closing over my breast, the other grabbing my butt. "The moment I saw you in the airport, I knew you still wanted me."

I froze. I wasn't really engaged in the wild groping, but at his words every molecule in my body recoiled. Flattening my hands to his chest, I shoved. He didn't move that far backward, but he did move. Enough for me to see the indignant confusion on his face as he stared at me. How had I been sucked in by him again? Where was my brain? What was I thinking?

Oh God, what was I—

"What's going on, Chase?" he asked, pulling his familiar composure around him.

I frowned. In my chest, my heart fluttered faster than a hummingbird's wings. "I was thinking we could go to the opening of the new exhibition at the San Diego Museum of Art tomorrow night?"

Donald regarded me, his eyes narrowing. "That's not what I'm thinking about at the moment."

I raised my eyebrows. "No?"

He studied me a fraction of a second longer and then smoothed his hands over my hips and pressed his body against mine once more, rubbing his crotch against the curve of mine. "We can talk about it later though."

"Later?"

"After," he said, lowering his head to close his lips on the side of my throat.

My stomach rolled. I turned my head away and pushed at his chest again. Again, he barely moved backwards, just enough for his groin to break contact with mine. Who would have thought that sensation would feel so right?

"Donald," I said, holding his stare. Oh, he was getting frustrated. Angry. "Why did you first call me, after we ran into each other at LAX?"

A muscle ticked in his jaw. "Because seeing you made me realize how much I miss you. Made me realize how much I want you in my future. Seeing you made me think about marriage. About what we had. How much I fucked up letting you go."

"Letting me go?" A throb in my temple intensified. I drew in a deep, slow breath, tainted now by Donald's cloying cologne. "*Letting me go* is a rather peculiar way of putting it. More like dumped me because I was defective. And marriage? The man who wouldn't even wear the signet ring I bought him, is now thinking about *marriage*? Really?"

"Chase," he crooned, sidling back against my body, a cajoling smile splitting his face. "Baby. I made a mistake. I messed up. I messed *us* up. But you know how much I—"

"Want me?" I interjected. "Or is it how much you don't want *someone else* to have me? You've become very determined to restart *us* since LAX, given we'd had no contact for weeks before that."

His hand on my hip grew tight, his fingers becoming hard points digging into my muscle. "I think you need to be quiet and let me remind you what we had, what we *have*, and get these silly ideas out of your pretty head that I'm just jealous of the Australian."

I burst out laughing.

Seriously, I laughed so hard I almost doubled over. My ribs began to hurt, as did my cheeks, and a part of me recognized the anger boiling in Donald's face, but the rest of me was lost to my laughter. Cathartic, soul-deep laughter.

Donald grabbed at my upper arms as he staggered back a step. "What the fuck, Chase?"

Even with my crappy hearing I couldn't miss the incensed confusion in his exclamation. Shaking my head, I waved a hand at him to wait. I had no chance of talking yet. Not while I was laughing so much.

His fingers dug deeper into my arms. He tried to make me stand up. "What's so funny?"

I stumbled a step to the side, still laughing. Finally, after Donald released my arms, I righted myself and wiped at my eyes. I was crying. "Oh man," I said, the words part chuckle, part breathless pant, "did I fuck up so bad."

Donald's eyes narrowed again. He studied me, clearly completely disconcerted by what was going on.

I leaned against the wall behind me and met his mystified – and suspicious – stare. "You really are a Grade-A jerk, aren't you?"

His mouth fell open. "I think you've got the wrong idea, Chase," he declared.

"You're right," I said. "Of course you're right. You don't just want me because someone else does, you want me because I'm incredible, right? Because you enjoy talking to me. Because you enjoy doing things with me. You want to marry me, right? Is that why you were at my parents' place today? To ask Dad for my hand in marriage?"

Something flickered in his eyes. He shook his head. "No. Your father doesn't . . ." He stopped, his Adam's apple jerking up and down his throat as he swallowed. "No one knows about us, but I'm ready to come out."

"Out?" I raised my eyebrows. "You and me? Together? Out in public? Right?"

"Right," he replied, closing the distance between us again, his hands finding my hips. He smiled, a wide triumphant smile. "Doing things with you is what I enjoy the most."

Let's go get some ice cream, I signed, watching his face. *And then go to a movie. The new Captain America movie is still in theatres.*

Puzzled frustration flashed in his eyes. Discontent twisted

his lips. "You know I don't understand when you do that, Chase."

I drew in a breath, my own smile curling my lips. "No, you don't. Why not? If you can't stop thinking about me, if you can't bear not to be with me, if you are contemplating marriage whenever the mere thought of me pops into your head, why haven't you learned to sign?"

He blinked. And then gave me another one of those smug, supremely confident smirks. "We speak *another* language," he said, tugging my hips to his. His erection was nowhere near as hard as it had been when he first pinned me to the wall. Funny, that. "It's the only language that matters for us."

I laughed again. "Oh God, were you always this clichéd?"

Venomous anger flashed in his eyes. "I'm not sure what you think you're doing but—"

"I'm over you," I said, pushing away from the wall. "Once and for all. And I'm going. That's what I'm doing."

He grabbed my arm as I tried to walk past him. Grabbed it hard.

I shook it off with a laugh. "Seriously, Donald. The alpha male act does not fit well on you."

"What *is* your problem?" he snarled. Although to be fair it was less a snarl and more a petulant whine. "I thought you wanted us to happen again. I'm willing to *marry* you, for Pete's sake. I thought you came here so I could—"

"Fuck me?" I finished for him.

He sneered. An honest to goodness sneer. Wow. Where was the poised, cool – in both senses of the word – art history professor who'd seduced me with his suave charm? I will freely admit I've got some Daddy issues, but was this really the guy I'd tried to sort them out with?

What the hell had been wrong with me?

"That's what you wanted, wasn't it?" he shot back. "For

me to fuck you? I mean, it's not like I wasn't getting any without you. And you were all over me back at LAX. I figured you needed a good fuck."

"I was all over you?" I burst out laughing again.

You know that sensation you get when you've spent the day bent over a desk, working or studying, and you stop and look up for some reason? That ethereal, indescribable sensation that the world is suddenly lighter, that with every little crack of the bones in your spine as you straighten in your chair, the fog falls from you and you can breathe?

That. I was experiencing that.

Right there, I got it. I understood it. Donald had been my poison. My fog. The pressure on my back as I bent at the desk, and the goddamn midterm paper sucking at my soul.

All those things, wrapped up in a package that had awed me, left me star-struck and flattered to be the focus of his attention.

I'd been greedy for that, craved it, but what I'd really craved was attention, the kind that validated who I really was. The kind a father gave his daughter. Dad hadn't given me that, and I'd gone searching for it elsewhere. I'd gone searching for the kind of attention that said it was okay to be different, witty, sarcastic. The kind that said just because I couldn't hear, didn't mean I didn't feel.

Every time Donald screwed me in his car, every time he felt me up between classes, telling me how hot I was, how sexy, I'd been amazed anyone could think that of me. But what I should have been asking myself was, when had I decided hot and sexy was enough?

It wasn't. I was more than a walking pair of tits and a pussy. I was more than a desperate defective person just needing someone to take pity on me.

I was Chase Sinclair. I was smart. I was talented. I was

creative. And I didn't need to be reduced to my body parts – those that worked and those that didn't – to be Chase Sinclair.

Throwing back my head, I laughed again. "Y'know," I said, looking at Donald as I wiped at my wet cheeks, "this has been the most enlightening night of my life. I'm so glad I came here. But now I have to go."

Donald ran a slow gaze over me. Uncertainty lurked in his eyes like a sludge of oil. "Go where?"

I didn't answer. Instead, I started for the door again.

"If I'd know you were going to be like this when I followed you to—"

He stopped his angry snarl dead.

I turned. Stared at him. "Followed me to where, Donald?"

My body thrummed. My stomach clenched. Had he just admitted what I thought he'd admitted?

He didn't answer. Instead, he stared like a deer caught in headlights.

"Followed me to where?" I repeated. "To LA? We didn't just happen to bump into each other at LAX, did we?"

His Adam's apple jerked up and down his throat.

I frowned. "And you didn't just happen to think about going to Disneyland with me for no reason, did you? You were there. When Caden and I were. You were following me."

Disgust mingled with contempt in my stomach, before an emotion far stronger swelled through me: pity. Not for me, but for him.

"Goodbye, Donald," I said. "It's been . . . fun."

I turned for the door, but once more he grabbed my upper arm. "Babe," he crooned when I swung back to him. "This hasn't gone the way I wanted. This is not . . . I mean . . ." He stepped closer, snaking his hand up the side of my face, to my ear.

I knew his fingertips had encountered my hearing aid when he stiffened and jerked his hand away.

I grinned. Donald had always hated my hearing aid. Whenever I wore it when we were together (huh!), he complained how unsexy it was, how it marred my beauty. By the time he dumped me, I was ashamed of the damn thing. Hated it.

I don't know why I'd put it on before coming here tonight, but perhaps on a subconscious level I was reclaiming the Chase I'd lost to his emotional and sexual manipulation of me. Maybe I was saying to the world, I remember who I am.

Or maybe the *real* me knew it was going to piss him off.

Maybe both.

"Oh Donny," I said, melodramatic sympathy lacing my voice. "Did you have trouble hearing me earlier?"

He blinked.

I smiled. *I'm over you*, I signed, moving my hands as slowly and obviously as I could.

And with that, I walked past him.

"What?" he called. "What?"

I didn't stop or turn back to him. I left his house, strode to the Speeding Dragon and dropped into the driver's seat. He yelled things at me the whole way. Things I'm pretty certain I would have found hilarious if I could hear them.

Starting the car, I reached up to my ear, removed my hearing aid and tossed it onto the passenger seat beside me. The battery was dead. Had been for the last three months.

But damn, it had been the perfect piece of costume jewelry tonight.

Ignoring the sight of Professor Douchebag's silhouette in his open front door, I threw the car into gear and drove away. It would take me roughly ninety minutes to get to LA. I'd need to get gas on the way (the Dragon was thirsty) and swing by

Amanda's place first to tell her what was going on. As much as I am the annoying, irritating little sister, I'm not so horrible as to not fill her in on the awesomeness of what just happened.

So a quick conversation with Amanda, a hug with Tanner, a pee break, and then on to LA.

I was at the end of Donald's street when it occurred to me I had no idea where Caden was. Was he still at the motel near Disneyland? Or would he have thought to relocate to a motel closer to the animal hospital? I would have. Damn it.

Digging in my bag for my cell, I checked it for incoming messages. Nada.

My stomach twisted. Surely he'd got a US SIM by now? So why hadn't he texted? Was he pissed at me?

If he was, why wasn't I getting his patented I'm-a-smartass-joker responses? The kind that drove me mental but, strangely, made me want to smile at the same time?

If he wasn't texting me back, was it because he'd given up on me? On us?

I couldn't believe that. Caden didn't do giving up. He'd told me as such. Of course, that was before I'd told him I didn't need him, or want him and abandoned him in LA all alone with a dying dog.

A raw sob tore at the back of my throat and I pressed my hand to my tummy. Oh fuck, I'd messed up.

I'd messed up and I didn't know what to do about it.

How would I live without any more of his sock puppets? How would I function without his jokes and sense of humor and . . . and . . .

A loud car horn blasting behind me made me jump. Shit, I'd stopped completely in the middle of the road. Face flooding with heat, I let out a yelp and slammed my foot to the pedal.

It didn't take me as long as it legally should have to get back to Amanda's place. Brendon and Tanner had returned, and my family was sitting down eating supper when I barged into their apartment using my spare key.

"Aunny Chase!" Tanner cheered as I sprinted across the living room to the dining table.

I scooped him up from his booster-seat and squeezed him in a hug. "Hey, Superman," I greeted him, jiggling him on my hip with a wide grin. "How's dinner?"

"Yummy," he declared, whacking me on the head with his fork. Something warm dropped onto my cheek. Yep. Mashed potato.

Chuckling, I replaced him in his seat, wiped the mash from my cheek and then sucked my finger clean. "Oh, it is," I said, smacking my lips.

"Ice cream is better," Tanner declared.

I nodded. "Agreed."

Something small struck the side of my head. I turned to find Amanda and Brendon regarding me. In Amanda's hand, pinched loosely between forefinger and thumb, was a green pea, primed and ready to fly.

"Ahem?" she said.

I dragged my hands through my hair and sighed.

"Oh, stop being a drama queen," she reproached. "I know you told Professor Perry to take a hike."

I raised my eyebrows. "How do you know that?"

She grinned. "You get that exact same look on your face when you tell Dad he's being an idiot."

"What look is that?" I asked, returning my attention to Amanda.

She pulled a face at me. Part vindictive grin, part triumphant smirk. On her it looked ridiculous. Amanda is the nice Sinclair girl. On me, I bet it looks incredible. It felt incredible.

What also felt incredible was seeing pride and happiness in her eyes as she smiled at me. My big sister was proud of me. Do you know what that feels like?

Let me tell you, it feels like nothing else in this life.

I crossed to where she sat on the other side of the table, dropped to a crouch and wrapped my arms around her. "I love you, Mandy."

Her chuckled hum vibrated through her chest into my cheek. That felt equally as incredible. "Love you too, Chase."

I'm not sure how long we stayed that way, but when I pulled away her eyes glistened with shimmering tears.

"I'm quite fond of you myself," Brendon declared. *After* launching a tiny green missile from his plate that completely missed me and landed in Amanda's hair.

I rolled my eyes at him and then grinned. "Thank you, oh Benign One. Now, is there any chance you could tell me where Caden is staying in LA and how I might go about making him talk to me?"

Caden

I can't believe not a single Telco in LA had a 24-hour shopfront that I could stride into and buy a local SIM. Not one.

I found a shop where I could get it changed tomorrow morning, although I was of the opinion its 10am opening time was a deliberate attempt to really push what little patience I had left. But patience was all I had. That and Buckley's of finding a store to get a SIM before 10am. (Translation for the non-Aussies: "Buckley's" means zero chance of it happening.)

Instead of going back to my motel room, a depressing and frustrating thought even with the tropical pool and obscenely large bath and pristinely clean kitchenette, I walked the few blocks to the animal hospital to check on Doofus. I'd received an iMessage from Dr. Adams while I was still at Denny's, to say Doofus was slowly – almost stubbornly – improving. He still wasn't out of the woods yet, and his kidneys were still not functioning the way they were meant to, but the antibiotics finally seemed to be taking serious affect. I took that as a good sign.

I also took it as an omen for my relationship with Chase. Lame, yes? But a bloke's got to hang on to whatever hope he can. Until I had a bloody US SIM in my phone I couldn't call her, text her . . .

Fuck. I could message her on Facebook. Damn it, why hadn't I thought of that before?

I yanked my phone from my back pocket and checked the Wi-Fi indicator at the top of the screen. It was gray. I had no net access, unless I could hop onto someone's unsecure network. Shit.

Okay, maybe I could sweet talk whoever was on duty at the animal hospital into giving me the password again for their network? Who could refuse a charming, cheeky Aussie like me?

Dr. Randolf Simmons, that's who.

When I got to Laguna Niguel, the last veterinarian on day shift was leaving. I'd met her earlier – a really nice woman who originally hailed from the UK. She let me in the building, told me Dr. Simmons was the vet on duty for the night, hollered out to an unseen Randolf that she'd let me in and that I was checking up on the Doberman-cross in recovery, and then stepped out the door.

Randolf had appeared a few moments after that, just as I

was heading around the empty reception counter. Our eyes met.

"G'day," I said, giving him a friendly nod and a smile. "I'm Caden O'Dae."

Randolf could have been Hagrid's twin, from *Harry Potter* – *sans* beard and sunny disposition. He'd looked me over from head to toe, and then grunted and stomped his way to the bathroom.

That was it. Nothing else was said to me. No other form of interaction.

I watched the door swing shut behind his cliff-face back. "I'll just go see Doofus, shall I?"

Accompanied by the sounds of the menagerie, I made my way to Doofus's cage, preparing myself for whatever I found.

His ears pricked as I approached. A good sign.

"G'day, mate," I said, keeping my voice low and soothing and calm.

I didn't even get the chance to say *How you going?* before Doofus not only raised his head but stood in his cage.

Stood.

Sure, it was a wobbly stand, what with the plaster cast on his front right leg and shoulder, and his deformed back left leg, and it only lasted a couple of seconds before he laid back down again. But in those few seconds he'd looked at me, tongue lolling out in what could only be described as a happy doggy grin, tail wagging with equal canine happiness.

Elation swept through me in a warm wave. A smile spread over my face. A big one.

"That good, eh?" I murmured, unlatching his cage with gentle, slow movements.

He barked at me, a low conversational *woof*. One of the best freaking sounds I've ever heard, trust me. He stretched his neck as I reached in to give him a pat, meeting my head with his muzzle. He licked my wrist, tail wagging faster, his tongue warm and wet. A happy tongue, to go with his happy tail and happy woof. A healthy tongue. Joy rushed through me, not a wave but a tsunami.

I continued to pat and stroke his head, giving him a gentle scratch every now and again, checking out his stitches and wounds. The intravenous antibiotic drip, I noticed, was gone. An awesome sign, to be sure. Doofus kept wagging his tail, trying his best to inch as close to me as he could, giving another conversational woof as he did.

"I reckon you're going to be okay, mate," I told him, kneading his ears as I examined the cast on his front leg. "Reckon we'll be playing fetch before you know it."

He gave me another happy bark. His tail was wagging with such gusto now his whole body was wobbling. You know a dog is happy when the whole-body wags are happening.

I let out a low chuckle, rubbing my forehead to his. "Chase is going to be so happy to see you like this."

He woofed. I chuckled again. "Yeah, she's a prickly one, I know, but she's deadset in love with you. Reckon that might be the way to get her to Australia. Tell her we need to do joint custody, and seeing as you're coming back to Oz with me, she'll have to come as well. What do you think? Plan?"

Doofus woofed. His tail whacked the sides of his cage.

"Plan," I agreed.

He strained his neck so he could lick my face. I laughed. And then jumped about twenty feet in the air, letting out a startled "shit" when a voice behind me said, "You know you shouldn't let dogs lick your face."

I turned to see Randolf watching us. "Yeah. But this guy's worth it."

He regarded me without expression before shrugging those massive shoulders of his. "Your funeral," he muttered, pivoting on his heel and making his way through the recovery area.

I watched him shuffle around, checking on the other animals in their cages – muttering the whole way about idiot Australians. If it weren't plainly obvious he was tender and concerned about his charges, if it weren't for the fact he lingered with each one longer than required, his voice as low and soft as he was hulking and imposing, I would have wondered what the hell he was doing here.

I stayed with Doofus at his cage, talking to him, massaging his ears, long enough my feet and lower back began to ache from standing. I told Doofus of all the incredible hiking trails we were going to do together back in Australia. Filled him in on all the games of rugby we were going to play in my mum's backyard. Described in detail the expanse of Brighton Beach on the Victoria coastline, and how we'd leave our footprints and paw prints on its pristine white sand as we jogged along its length.

By the time I realized I needed to go to the loo, I'd decided Doofus was going to be a permanent fixture in my own vet practice when I established it. After we returned to Australia and his stint in quarantine, he'd join me in my internship at Dr. Phillip's clinic.

He'd start out as a regular guest on her television show, no doubt wooing the audience with his doggy awesomeness and plucky nature, before his fame became too big for her show to contain. Then, with his Twitter followers numbering in the millions, he'd become the face of Dr. Caden O'Dae, Animal Doctor, a practice that would specialize in caring for rescued animals.

Doofus listened to my grand plans as I relayed them to him, his head tilted, his ears pricked, the occasional encouraging woof thrown into the conversation, his tail wagging.

"Of course," I chuckled, giving the side of his neck a scratch, "Chase will no doubt feature you in all her art works. So you'll be famous that way as well. Hey, maybe yours will be the first dog portrait to win the Archibald prize?"

Doofus woofed, gaze fixed firmly on me.

It was a moment of fantasy, my conversation, but it calmed me. I had no idea if I would be able to get Doofus into Australia. Our quarantine laws were infamously strict, even with domestic animals. I also had no idea if Chase would be remotely interested in moving there, even if we did get our . . . relationship sorted out. But sometimes a guy's got to allow himself a fantasy, for his sanity's sake. Or at least, for the sake of making it through the next few hours.

"Okay," I said, giving him one final neck scratch before closing the cage, "I gotta go take a leak."

His ears drooped. His wagging tail did the same.

"Ah, don't make me feel bad," I scolded gently. "I'll be back. Promise," I added, before turning and heading for the door.

His answering woof told me in no uncertain terms to hurry the fuck up.

I crossed the empty waiting room to the bathroom. I felt good. Like I'd been mainlining whatever it was Brendon was on to be so positive. Now, if only it would hurry up and be 10 am so I could get my butt into the Telco shop, get a US SIM and get Chase on the phone. I could have called her on the clinic's phone, I know, but it was late now and I didn't want to wake her if she was asleep.

Pushing open the bathroom door, it occurred to me I could probably just ask Brendon to get her to call or text me on his phone. As awkward as that would be, at least we could communicate. The first step.

I pulled my phone from my back pocket and quickly

tapped out a message to Brendon: *Sorry for texting so late, but when you see or speak to Chase next, can you get her to text or call me on your phone? Even if it's tonight. I can't get a US SIM until tomorrow morning. Thanks, dude.*

Feeling like I was thrumming, I slipped my phone into pocket. And then jerked my head around at the soft tap of knuckles on glass.

My throat seized up.

Chase stood on the other side of the main entry door, looking at me.

For a moment – just a moment, but a bloody stupid moment – I didn't move. Stood rooted to the spot, staring at her. The exterior lights played with her hair, turning it to a halo of vivid cyan blue that was almost surreal.

I blinked. Was she really there?

Let me in, you over-protective moron, she signed, lips curling into a devilish smile.

A short, startled laugh burst from me. *Well, if you're going to be that way . . .* I signed back, staying exactly where I was.

Well, most of me was staying exactly where I was. My heart was well and truly on its way to thumping itself out of my chest.

If you don't let me in I can't show you how sorry I am for being a moron myself, she signed.

Sorry, I signed back, forcing my expression to be serious and aloof. *But the only people allowed in here this time of night are those coming to see their animals.*

Her eyes narrowed.

Their not-dying animals, I continued. I know I stumbled over the word *dying*. For some reason my hands were shaking. Maybe because I was on the verge of bursting into song and dancing around with sheer joy. Mind you, I'm not *that* good a dancer. If I *had* done that, Chase might very well have bolted.

She frowned. And then the frown turned into an expression of hesitant hope. Her hands moved: *Do you mean . . .*

Yep.

"Fuck yeah!" her muffled shout came through the glass. What wasn't muffled was the sheer delight in her voice.

I grinned.

She grinned back. And then a heartbeat later, signed, *Well? Are you going to let me in?*

I ran to the door, unlocked it and yanked it open. Before she could ask or say whatever her mouth was opening to ask or say, I hauled her to my body and kissed her. It might have been a tad presumptuous, but fuck it. She was here, not with Donald the Dude, and I was going to kiss her.

The heavy glass entry door whacked into my back, knocking us both off balance. Laughing, still holding each other, we moved away from the door. It took a second for us to regain balance, another second to stare into each other's eyes, and a third to return to our kiss.

And holy hell, did we *kiss* each other. Our tongues and lips and teeth spoke of every desire and passion and need we had. I completely lost myself to the wonder of her lips on mine, far more potent because I had spent a great deal of the day thinking it was never going to happen again.

When we finally tore apart, the separation lasted barely a second before I cupped her face and kissed her again. And again. Over and over. I couldn't get enough of her lips, of her smell, her taste.

Finally, all too aware that if we didn't stop we'd end up breaking the laws of decency right there in front of the animal hospital, under the glaring entry lights, I dragged my mouth from hers.

"So . . ." I said, catching my breath. "That just happened."

Chase laughed. Raking her fingers through my beard, she

closed her eyes and smiled. "Yes, it did. And it was *wow*. So much *wow*."

"Wow is an understatement." I wanted to ask her what had happened between her and the Douchebag. The need to do so itched at the back of my skull like a hive of ants. I ignored it. Just. She may have just made fun of my over-protectiveness, but I wasn't prepared to push the point. Not yet, at least. Not until I finished basking in the fact she was here with me now.

I smoothed my hands up and down her back and waited for her to look up at me. "How did you know I was here?" I asked.

She shook her head. "I didn't. My plan was to drive to the last place I saw you, then ring Brendon and have him tell me where you were."

I chuckled. "I love your impulsiveness."

"And my sarcasm?" she asked. "I think I just sarcasmed my way out of ever being a student at SDSU again."

A hot lump filled my throat but I smiled all the same. "I love your sarcasm."

She chewed her lip, a hesitant uncertainty falling over her face. "Do you?"

"I do." I searched her eyes. "And your courage and your independence and your strength."

"Independence?" she repeated, her voice catching. "You know that's a big one for me, don't you? I mean, I'm not a little girl who can't look after herself. I'm allowed to make my own decisions. And I'm definitely allowed to run across a busy road if I want, and you're not allowed to freak out and try to protect me."

"You know I'm likely to do just that," I countered. "And it has nothing to do with your hearing and everything to do with me being terrified you might get hurt. Hell, I'd freak out if

Brendon tried to sprint across that road you took on. Might not shout at him though. More likely to punch the bastard in the jaw for freaking me out."

She watched me. I could see her mind working.

"You know," she went on, the words slow, considered, "if someone is being horrible to me, I'm perfectly okay with taking care of it."

Donald the Dude. We were talking about Donald the Dude. His name didn't need to be mentioned to know that.

Anger and jealousy threaded through my happiness. I swallowed. The need to be flippant, to toss out a joke instead of address those emotions, crushed down on me. "And if *I* want to take care of it?" I finally said. "If someone is being a dick to the woman I love, I'm allowed to let them know, right? And to tell them to fuck off? Or is that being too protective as well, because if it is, Chase, I . . ." I stopped, shaking my head. My pulse thumped in my ear, a cannon of drilling volume.

"I should have told you sooner I answered Perry's call," I said, stepping back from her and rubbing at the back of my neck. "It was wrong of me not to."

She caught her bottom lip again. "It was."

Dragging my hand up into my hair, I clawed at my scalp.

It's okay to get angry, Brendon had said. *You don't have to smother everything in a joke.* But a lifetime of suppressing any agitation I experienced, of keeping my calm and not getting ruffled . . . it was hard to not fall back on that. Especially when I suspected things needed to be said that would hurt. Both her and me.

"Why *did* you answer his call, Cade?" she asked, her stare holding mine. "Why didn't you tell me?"

"Why didn't you just tell him it was over, Chase?" The question – the accusation – burst from me before I could stop it, or cut it off with a self-deprecating joke. "Why did you go to his place? After everything we've . . . Fuck, I don't . . . I don't know . . . You . . ." I broke off again, jerking my gaze everywhere around us but to where Chase stood, watching me. "After everything that happened between us, why did you go to his house?"

"I had to," she said, the words husky.

Hot disappointment sheared through me. I finally looked at her. "And?"

"And I'm here, aren't I?" she said. "I'm here with you. Not there with him."

Here with you. A rush of concentrated relief and joy at those words flowed through me. Followed by an undeniable need for clarification. "You told him it was over? To stop calling you. You told him you're done with him?"

She nodded. "Yes. Quite emphatically, in fact. There was shoving involved."

I sucked in a sharp breath, my fists balling. "He shoved you?"

"No, *I* shoved him." A frown knitted her eyebrows. There and gone just as quickly. "For a while he didn't want to take the hint. And then I laughed at him."

I should have been listening to her. I should have focused on the "laughed at him" part of her declaration. Instead, I was seeing red, and there wasn't a joke or witty comment to be had. "He touched you? Tried to . . . to what? Force you?" Rage turned my blood hot. I ground my teeth. "I should have dealt with the prick when I was on the phone with him."

Chase's jaw clenched. Dark tension flared in her eyes. "Why? Because I wasn't capable?"

"No," I almost shouted. "Because I love you. Don't you get that? I love you and I hate the idea of anyone, *anyone*, upsetting you or hurting you. I hate it. I hate that I did it, I hate that Perry did it, I hate that your father does it. The whole point of being in love with someone is to make sure their life is the best life it can be. It's not about being selfish. It's not about how great that person makes *your* life, it's about making *their* life wonderful. And I couldn't do that. I *didn't* do that for you. I yelled at you and I betrayed you and I made jokes when I really wanted to scream."

Chase stepped toward me. I fisted my hands in my hair, watching her.

"I've loved you from the second I saw you, Chase," I said. When had someone lined my throat with hot sandpaper? "It's lame and corny and you can roll your eyes all you like, but it's true. And I know I'm probably going to piss you off a lot because I *will* try and protect you when you don't want me to, but I can't help that. Just like I can't help being in love with you."

I stopped. My breath squeezed from my lungs in shallow breaths. I felt giddy.

"And I swear," I croaked, my voice little more than a scratch, "if Donald the Dude calls or texts you one more time I will find out where he lives and shove his phone up his arse."

"I don't need you to protect me, Caden," she said, looking up at me. I can only assume she'd read my lips because there wasn't a hope in hell she could have heard me. "But I think . . ." She touched her fingers to my chest. "But I think I'm going to like that you want to."

I swallowed.

A smile curled her lips, small, almost shy, but a smile. "I'm going to tell you that I love you now, Caden O'Dae. Promise you won't freak out? Or make a lame joke?"

My pulse detonated in my throat. "Promise."

Happiness danced in her eyes. "I love you."

Drawing in a steady breath, I smoothed my hands over

her hips. My heart pounded in my throat, my ears. "I'm going to kiss you now."

"If you don't," she said, "I may have to beat you."

I kissed her. Quite a bit.

When our lips finally separated, I cupped her face in my palms and smiled down at her. "We can make this work."

She smiled back. "We can."

Releasing a ragged breath, I smoothed my hands up her back. "So, want to go in and say g'day to Doofus?"

Hesitation fell over her face. "Is he okay? Really okay? Or 'vet boyfriend who doesn't want to upset his girlfriend' okay?"

Boyfriend.

Girlfriend.

Do you have any idea how I felt hearing those words? I don't think I've got a hope of describing it, to be honest.

"Really *really* okay," I answered. "He's still got some recovering to do, but he's going to make it."

"Yes!" She launched herself from the ground, wrapped her legs around my hips, and her arms around my shoulders, and kissed me again. This kiss fell somewhere between we're-going-to-be-arrested, and stolen-but-meaningful. Plus it had the added advantage of Chase's sex being *very* close to my groin. Those kinds of kisses are bloody awesome.

When it ended, I threaded my fingers through hers and grinned. "Let's get in there," I said as I turned to open the door.

Only to find it locked.

"Shit," I muttered, a second before Chase chuckled and tapped me on the shoulder.

I looked up from the door handle and burst out laughing. There, on the other side of the glass, perched on the reception counter watching us, was Dr. Randolf Simmons. And sitting beside him, grinning at us in interminable doggy happiness, a plastic protective cone around his neck to stop him messing up his stitches, and a new bright blue collar, was Doofus.

Randolf regarded us, expression completely serious, and then his wide face broke into a wide smile and he lifted his hand and gave us a thumbs up.

Veterinarians. We're a very special breed.

TEN

"What counts is not necessarily the size of the dog in a fight – it's the size of the fight in the dog."
~ Dwight D Eisenhower

Chase

After the reunion to end all reunions – and I'm talking about my reunion with Doofus, who I had been convinced was going to die and take my heart with him – we sat on the waiting room floor together, his head in my lap, while Caden and Dr. Simmons talked veterinarian stuff, Doofus's progress, and his treatment.

Whenever I stopped patting him to answer Amanda's text (yes I'd got to LA okay and yes, I'd found Caden and yes, we were *together* together), or to answer Mom's text (yes, I was okay and yes, I was in LA and yes, I was coming home eventually), Doofus would give my hand a nudge and I'd pat him again.

It was nice. More than nice. I was lovely. I couldn't wait to take him home. To introduce him to Tanner. To love him the way he deserved to be loved.

Finally, Caden's gaze found mine and he gave me a smile. "Any chance you're ready to get going? Or do I have Buckley's of dragging you away from Doofus?"

Before I could answer a frantic woman started banging on the glass door, a writhing cat in her arms. She was rightfully frantic because her cat – the fluffiest white Persian I've ever seen – had somehow got its head stuck inside her daughter's Mr. Potato Head.

Both Caden and Dr. Simmons hurried to the door at the same time, expressions calm and determined. Watching Caden as he helped Simmons deal with the distraught woman and her very angry cat, I couldn't help but notice just how relaxed and completely at home he was in the situation.

It was clear he was born for this line of work. He loved me – to be honest, I think I'd known that for a while – but watching him work in the animal hospital, I realized just how much he loved being a veterinarian. Or almost one. He still had one year of his studies at Melbourne University to complete.

That's Melbourne, Australia. A country situated on the other side of the world from the US.

Goddamn it. How the hell were we going to work *this* out? As far as long-distance relationships go, this was pushing it to the max. There was no way my wages at the exotic pet store would cover the cost of numerous international flights. Which meant we'd only physically be together whenever Caden could fly to America. And with the pressure he was under due to exams and studies I doubted he'd have that much free time to fly to the States.

Trust me to go and fall in love with a guy who didn't even

live in the same country. A knot bigger than Mount Rushmore twisted in my belly.

"Ready?"

I blinked, the question bringing me back into the waiting area.

Caden smiled down at me, duffle bag slung over his shoulder. "Randolf's got the cat situation covered. We can go now." He slid a grin at Doofus. "That is, if you can say goodbye to this guy for the night?"

Doofus raised his head from my lap and let out a happy bark, his liquid brown eyes fixed on Caden. Tummy fluttering, I let out a soft chuckle. I wasn't the only one completely and utterly lost to Caden O'Dae.

"Well," I said, a warm sensation of happiness and anticipation rushing through me. "If it's just the night . . ."

Caden's gaze found mine, a silent message in his eyes, one that detonated an excited fluttering in my girlie bits, before moving his attention to Doofus. "Okay, mate, time for you to go back to the recovery room."

Doofus let out a soft bark. His tail wagged faster. He started to get to his feet, and Caden dropped into a deep crouch, gently sliding his arms beneath his belly and ribcage and lifting him from the floor. Doofus's tail continued to wag. He tried to lick Caden's face, the plastic protective cone around his neck stopping him. I looked up at them both from where I still sat cross-legged on the floor.

My future. Right there. For the first time in my life, my *entire* life, I knew exactly what I wanted. This Australian and this dog. It didn't matter where we were going, as long as we were going together.

"I love you," I said, when Caden looked at me over Doofus's shoulder.

"I know," he said, and then grinned.

I threw back my head and laughed. Yeah, trust Caden to use a *Star Wars* quote in response.

"Just let me put Doofus back in his cage," he said as I got to my feet. "And I'll let Randolf know we're going."

I nodded. Inside, my tummy had turned to a cage of frantic butterflies. Not because I was nervous. There was nothing to be nervous about. Because I was excited.

I knew.

I freaking knew what was going to happen for the rest of my life. Caden and I were going to be together – somehow we'd work out the geography – and things were going to be awesome. I knew it. I felt it. In my heart.

Wow. I mean . . . wow.

"See you tomorrow, Doofus," I said, giving him a gentle scratch behind his ear. He tried to lick me this time.

Life was good. So good.

Caden returned a few moments later, the strong scent of disinfectant and soap clinging to him. He crossed the waiting room floor to where I waited at the door, stopped directly in front of me, threaded his fingers into my hair and kissed me. My knees trembled. Have you ever been kissed so beautifully and perfectly that your knees tremble? I didn't want it to end even as I wanted it to hurry the fuck up and end so we could get out of here. So we could get to wherever Caden was staying, and do what people who are in love do when they finally stop being idiots and admit that's exactly how they feel.

Finally, Caden lifted his head and smiled down at me. "My motel is just down the road."

I let out a ragged laugh. "That's good, otherwise we'd be doing it in the Speeding Dragon in the parking lot."

I still don't know how we actually made it into Caden's motel room, but we did. We fell through the door kissing, and trying like hell to undress each other, our feet tripping and stumbling, our tongues tangling.

The end of the bed halted our frenzied progress. The backs of my calves struck it, toppling us both over. We hit the mattress together in a tumble of arms and legs and laughter. And then we were both naked, our clothes discarded with wild abandon, our bare skin sliding together, our breaths mingling.

When I flattened Caden to his back, straddling his hips, my sex rubbing against his naked erection, he let out a groan I felt all the way to my soul.

"Wait wait wait," he said, pleasure etching his face. Without warning, he flipped me onto my back.

I squealed with delighted surprise, the sound becoming a groan as forceful as his when he dragged his lips down over my belly to the junction of my thighs. He explored every inch of my flesh down there. Every. Inch. He propelled me to the very heights of pleasure with his tongue, over and over, keeping me balanced there, like an inferno burning on the tip of a pin, until I begged him to make me come.

He didn't. Instead, he rose up over my body and turned his masterful mouth to the rest of my body. My breasts, my throat, my belly button, my hips, the inside of my elbows.

I writhed on the bed, on the tip of the pin, burning up, on the cusp of eruption. It was too much. Too much. Hooking my thighs around his hips, I snared two fistfuls of his hair and yanked his head up.

"We have the rest of our lives for long foreplay, O'Dae," I declared, holding his gaze. Oh man, his eyes were so ablaze with desire and need I almost came staring into them. "Right now, I want you inside me."

"Condom," he groaned. I didn't hear the word, only felt its vibration in his chest and saw it form on his lips. His voice was too strained, too hoarse for me to hear. I didn't care. I knew what his voice sounded like. I knew how his accent would make the word sound. I knew how the vowels would form in the back of his mouth, how the consonants would form on his tongue. I didn't need to hear it to love it. It wasn't necessary. And neither was . . .

"I'm protected," I said, watching his eyes. "And I trust you."

He grew still. Every part of him. Every part except that which nestled against my sex. It throbbed, each pulse nudging my folds with gentle pressure.

"Are you . . ." he began, and then stopped to let out a choppy breath. His hips rested against mine, his long sinewy legs framing my thighs. I reveled in the weight of his body on mine, its strength and warmth and connection. "Are you sure? The box of condoms you bought are in my bag. If you want I can—"

"Do *you* want?" I asked around my pounding heart.

Another raw groan vibrated low in his chest and he closed his eyes. "Chase, the thought of sliding into you with nothing between us . . . the thought of being naked inside you . . ." He opened his eyes again. "I want that fucking more than I can say."

I smiled, and touched his cheek with shaky fingers. "Me too."

He gazed down at me. "Everything you are, Chase Sinclair," he said, "is everything I want and love."

Sheer, pure happiness flooded through me, and then exquisite concentrated pleasure replaced it as Caden buried himself inside me in one fluid stroke. We moved as one, our bodies joined in the most intimate of ways. He filled me, stretched me, making my head spin and my body burn with pleasure. I arched beneath him, my legs encircling his hips, my lips on his throat, his collarbone. The salty heat of his sweat-slicked skin stirred a carnal lust in me. I clawed at his back, wanting more of him. Needing more of him.

I cried out his name, undone and remade in the pleasure he wrought on me, created in me.

My release crashed through me, wave after wave, and then Caden came and I erupted again, his hot breath on the side of my neck, the smell of his body, the sensation of his orgasm flooding into me detonated another orgasm in me, more powerful than any other.

We finally slumped on the bed together, the shuddering pulses of our climaxes fading, until at last we were still and breathless. I rested my cheek on his chest and draped my thigh over his hip, my hand loosely cupping his shoulder. He drew languid circles on my back with his fingertips as we lay there, neither of us talking.

And that was when I felt it. Or heard it? Or both.

His heartbeat. In my ear. So soft I might have been imagining it. Lying there with my cheek and ear pressed to his chest, I experienced his heartbeat. It was everything I knew it would be.

"I love you," I said, the words growing more powerful more significant every time.

"Of course you do," he answered against my cheek. "Took you freaking long enough to admit though."

I lifted my head to grin at him. "Hey, you think something as amazing as *this* –" I waved my hand up and down the length of my side, "– was ever going to be easy?"

"It was bloody expensive," he answered with his own grin. "Do you have any clue how much flights to LA from Melbourne cost? I've been pulling in hours and hours of intern work just so I could fly over here as often as I could, just to have you scowl at me."

I arched an eyebrow at him. "I have a feeling that veterinarian you work for back in Melbourne wasn't upset about all those extra hours. I've seen the posts she tags you in on Facebook. If you were a Tootsie Roll she'd be tearing off your wrapper and eating you."

He burst out laughing. Like his voice, it radiated through my body in a sensory caress I absolutely loved. "Is that jealousy I hear in your voice, Chase Sinclair?"

I twisted my lips into a righteous pout. "Hell yeah. You're my property, O'Dae. She's just going to have to find another Tootsie Roll."

"We don't have Tootsie Rolls in Australia," he pointed out.

"Well," I said, snuggling back down against his chest and tightening my leg around his hip, "she sure as hell can't have mine."

We stayed that way for a long time, just lying together, breathing in perfect harmony. Eventually, as I began to feel my eyes grow heavy with sleep, I raised my head and met his gaze. "Thank you."

"For what?"

I shrugged. "Not giving up on me."

"Ahhh," he said, trailing his fingertips over my back. "That. Yeah, that was never going to happen. Mind you, I had pictures in my head of us old and grey and wrinkly with walking-frames and you *still* pretending you didn't like me."

I snorted.

He grinned. "Actually, you were a pretty damn sexy old lady. The only one in the nursing home with her eyebrow pierced, a butt tattoo and wearing Doc Martens."

I couldn't help but giggle.

"And I was a very dirty old man," he finished.

"I bet you were."

We fell asleep in each other's arms, and I came to accept that falling asleep in Caden's arms was the only place I wanted to fall asleep, with my cheek on his chest, feeling his heart beat in rhythm with mine, imagining us growing old together, me and my dirty-old-man husband.

Caden

My fourth morning of waking up in America was my favorite one of all.

Chase was beside me when I opened my eyes, she was gloriously naked, she was smiling in her sleep, and she loved me.

I'd suspected she did for some time but I'd only been ninety-nine percent convinced of it. Well, maybe ninety percent. Then, when I'd seen her with Donald the Dude in LAX that percentage had slipped a little. Yesterday afternoon, when she'd headed back to San Diego that percentage had slipped some more, but it had stubbornly stayed above fifty percent.

Now, lying here with her by my side, studying her face as she smiled in her sleep, I knew one hundred percent she loved me.

Fuck a duck, it was a good feeling. The best.

I didn't wake her, I lay still and watched her sleep, loving the fact I could. Loving her.

She finally stirred a few minutes later, stretching and arching on the bed like a cat, yawning and scrunching up her face unabashedly.

"Good morning," I said as her heavy-lidded eyes found mine.

Her smile grew wider, soft with sleep. "Morning."

"Wanna go for a swim?"

A husky laugh fell from her. "I don't have my swimming suit here."

I flashed a grin at her. "Well, in that case, may I suggest some other form of morning exercise?"

"Hell yeah," she answered, before pulling my head to hers for a kiss that made it loud and clear the morning exercise I had in mind was exactly the exercise she had in mind as well. I'm not sure, but I think we may have woken the guests in the rooms either side of ours. There had to be some reason for them banging on the walls, right?

I was rubbing my hair dry with a towel after my shower when Chase entered the bathroom and perched her butt on the edge of the basin, her gaze contemplative. "I had an epiphany when I walked out of Donald's place last night."

Her words made me pause. "K."

She let out a ragged breath, and dragged her hands through the spikey blue mess of her hair. "I think it explains why I was so stupid about him, and I need to tell you."

Throat thickening, I nodded. "Shoot."

Her answering laugh was wry.. She scraped her fingers over her scalp again and then looked at me. "You know what my dad is like, right?"

I had to bite back the words, *You mean a wanker?* He wasn't. Well, not really. He was . . . hmmm, let's go with an elitist. He'd done everything in his power to make Brendon's life hell. During Tanner's fight with leukemia, Charles Sinclair had started legal proceedings to have Amanda and Brendon declared unfit parents. He had a vision for his daughter and his grandson that didn't include an Australian personal trainer, regardless of how great a guy that Australian personal trainer was. When his vision unraveled, Charles became an angry, bitter father and father-in-law.

I've yet to see Charles meet Brendon's eyes. They are rarely in the same room together. From what I understand, last Thanksgiving he refused to go to Amanda and Brendon's home, thereby not seeing his daughter and grandson on a day that's meant to be all about showing your thanks for those you love.

That's the kind of behavior that illustrates his candidacy for Wanker of the Year in my opinion, but he's also been less than welcoming to me. You'd think, given my bone marrow helped save his only grandson's life, he'd be a little more open, but I barely get more than a grunt from him whenever we come face to face.

I can deal with that. My father – absent in my life since I was twelve – isn't exactly in the running for Dad of the Year. I know what fathers can be like. What I didn't like was the way Charles spoke to Chase. The last time I was in the same room as Charles, he'd told Chase she had to get her life sorted out and stop using her hearing impairment as an excuse for being pathetic.

I don't think the word *pathetic* could ever be attached to Chase, in any way. But I bit my tongue back then, just as I did now. A guy didn't tell the girl he loved he thought her father was a dick, no matter how much evidence supported the opinion. That's just not the right thing to do. I also had to believe Charles loved his daughters. I had to believe what he did to Amanda and Brendon came from a place of love, no matter how misguided and deluded. I have to believe the way he treats Chase comes from that same place. Otherwise, I'd be likely not to bite my tongue any longer, and no amount of joking would save me from destroying any civil relationship I'd have with the man I hoped would one day be my father-in-law.

"Yeah," I said now, draping the towel over my shoulders. "I know what your dad is like."

Mischief twinkled in Chase's eyes. "Love your diplomatic tone, O'Dae."

I grinned.

"Anyways," she went on, hoisting herself up onto the cabinet to swing her legs a little, her heels striking against the doors in gentle thuds, "Dad gets under my skin a bit."

I had no hope of stopping my snort at that understatement.

Chase pulled a face at me. "Yeah, yeah. I know what you're thinking." She sighed, a sadness filling her face for a moment. "We don't always see eye to eye. I know he loves me, I don't doubt that, but he also . . . cripples me, if that makes sense. I don't think he means to, but I've grown up with him telling me I'm defective."

I ground my teeth, fighting to keep the emotion from my face. Defective? What kind of father called his daughter defective?

"Because of that defect, he's been over protective. Like, big time over protective. You remember when I lost it so much on the road when you yelled at me? I suspect I probably wouldn't have reacted the way I did if it wasn't for Dad telling me my whole life I couldn't do the things normal kids do because of my hearing. So yeah, he kind of messed me up a little that way." She gave me an almost shy smile. "In case you hadn't noticed."

"Hmmm," I responded, with my own small smile. "Might have. Maybe."

She laughed. If you asked me for an example of melancholy, that laugh was it.

"In Dad's opinion," she went on, studying her toes, "the way to beat my defect was to excel academically. He told me it was my brain that would make me stand out in the world. I grew up thinking I had no chance of being anything but a defective smart person. When I decided not to study English Lit at college, Dad was disgusted. Mortified in fact. Art, and anything relating to art, isn't a real subject in Dad's not-so-humble opinion. Hell, even when my old school principal suggested I submit my college application essay about art as therapy to a national writing competition, Dad wasn't appeased. So when . . ." She paused, a frown pulling at her eyebrows. "So when I went to college, I threw myself into my practical studies and neglected my theory ones. Just to piss Dad off."

Lifting her gaze to me, she chewed her lip. "I know deep down I was hurting myself, but at the time, I just wanted to hurt him. Does that make sense?"

I nodded. Every joke I'd made at my parents' expense about their separation had been about doing the same thing: hurting someone. Although to be fair, that pain wasn't directed at them, but rather myself.

"Everything changed," she said, frowning again, "when I started Donald's class. He didn't treat me like I was a little girl, or broken, or needing special attention. He treated me like I was normal. Like my thoughts mattered." A tear slipped from her eye but she rubbed it away with the back of her hand before I could move, returning her gaze to her toes. "I needed to know that more than anything else. What's a girl to do when she knows her thoughts, her life, the decisions she made about that life, aren't good enough for her father? She goes looking for a father figure they *are* good enough for, and unfortunately I found that father figure in Donald. So then, when he first told me I was the sexiest thing he'd ever seen," she continued, her cheeks red, her eyes downcast, "it made me feel like I was actually a real woman. Which basically means

I'm a walking, talking cliché. You want to see what classic textbook Daddy issues look like? I'm the living example, right here."

I waited for her to raise her head before speaking. It was hard to keep my voice calm, but I did. For her, I did.

"A real woman isn't about being sexy, Chase," I said when she looked at me. "Not in my opinion. A real woman doesn't need to be sexy. She needs to be herself. Believe in herself. Be true to who she is. That's what makes a woman gorgeous. That's the reason *I* fell in love with you."

She regarded me, anguish shining in her eyes. "I wish I'd met you before Donald and I . . ." She broke off, gazing at the space above my head. When she looked at me again, another tear was trickling down her cheek. "I was in awe of Donald. He was the popular professor, and lots of girls in my class lusted after him. But it was me he chose to have a relationship with."

Her voice cracked on *relationship*. My heart thumped fast as another tear trickled from her eye.

I wanted to go to her, but I know Chase. She wasn't ready for me to go to her yet. So I stood my ground, as hard as that was, and waited.

"It wasn't until he began to complain about little things," she said, her wet eyes finding mine again, "like the fact I tend to speak louder in crowds, or my speech is hard to follow sometimes, that I started to realize his idea of sexy had little to do with my personality. By that time, I was addicted to him." She sighed. "And that's the single most miserable thing I've ever confessed in my life. But it's the truth. I was addicted enough that when he dumped me because I wasn't suitable *serious relationship* material, I begged him to change his mind. Pleaded with him not to end us."

Another sigh escaped as she shook her head and raked her

fingers through her hair. Disgust etched her face. "It took finding him with another student for me to wake up," she said. "I might have been addicted to him, but I'm not stupid."

The hot anger I'd felt for her father narrowed to an icy cold knife of fury at Donald the Dude. No, Donald the Dude was the wrong name. Donald the Dick.

Chase gave me a lopsided shrug. "And then you came crashing into my life, with your sock puppets and sense of humor, and obvious interest in me, and I had no freaking clue what to do."

My throat grew thick. "But now you do?"

She levered herself off the basin and smoothed her hands around my waist. "I do."

I smiled back at her. "Good. You do realize, however, if I ever come face to face with the fuck knuckle, I'm going to break his nose, right?"

She chuckled, the sound wobbly, but warm with happiness all the same. "I do."

I cocked an eyebrow. "That goes for your dad as well."

She rolled her eyes. "It's really going to take me a while to get used to your particular brand of protectiveness. Now, enough with the caveman chest-thumping. I'd like to kiss you, if I may?"

"Hell you may," I answered, pulse quickening.

She rose up onto her tiptoes and brushed her lips over mine in a gentle kiss.

I was having none of it. Gentle my arse.

We *christened* the bathroom, for want of a better word. As it turns out, the cabinet was the perfect height for all our respective bits to line up the way they're meant to.

As our bodies joined, I told her over and over how much I loved her. She told me back. I think the entire motel heard. I have no problem with that whatsoever.

By the time we finished our neighbors in the next room were banging on the wall again. Which when you think about it is kind of perfect. Banging due to our banging.

Yeah, that was lame. If my career as a vet ever crashes and burns, comedy will not be my go-to second job option.

I received a text from Dr. Adams while we were getting ourselves back in some semblance of order.

Doofus was ready to be released. It was early, but because I pretty much knew what was going on, and would have no problems administering his medication and changing his dressing when required, Dr. Adams believed the best place for him to recover was with those who loved him.

I'd say *come home* instead of *released* – that was the normal term a vet used to inform an owner their pet was well enough to leave the clinic – but in Doofus's case *home* was a fluid state.

For starters, my home – which was where I wanted *his* home to be – was almost thirteen thousand kilometers away. For another thing, Chase might very well want him to stay here in the US. For a third thing, Chase might very well want me to stay here in the US.

For a fourth, what the hell did I do if she did?

I looked up from my phone and gave her a grin. "What are your thoughts on moving to Australia with me?"

Hey, I've never been one for holding back. Subtlety wasn't one of my strengths.

She looked at me and frowned. *Her* phone chose that moment to vibrate into life. The fact it wasn't Pink singing filled me with a happiness I can't really describe. Chase pulled it from her bag and answered the incoming call.

"Sis," she said. "What's up?"

Whatever Amanda said, Chase rolled her eyes. "That's so funny. What's really up?"

Chase flicked more than one glance my way as her sister talked to her. Something in her eyes told me she wasn't completely focused on what Amanda was saying.

"Uh huh," she said. "Uh huh . . . wait. What?" Confusion filled her face, followed by frustration. "Oh for the love of God, Dad can stick it in his ear."

I raised my eyebrows.

"Tell him," she went on, "we'll be back in San Diego whenever we're back in San Diego. And if he doesn't like it, he can find a new daughter."

I'm pretty certain the noise that wafted through the connection was Amanda laughing herself silly.

"Sis?" Chase said loudly in an attempt to get her attention. "What's the situation with Tanner and dogs? I know they had to be kept away from him when he first came out of hospital but what about –" She stopped, obviously listening to Amanda.

Whatever the answer was, it made her frown. "S'okay," she said into her phone with a nod of her head and a roll of her eyes. "Looks like Dad will be seeing us earlier than I'd planned after all. Won't he be happy?"

Amanda said something that made Chase laugh.

"A dog and an Australian," she said, regarding me with a devilish smirk. "There goes any chance of me becoming the favorite daughter again."

I couldn't help but snort out a laugh. The thought of antagonizing Charles Sinclair instilled zero fucks in me.

Chase hung up and dropped her phone into her bag. "Let's go get Doofus," she said. "We can discuss future living arrangements—"

"At the end of my time here in the States," I said. "Who knows, some clever sod somewhere may invent a portal for traveling from one side of the world to the other in thirty minutes by the time I'm due to leave."

Chase grinned. We were dodging the inevitable. At some point we would have to have the conversation about how were we going to deal with the vast distance between us. I was serious about Chase moving to Australia, but I had little doubt she'd also be serious about me moving to the US.

Of course, I could be totally putting the cart before the horse here. We'd only just declared our love for each other, Chase had only just purged Donald the Dick from her life. Rushing was the last thing she needed now.

But fuck a duck, the thought of returning to Australia without her . . .

I bit back a ragged sigh.

"Hey." Her soft exclamation drew my attention to where she now stood, directly in front of me. "Stop your stressing, O'Dae. We'll work it out."

Her kiss told me exactly how confident she was on that statement. I really wanted to feel the same.

We collected Doofus from the hospital after swinging by one of the biggest pet supply stores I've ever seen. In my opinion, the one thing the Americans know how to do better than any other country on the planet is super-size. Shopping for a collar, lead, bed, food and water bowls, chew toys, and other equipment with Chase was one of the most enjoyable times of my entire trip here so far. For her part, Chase glowed. I mean, she *glowed*.

She was almost giddy with excitement when she called our friendly Californian Highway Patrol officer, Gibson, and filled him in on Doofus's condition, promising we would send pictures of Doofus often. She stayed happy way right up until we pulled to a stop out in front of her parents' house.

Doofus barked, his head hanging in the space between

our seats, the protective plastic cone around his neck thunking against the sides of our seats, his attention fixed on the man climbing out of the bright red convertible Porsche parked directly in front of us.

"Fuck," Chase muttered, her grip on the steering wheel turning white.

My own knuckles, I suspected, were white, what with how tight I'd balled my hands into fists.

Donald the Dick was striding along the footpath, heading for the Speeding Dragon's driver's side door.

Doofus barked again. Hot anger crashed through me. I ground my teeth. Sucked in a sharp breath.

Doofus growled.

Have you ever heard a Doberman Pincher growl? It's a menacing sound. Now Doofus was only part Dobe, but the rest of him – Great Dane and God knows what else – was equally as intimidating. I gave his neck a quick scratch, even as I kept my eyes on Donald, who was now at the nose of the Speeding Dragon. "It's okay, mate," I told Doofus, forcing my voice to be calm. Not an easy task, let me tell you.

The man taking up almost my entire focus had hurt the woman I love. In turn, I wanted to hurt the fuck out of—

Chase opened her door and climbed out.

"I've lost my job thanks to you, you little whore," Donald snarled.

Right. That was it. I wasn't putting up with this shit any longer. I opened my door.

"Someone *anonymously* told the Dean I was fucking a student," Donald went on, childish petulance in every syllable. "And now I've been—" He stopped as I got out of the passenger seat.

"G'day," I said with a cold grin. "Care to take a step back before I have to help you?"

"Caden," Chase said to me. "It's okay. I'll deal with him."

Donald grabbed her upper arm. Hard. "I'm going to talk to you in private, Chase. And you'll hear every fucking word I say, you deaf dumb—"

I stormed at Perry, Doofus growling behind me. A part of me knew if he was physically able, he'd be out of the car and showing Donald the Dick exactly what he thought of him. Movement in my periphery told me someone had exited the Sinclair house, but I couldn't pull my stare from the art history professor strutting toward us.

"Caden," Chase called my name, shaking her arm out of Perry's grip as I bore down on them both. "He's not worth it."

He wasn't. But she was. And I may have promised her I wasn't going to be over-protective, but I sure as hell wasn't going to stand by while a wanker insulted her.

"Caden," she repeated my name when I reached them, flattening a firm palm to my chest. "Don't."

I dragged my stare from Perry's. Chase looked at up me, her expression calm. "Mom and Dad are watching. Actually, Dad's coming over her now. Let's keep this—"

"I told you I wanted you to marry me, Chase," Donald cut her off, reaching for her arm again. "What's this boy going to give you that I don't?"

"Respect," she answered. "Love. And a whole lot of sex that is so good I can't even describe it."

Hate and contempt burned in Donald's eyes as he slid me a look.

"And as for you fucking a student," Chase went on, "it hasn't been me for over a year. So if you're looking for your anonymous source, I'd be checking with the student you replaced me with. Or have there been more since?"

Donald's lip curled. His eyes narrowed.

Chase pointed over his shoulder to his Porsche. "Now I'm

suggesting you get in your car and get out of my life once and for all. Before I let this *boy* deal with you."

Donald looked at me again.

Chase did the same. And then she signed *Scare the crap out of him if you like.*

Clenching my teeth, I stepped toward him. Just as Doofus appeared at my side, growling.

It had taken him a while, but it seemed he'd made his way out of the Speeding Dragon after all.

Donald stared wide-eyed at Doofus, and back at me, and then scrambled away. I could be wrong, but I'm pretty certain a patch on the front of his trousers suddenly got darker. He ran. Actually, he scurried and tripped and stumbled his way back to the Porsche. He didn't look back.

If he had, he would have discovered Doofus wasn't chasing him. He would have seen Doofus sitting beside Chase, his tail wagging.

If he had, he would have seen *me* following. Not running. Just striding. Making sure he didn't turn around. Making sure he didn't even get the chance to look at Chase again.

But he didn't look back. He threw himself into his car and tore away, leaving nothing behind but a billowing cloud of tire-tainted smoke and his dignity.

I waved my hand in front of my face. Both his dignity and the smoke stank.

A cold wet nudge against my elbow made me look down. "You are the best dog in the world," I told Doofus.

He woofed up at me. And then woofed up at Chase. "And you are the best guy in the world," she said.

I grinned. Preened. Couldn't help it.

And then I turned my head to find Charles and Jacqui Sinclair standing on the footpath, watching us.

"So . . ." I said, smoothing my arms around their daughter

and drawing her even closer to my body. "Aren't you glad she picked me?"

CHASE

"So you're the student he's been sleeping with," Dad said, ignoring Caden.

The butterflies that had taken up residence in my belly the second I saw Donald's car turned insane. I stared at my father. He stared back. My brain identified the emotion boiling on his face but my heart refused to believe it.

"I have never been more disappointed in my life," he declared.

Hard to deny *that* level of negative emotion from one of your own parents when it's so openly declared.

Damn. Anger cut through me, turning my pain into something dark and snarky. Of course. "Why?" I shot back, disengaging from Caden's arms to ram my hands on my hips. "Because your defective daughter actually had the audacity to have a sex life? Or because it was with someone almost as old as you?"

"Chase," Mom said, stepping forward. "Charles. Stop it."

Dad ignored her. "Haven't you embarrassed yourself enough already, Chase? What with dropping out of school, the ridiculous hair, the ridiculous car. And now we find out you were sleeping with your professor?"

"Really, Dad? Who are you thinking of, right this very minute? Me? Or you?"

"*You!*" Rage engulfed his face. Mortified, indignant rage. I didn't know whether to laugh, or cry. So instead, I stood motionless. And numb.

Beside me, Caden took my hand, working it out of its

aching fist to thread his fingers through mine. Pressed against my thigh, Doofus whined. I didn't hear him, but I felt the vibrations of the sound through his ribs.

"Charles!" Mom snapped. Man, was she angry. When had I seen her like this? Oh yeah, that's right. When he'd threatened to declare Amanda unfit as a mother.

When had my father, the man who once gave me piggy-back rides up and down the supermarket aisle, become such a . . . such a prick?

He looked at Mom, incensed. "Perry asked the Board if he was married to this student would his suspension be upheld. He was here the other day asking if I'd act as his character witness for the meeting with the Dean and the Board. If I'd known he was talking about you, I would have broken his jaw. Thankfully, I didn't. In both cases."

My stomach dropped. Caden's fingers tightened on my hand.

Jesus. Was *that* what Donald had been doing? Trying to restart our relationship so he could keep his job? Oh God, I think I wanted to be sick.

Dad fixed me with a level stare. "I can't believe you were . . . were . . ." He stopped, swiping at his mouth with a shaking hand. "Why, Chase? Did he pressure you?"

"Charles," Mom said, stepping up to put her hand on his arm. "Perhaps out here isn't the best place to have this discussion. Nor is it perhaps the best time. Can't you see Chase is stressed?"

Dad let out a terse breath. "When *is* going to be the best time, Jacqueline? When she's forty and has wasted her life?"

"Enough, Charles," Mom snapped. God, I loved her right then. More than I can articulate.

Swinging back to me, Dad ran a narrowed-eyed gaze over

me. "Seriously, Chase. If I'd known you were . . . you were . . ."

"Say it, Dad," I said, feeling numb. "C'mon, you're a man of words. How would ol' Bill Shakespeare put it? 'Making the beast with two backs' with him?"

"*Chase.*"

I flinched at Mom's reproach. Caden held my hand tighter.

My stomach rolled. My throat seized, a hot lump choking me. Tears stinging at my eyes, I stared at Dad. "In the absence of fatherly love and respect, I went looking for the next best thing. I came up short, clearly, but whoa, did I learn a lesson. And isn't that one of the things you've longed for me to do? Learn? Use my brain?"

Something dark flickered over his face. Something tormented and haunted. "Absence of fatherly love? Do you honestly think I don't love you, Chastity? Do you honestly think I would get so stressed and agitated about you, about what you're doing if I didn't *love* you? You need to stop wasting your life and get back on track."

A scratchy breath tore from me. "You know, Dad, if you really took the time to understand me, you'd know I've never wasted a second of my life. I've lived it, for better or for worse, true. But I've lived it. I've been brave, I've been foolish. I've been scared." I looked at Caden, my smile for him and him alone. "I've been wrong and I've been right. All those things I've been because I've lived. I thought one day you'd finally understand that. But it has nothing to do with me, has it? The way you treat me, the way you think about me, has everything to do with *you* and your expectations and elitism."

"Enough," Charles stamped his foot. Yes, the foot had gone down. We'd reached that level of fatherly engagement. "Of course I speak from worry. You've been screwing your art history professor for who knows how long, and now you turn up after three nights with this *Australian?*"

My eyebrows shot up. "Careful, Dad, your American elitism is showing again."

He threw up his hands, exasperation warring with disbelief on his face. How many nights of my life had I looked up at that face when I was young as he read story after story to me? This was the man who had given me my love of Shakespeare, had taught me my appreciation of Chaucer. This man introduced me to the surreal perfection of Dr. Seuss and the dark humor of Roald Dahl. And now, this was the man questioning everything I had become. Everything.

"This is not the time for your sarcasm, young lady," he declared. "It's time for you to wake up and start living up to your true potential again."

And there it was. His openly mortified dissatisfaction with how his daughter had turned out. Talk about home truths hitting hard. Donald had nothing on Dad for making a girl feel good about herself.

Nothing.

Meeting his glare, I shook my head. "No, it's the *perfect* time for my sarcasm. Gee, Dad, so glad to see how ecstatic you are that I'm finally happy. And I *am* happy, Dad. This guy right here, holding my hand? Caden O'Dae? The guy who saved your grandson? He makes me happy. *Really* happy. It took me longer than it should have to see the light, but I did. And I came back here, to my home, to my parents, to share that with them. And instead, I'm facing you down on the sidewalk as you lecture me again about how crappy I'm living my life. Father of the Year award goes to Charles Sinclair."

"Chase," my mother said, stepping forward.

I shook my head, tears hot on my cheeks. "No, Mom, I need to say this. I really do." I turned back to Dad. "Think about that, Dad. You pride yourself on raising intelligent daughters, but when we have the audacity to use our brains in any way you don't see fit, your disappointment is palpable. Why can't you look at me, really look at me, and see *me*? Your daughter? Who has achieved so much more in her life than a simple piece of paper could ever encompass?"

His jaw bunched. His nostrils flared. I don't think I've ever seen my father more angry. "One second you're sleeping with Perry," he said, voice devoid of all emotion, "and the next you're shacked up in a motel with this . . . this . . ."

"Veterinarian." Caden's relaxed voice filled the air. He released my hand and smoothed his arm up my back and around my shoulders. "Well, almost. I've got my doctorate of Veterinarian Medicine to finish at Melbourne uni. But given you've known me for a while now, given you had Brendon investigated when he came back into Amanda's life, I'm sure you already know that, despite how hard you've tried to pretend I don't exist."

I gasped, and then gaped at Dad.

"Investigated?" Mom asked, her face as shocked as I felt. "You had Brendon *investigated*, Charles?"

He ignored her. He studied Caden, his eyes unwavering.

"You probably already know what my midterm exam results are," Caden went on. I'd never heard him speak so calmly. It was like he was having a chat with the guy packing his groceries. "And I'm okay with that because I know they're pretty bloody good." He threw me a quick glance. "They are. Top of all my classes. Proud of me?"

Before I could respond, he turned back to Dad. But he didn't let go of my hand. Instead, he drew me closer to him. That simple move made me love him all the more. Despite this fucked-up situation he was still here. Still standing beside me. Still standing *with* me.

"As for the Australian thing?" He scratched at his beard, a lopsided grin on his face. "Well, there's nothing I can do about that except say *Fair suck of the sav, mate*. Oh and this – which is probably the *worst* thing I can say at this point in time, but I don't give a rat's arse – you're a bloody wanker, Dr. Sinclair. My cousin is too nice a bloke to say it, but I'm not. Too nice, that is."

"Caden," I whispered, my stomach clenching.

Dad watched him, silent.

Caden let out a dry snort. "I get that you're protective of your daughters, sir. I truly do. I understand the whole being protective thing. Ask Chase, she'll tell you. But you've got to take a chill pill. Trust me, I know. Otherwise you're going to mess everything up and you might never get a second chance to make things right again. And from everything I've seen, both Amanda and Chase are doing okay."

I swallowed. Not just at Caden's words, but at Dad's expression – contemplative. Guarded, to be sure. But contemplative all the same.

"Maybe," Caden said, letting go of my hand to smooth his over my hip, "if you just step back a little and see them for who they are . . ." He looked at me. Smiled at me. "See how amazing and courageous and intelligent and beautiful and perfect they are . . . *she* is . . ." He returned his attention to Dad. "You'll see all your stress and worry and freaking out is for nothing."

Dad stood motionless. So did Mom, chewing on her bottom lip.

I am *so* her daughter some times.

"Dad," I said finally, walking over to them both. "I love you, I really do. And I know it's your job to be dogmatic some-times, just as it's mine to sometimes be a pain in the ass. It's the whole father-daughter dichotomy. But you're destroying this family. Can't you see that?"

His eyes narrowed, and his chest swelled with an intake of breath I didn't need to hear to know was shaky. "I just want the best for my daughters," he said.

Mom touched his arm, worry eating up her face. "Caden is correct, Charles. Your daughters are incredible women. They have grown into amazing young adults, thanks in part to you. Now it's time to let them find their feet completely."

I gave Mom a grateful smile. I wasn't going to cry and spoil the moment. The moment didn't need tears. The moment needed strength, understanding. Forgiveness.

Acceptance.

Dad studied me, his expression enigmatic. *The Australian is not sharing your bed with you while he's here*, he signed at me. *Neither is the dog.*

"The Australian wouldn't disrespect you with the assumption he was going to," Caden answered from behind me.

I barely heard the words, but they made me smile all the same. They also made Dad's eyebrows rise as he turned his gaze on Caden.

"I'll be staying with my cousin," Caden continued, now at my side, "until I go back to Australia. Why don't you all come around for dinner one night?"

Dad looked at him. Looked at me. Looked back at him. I could see his brain processing it all. I know my father well. We may not exactly get along, but the one thing I've always admired about him is his intelligence and his ability to navigate through a problem. Well, except when the problem was me. Or Amanda.

"So you really love my daughter?"

My pulse jumped at the question. It wasn't what I'd been expecting at all.

"I do." Caden took my hand. At my knee, Doofus let out a happy bark.

"Enough not to expect her to leave the US when you do?"

My stomach twisted. But as much as I didn't want to admit it, Dad was right. Geography was not on our side.

"Enough to expect her to make the right decision for her future herself," Caden answered. "And to accept it when she does, whether I like it or not."

Dad's eyes narrowed again. He regarded Caden with silent contemplation, and then turned his attention to me.

"I know you and your sister don't believe me," he said, signing the words at the same time. I'm glad he did. It was hard to see his lips through the tears suddenly prickling my eyes. Or to hear him clearly through the choked timbre of his voice. "But I've only ever wanted what's best for you both."

I nodded. Damn, my throat was thick. Tight. *I know, Dad,* I signed back.

"I've just got to get my head around what *best* is," he said. "And that you're both old enough, responsible enough to know what it is, even when I don't."

"I love you, Daddy," I said. Okay, *said* is probably not the right verb. *Croaked* might be better. *Rasped* more accurate.

"I love you too, kitten," he said.

Wow, when was the last time he'd called me kitten? When I was nine? After I'd gotten in trouble at school for arguing with a substitute teacher who'd accused me of whispering in class? Dad had stormed into the principal's office, guns blazing, and told them he'd make sure every single one of them lost their job if they treated his kitten that way again.

I remember being so embarrassed.

We looked at each other. The chasm between us wasn't

even close to being bridged, and the chasm he'd created between him and Amanda might never be, but at that point, I found myself believing one thing: he'd behaved the way he had out of love. It was hard to be pissed at him for that.

Do you mind, he signed, *if I hug you?*

I opened my mouth to say I didn't mind at all, and stopped when Brendon's SUV pulled into the driveway behind Mom and Dad.

Mom turned. Dad did the same. Caden took hold of my hand again. I shot him a quick glance, for a moment completely tongue-tied. What he'd said to Dad, what he'd done . . .

Frowning, I shook my head. *I don't know what I did to deserve you*, I signed.

He grinned. And then quickly snatched a kiss. *Be you*, he signed back.

"What's going on?" Amanda asked, alighting from the car and frowning at us all, as Brendon opened the back passenger door.

Before any of us could answer, a little blur of color shot from the car.

"Cade!" Tanner cried, delight dancing in his voice as he ran straight for Caden.

"Hey, little dude." Caden scooped him up, swinging him around with gusto. "'Bout bloody time I saw you."

"Language, cousin," Brendon scolded with a grin, walking over to join us. I didn't miss the quick glance he gave my father. Nor did I miss the tension in his body.

"Yeah, Cade," Tanner echoed, laughing. "Bloody language."

I covered my mouth with my hand, desperate to hide my smile.

Caden didn't bother. He grinned some more, first at

Brendon – who shook his head with his own smile – and then at Tanner, now resting on his hip. "Oops. I'm bad."

"You *are* bad," Amanda agreed, placing a kiss on Mom's cheek. "Hey, Mom. Dad. Any reason we're all out on the sidewalk?"

"Doggy!" Tanner squirmed out of Caden's arms, before any of us could answer. He reached for Doofus, currently standing at Chase's ankles, tail wagging. "Doggy!"

Amanda and Brendon both moved toward their son with the kind of speed I recognized all too well: that of a parent in protective mode. "Tanner," Brendon shouted.

Before either could reach him however, Tanner wrapped his arms around Doofus's body, his face beaming with joy, his cheek mashed to Doofus's side. "Doggy," he repeated, eyes closed.

Every instinct I had screamed at me to disengage my nephew – so recently recovered from leukemia – from the dog I'd so recently fallen in love with. I almost did. And then stopped when I saw Caden lower to a crouch beside Tanner and Doofus, his smile relaxed. He reached out, placing his palm on Doofus's side. Doofus looked at him, a happy pant making it appear as if he was smiling. The protective plastic cone around his neck, and his front leg cast pressed to Tanner's shoulder, didn't seem to diminish Tanner's joy at all.

"He's a cool dog, isn't he, little dude?" Caden said, smiling at Tanner.

I flicked my sister a quick look. She stood beside her son, watching him and Doofus and Caden like a hawk. Brendon did the same, although he was more at ease than Amanda. This was Brendon after all.

"He's a *bloody* cool dog," Tanner agreed.

"You know," Caden said, giving Doofus's ear a gentle scratch, "I'm very much of the opinion that all boys need a dog to love, just as much as all dogs need a boy to love. What do you think?"

Tanner nodded against Doofus's side. "I want a dog to love," he declared with all the emphatic force of a three year old. "Mommy and Daddy say one day."

Caden closed his eyes, brow furrowing for a heartbeat. And then he opened his eyes and smiled at Tanner again.

"If your Mum and Dad said it was okay," he said, moving his hand to Tanner's head, "would you look after Doofus for me? When . . ." He gave me a very quick look. "When *I* go back to Australia?"

Tanner pulled away from Doofus. If I hadn't already thought Doofus was the best dog in the world, I did now. He stood still and calm, his tail wagging, as if aware the little person hugging him was fragile.

Eyes wide, Tanner studied Caden with solemn intensity before swinging his stare up to his parents. "Can I?"

I swallowed. I remembered what Amanda had told me on the phone earlier today when I'd asked her whether Tanner was medically well enough to have a pet. I remembered her answer very clearly: "I don't know. I'll have to check with Parker."

"I don't—" Dad began, making me jump. He made Mom jump as well.

Brendon, however, didn't jump. Nor did Amanda.

"Of course you can, buddy," Brendon said, giving Tanner a wide smile. "Mummy spoke with Doctor Waters today and he said a dog is a good thing, an *awesome* thing for you to have. So whenever Chase and Caden need someone to look after Doofus, that someone can be you. How's that sound?"

Tanner grinned up at me, and then hugged Doofus again. Gently. Was he aware Doofus was fragile as well? It's likely. When you've battled leukemia at the age of two, you become far more aware of what it means to be sick. And what it means to be well. "Are you going to Australia too, Aunny Chase? With Cade?"

My heart thumped faster in my throat. My breath seemed to feel heavy. I opened my mouth. And then shut it. I had no answer to that question. None.

Not yet.

Goddamn it, just when you think you have all your ducks in a row, one of the bastard ducks turns out to be from the Southern freaking Hemisphere, and another one of the ducks is a dog.

"Hey, Tanner?" Mom suddenly said, doting grandma voice in full affect. "I bought a new tub of ice cream today. Want to help me eat it?"

Just like that Tanner shot to his feet. "Ice cream!"

Amanda laughed. Mom did the same, holding out her hand to Tanner. "Come inside, champ."

"Ice cream," Tanner cried again, the words a joyous song, as he took Mom's hand with excited eagerness.

Amanda looked at me. At Caden. At Dad. "See you inside," she said, her smile understanding.

Doofus barked his farewell.

Brendon chuckled. "Ice cream," he said, shaking his head. "Guess that's another hour on the treadmill coming my way."

I tried to laugh. Instead, I moved my gaze between Dad and Caden. Caden watched Tanner, Mom and Amanda enter the house, his hand resting on Doofus's head. Dad slid his gaze back and forth between Caden and Brendon.

My chest tightened. I turned to Brendon. "Are you sure?" My voice cracked.

He nodded. "We're sure. What about you?"

"Couldn't be surer," Caden answered. "Every boy needs a dog."

Before I knew what he was doing, Brendon grabbed Caden in rough hug.

I think Caden may have chuckled out a laugh, but I couldn't hear it if he did. I watched Brendon squeeze Caden and then, it was me in his arms, as he hugged me in an embrace that should have been crushing, but instead was gentle. For a guy with muscles bigger than The Rock's, Brendon sure knew how to do tender.

I'd just started to return the unexpected hug when he let me go and smiled. "See you both inside."

With a quick nod to Dad, he turned.

And stopped when my father said, "Brendon?"

I swallowed. A distant part of me noticed Caden had taken my hand again. God, I loved the feel of his fingers threaded through mine. Loved it almost as much as I loved him.

Shoulders tensing, Brendon turned back to Dad. "Charles?"

For a moment, just a moment, Dad didn't move. And then he held out his hand. "Thank you," he said, looking Brendon in the eye. "Are . . . are you staying for lunch?"

Brendon blinked. He dropped his gaze to Dad's extended hand. His Adam's apple slid up and down his throat. "We are," he said, completing the timeless gesture with a firm shake. "Thanks for the invite."

A breath fell from me, shaky and close to a laugh. I didn't know what else to do.

Dad smiled. There was still conflict and uncertainty in his eyes, but he smiled. At Brendon. At Caden. At me. "Let's go see what's on offer, apart from ice cream, shall we?"

Brendon nodded. "Sounds like a plan."

Dad turned to Caden. "You know, I've heard it said that

San Diego is the closest you can get to life in Australia without living in Australia."

And with that, he made his way to the house without another word to us, Brendon walking at his side. If you'd told me I would have witnessed such an occurrence a few days ago, I would have laughed in your face.

Caden and I stood shoulder to shoulder, watching them enter the house. My house. My home.

The place I'd spent the surreal, insane journey that was growing up. The place I'd fully intended to remain my home for quite a few more years, at least until I knew what I was truly doing with my life.

Which I did now, right?

"You know what we need?"

I turned at Caden's question.

"Ice cream," he said.

I chewed my bottom lip and then drew in a deep breath, my heart wild. "Know any good places to get ice cream in Melbourne?"

He grew still. So very still. "I do."

I smiled. "Let's go then."

And then I rose up onto tiptoe and kissed him.

Cause that's what you do when you're about to start a whole new life: kiss the person you're going to live it with, to let them know it's begun.

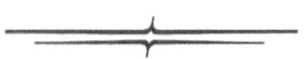

THANK YOU FOR READING

My best friend's second daughter was born partially deaf in one ear. Another close of friend of mine's third daughter was born deaf in one ear and partially deaf in another. Over the years, I've watched these two little girls grow into strong, fierce, independent young women who take on the world.

I can't even begin to image a life without listening to it, but I know Cate and Charlotte have never let it slow them down. Right now, just take a moment to stop, close your eyes and listen to the world...

If you enjoyed **Undeniable**, follow me on Bookbub for pre-order, sales, and new-release alerts, sign-up for my newsletter, the Lexxicon. You'll receive a free copy of my (erotic) paranormal short story, **The Cavern**, plus never miss out on exciting announcements and giveaways!

Unconditional
—— Always Book 1

LEXXIE COUPER

FIRST CHAPTER PREVIEW: UNCONDITIONAL

HEART OF FAME BOOK EIGHT

There's no such thing as unconditional love, right? Right?

Unconditional
(*Always*, Book One)
Available Here

Australia was not what I was expecting. Sure, I hadn't even made it out of the airport, but still, where were the kangaroos? The koalas? Where were the hot guys walking around in Speedos? Where were the Tim Tams? Didn't those delicious chocolate cookies fall from the sky over here? I'm sure I'd read that somewhere? Or maybe I'd dreamt it.

I must admit, the second I'd learned I'd won my college's scholarship to study Environment Studies abroad—and by abroad, I mean a gazillion miles away from Plenty, Ohio, my hometown and the only world I'd ever known—I'd been experiencing weird dreams about Australia.

In one, I was dating a kangaroo that sounded like Chris

Hemsworth. I remember waking in the morning stroking my pillow with the words "You had me at g'day," whispering through my head. In another dream, a shark called Bruce kept trying to take a bath with me.

See what I mean? Weird dreams. I chalked them up to nerves. Winning the scholarship, partly funded by Plenty's only college, partly funded by the University of Sydney, was a double-edged sword.

On one razor-sharp side there was the awesomeness of winning the scholarship in the first place. Mind you, winning makes it sound like luck had something to do with it, which it didn't. Hard work, long hours studying, zero time socializing, movies missed, days and days researching, so many days I sometimes forgot what the sun looked like. *That's* what earned me the scholarship. That, and my passion for the environment.

I'm what my folks call a tree-hugging greenie. Well, my *mom* calls me that. My dad—who had grown up in Australia and moved to the US when he met Mom during a vacation in LA—has been dead for over three years now. Killed when a drunk driver ran off the road and struck him and our dog as they were jogging.

I was a tree-hugging greenie wrapped up in the unassuming guise of a twenty-two-year-old hometown girl who still had bangs and wore pigtails on the weekend. Who still ate peanut butter straight from the jar and loved watching *Sleepy Hollow* and *Glee*when she wasn't studying environmental degradation and its impact on wildlife the world over.

On the other even sharper side of the damn blade was the fact I had to fly a whole day to get to Australia. Did I mention I'd never been outside of Plenty? I *did* mention a drunk driver killed my dad and my dog only a few years ago, right? Leaving my mom a widow?

Did I mention my mom suffers from Parkinson's disease?

Did I mention I do as well?

No on the last two, huh? Sorry about that.

Yeah, I'm a shaker. But I've got it under control. Good meds, meditation, tai chi, and did I mention good meds? Add them together and I'm okay. Mom, however, isn't. And with me being on the other side of the world, who's going to help her up when she falls down? Which she does. Often.

She told me to go, that's why I'm here. She *demanded* I go. But being this far away from her ... God, I don't even ...

Sorry. Didn't mean to get maudlin. Long and short of it, Mom has Parkinson's. She's alone and I'm here because I've never seen her so proud as when I won that scholarship. How could I not go?

But now that I was here—and I was excited to be, I really was—where were the kangaroos? Even a stuffed one on a pedestal or something. And more to the point, where was my passport?

Oh my God, where was my passport? I was about to go through Australian customs in about twenty seconds and I couldn't find my passport. It was in my bag on the plane. So where was it now?

"Next."

I started at the deep, authoritarian command, and shot the man behind the counter a harried look.

I shook my head.

He raised his eyebrows and beckoned for me to approach.

I swallowed. Suddenly aware my fingers were shaking, I clenched my fist. Was it nerves? Or—

"Miss?"

The customs official was now frowning at me. A prickling pressure at the back of my neck told me my fellow travelers were probably glaring. Why wouldn't they be? I'd be glaring too at the idiot who was rooted to the spot and holding up the line that allowed you to enter the country you'd just flown over nineteen hours to get to.

I swallowed again. Cleared my throat. Squeezed my fist—crap, I really *was* shaking—and stepped forward.

The man behind the counter gave me an expectant look. "Passport?"

During the nineteen-hour flight over, I'd passed the time by imagining my first few moments in Australia. In my admittedly sleep-deprived fantasy, the customs official who granted me access would sound like the kangaroo I dated in my dreams. Yes, I will admit now, I have a thing for Chris Hemsworth. But how could I not? Have you looked at him? Is there a sexier, hotter guy on the planet? No, I don't think so. Anyway, the customs official of my dreams would smile at me and tell me I looked amazing after such a long flight.

I didn't, by the way. My hair was flat and greasy, my eyes were scratchy and puffy, and I'd managed to spill most of the coffee the flight attendant had given me somewhere over the Pacific Ocean, somewhere around three am, all over my shirt. Or maybe it had been two pm? Who the hell knew? Helpful tip if you're planning on any long-haul flights—don't wear a white T-shirt, no matter how cute you think you look in it. It's a bad idea.

So, going back to my mid-flight fantasy ... I'm greeted by a super-hot customs official who tells me I look amazing, just as a camera crew from one of those travel shows runs over and asks me if I mind being interviewed about being an American college student in Australia. Added to that, they also inform me Chris Hemsworth is in the airport and wonder if I'd like to meet him. He's researching a role in a movie about the plight of the dingo in the outback and has read my paper about the environment and native animals online and wants to talk about it with me.

In *that* fantasy, I had my passport.

In reality, I had no idea where it was. God, how could I lose it between the plane and—

"Passport, miss?"

I gave the official—who didn't appear inclined to say anything that sounded like "You look amazing"—a weak smile.

Would they arrest you in Australia for trying to enter the country without a passport? I suspect so. I opened my mouth. A sound that may or may not have been a strangled squeak emitted from my throat.

The official's frown deepened. I couldn't help but notice his right hand slipped under the counter.

"I've lost my passport," I said, although I think I may have mouthed it. For some reason, my voice had disappeared. Maybe it was with my errant passport? Perhaps both were on their way to Paris?

The man behind the glass leaned forward. "Please repeat that, miss."

"I've lost my passport," I said again. Louder this time. With less silent asphyxiation.

His eyebrows shot up. "Since you boarded?"

I nodded.

"What flight?"

My mind went blank. Oh God, I was doing an appalling job of representing the USA at this point in time. "Err," I said. "Big plane. Had a ... a kangaroo on the tail."

The man's forehead furrowed. "A Qantas plane?"

Relief flooded through me and I nodded, looking, I'm sure, like an unhinged bobble-head. "That's it. Qantas."

"So you've just disembarked a Qantas flight from ..."

His silence told me I was meant to supply the answer. "Plenty," I gushed. "I mean Dallas."

Tears prickled at the backs of my eyes. I ached for Mom so badly my heart felt like it was being torn out of my chest. What the hell was I doing here? Where was my brain?

"I'm sorry." I rubbed at my eyes with the backs of my hands. My vision went that special kind of blurry that happens when you put too much pressure on your eyeballs, and I blinked. I needed to get a grip. Or a passport. A passport would be nice.

I wondered for a stupidly surreal moment if the traveler behind me would let me borrow hers. Only until I actually got *into* Australia. Then she could have it—

"Are you Maci Rowling?"

A deep male voice with an obvious Australian accent caressed my tired, overwrought mind, and I jerked my head around, my heart pounding fast.

An elderly gent, who had to be at least ninety in the shade, was standing at my elbow, holding what looked to be an American passport in one hand. In his other, he held a cane. Truth be told, it was the cane doing most of the holding, keeping the gentleman vertical.

"I found it on the floor in the line a second ago," he said, a friendly smile on his wrinkled face. "Think it might be yours."

He was old and feeble and holding a passport.

And if he knew my name, it meant it was *my* passport.

What else could I do? I threw myself against his frail body in a massive hug.

Knocking him to the ground.

Three hours later, I was allowed into Australia.

It's insane how long it takes to apologize sufficiently to an elderly gentleman you've just injured in your enthusiasm to thank him for finding your passport. Who knew it would be so easy to knock an eighty-two year old to the floor with a hug? I didn't help that my hug was pretty ... enthusiastic. Of course, *after* the poor old guy was taken away in a wheelchair, I received a rather stern lecture about my "enthusiasm" from the airport police. One of whom seriously looked like Russell Crowe. If Russell Crowe was fat. And older. And a woman. And after *that* I received an even sterner lecture about passport security from the same humorless officials.

Finally, with the public humiliation over and done with, I was allowed into the country.

Only to wait at the luggage carousel, watching it go round and round until I was the only person left, with no sign of my luggage on the conveyor belt.

Thirty minutes later, I accepted the fact that my luggage —with all my clothes, including my Victoria's Secret bra and panties I'd saved for freaking months to buy just for this trip— wasn't going to appear through the clear flappy-plastic opening in the wall.

Yay.

I made my way to the service counter only to be informed the airline had no clue as to the current whereabouts of my suitcase.

"I'm very sorry," the cheery attendant behind the counter said, beaming up at me. "We shall contact you as soon as we locate it. Welcome to Australia."

Welcome to Australia? Yeah, right.

Suffice to say, I wanted to go home.

There and then.

Badly.

So badly I actually pivoted on my heel to head back toward the customs counters. And then I stopped when I realized I was being silly.

Okay, confession time. I'm not exactly emotionally ...

stable. I mean, I'm not insane or anything. In fact, I'm quite intelligent and at times grounded—Mom's word, not mine. But more often than not, I'm impulsive. I'm also sensitive, self-conscious, uncertain and ... well, to put it bluntly—broken.

It happens. When you spend almost ten years of your life watching your mother slowly being devoured by a disease with no known cure, a disease that was robbing her of her ability to smile, her ability to cut her own food, button her own buttons, talk at a normal volume, have normal bowel movements—hell, have *any* kind of normal movement, even something as simple as blinking and swallowing—and you know one day that disease is going to do all those things to you, you get a little screwed up.

That's what Parkinson's disease does. It screws you. Messes with you. That's what it'd done to *my* family, at least.

I had to tell people Mom wasn't drunk at my father's funeral, that it was just her muscles refusing to allow her to walk without staggering about because her brain was betraying her. That messed with *me*.

I'd sit opposite her nightly at the dinner table, on edge—terrified even—that her throat muscles would stop working halfway through her eating, causing her to almost choke to death, an event that had happened at least three times.

It was bad enough for me to learn my mom had Parkinson's when I was twelve. Try being told when you're twenty-one that you have the same disease.

I'd been living with early-onset Parkinson's disease for a year now, and it wasn't getting easier. Twenty-two was not meant to be like this, it was meant to be lived large, partying, meeting new people ... not new doctors and specialists and medical-insurance representatives.

Jesus, I sound miserable, don't I?

I'm not. Honest. I try to laugh about it. I tell Mom I'm

racing her to complete neural shut-down. Whoever gets there first wins. And what does the winner get?

A complete loss of dignity and—

Holy shit, sorry. I truly didn't mean to go there. It's a bleak place, my self-pity, and I hate it. Let's try not to go there again, okay?

I forced myself to turn back around, hitch my carry-on bag—containing a spare pair of panties, thank freaking God— farther up my shoulder, stride through the last stage of customs. I had no food to declare. No insects, reptiles, items made of wood or animal body parts. I passed over my declarations card to the smiling lady collecting them, and stepped through the gates and into the Sydney International Arrivals terminal, surrounded by excited people waiting for their loved ones.

It was then I realized I needed to pee. I hadn't peed since somewhere over Hawaii.

Oh boy, did I need to pee.

And the second I acknowledged I needed to pee, the more I needed to go.

Searching frantically for the restroom sign, I spied what I thought was the ladies' room and ran for it, head down, fist gripping the strap of my bag as if it were a lifeline to bladder relief.

So of course, when I slammed into something rock-solid but warm and firm as well, the first thing I thought was I was going to pee myself. Not, argh, I've just run into someone and I need to apologize.

I stumbled back a step, flinging the poor woman in my way a harried glance. And froze when that harried glance found not a poor woman, but a tall, broad-shouldered, stunningly hot—no, change that—stupefyingly hot, gorgeous guy with shaggy dark-brown hair hanging over equally dark-brown eyes so intense and beautiful and sexy and—

He wrapped strong fingers around my upper arms and steadied me before I could fall completely on my ass.

"Hey, I think you're heading into the wrong loo."

I gazed up at him and didn't say a word. I'd've liked to have blamed sleep deprivation and jet lag for my ridiculous silence, but they weren't the culprits.

The guy holding my arms, keeping me upright, was stunning. Gorgeous. Hot. Like a brown-haired, brown-eyed version of Chris Hemsworth. Only sexier.

I didn't think that was even possible, but there you go. Tall, with a crooked grin that made my heart skip a beat and a goddamn divine body, all muscular and sculpted and perfectly proportioned with the broadest of shoulders, all wrapped up tight in a snug white T-shirt and snugger faded jeans.

And he had an Australian accent.

Oh boy.

I gaped at him, my heart thumping in my throat.

"Can you speak?" he asked.

I caught my bottom lip with my teeth and shook my head.

His eyebrows shot up. "You can't?"

"I can," I blurted, nodding this time. Talk about being a mess of contradictions. "I'm just ..." I paused, stopping myself from telling him I was falling in lust with him. Yeah, not exactly cool behavior. Gushing all over a complete stranger on the way to the bathroom? Welcome to Australia.

"I'm just ... desperate," I finished, ducking my head. I sounded like an idiot.

He gave a warm, friendly laugh. "To go to the loo?"

I peered up at him through my bangs. "Yeah."

That crooked grin returned to his face. As before, it made my body do things I wasn't entirely used to.

"You better go then." He stepped aside and held an arm out, directing me deeper into the men's restroom.

Oh my God, was I blushing? I shuffled my feet, frowning.

Devilment danced in his dark-brown eyes. "Something else you're desperate for?"

Something else? Was he serious? A guy that looked like him, asking me what I wanted? If I were the brave, take-no-prisoners kind of girl, I'd tell him straight up. *Something else I'm desperate for? Hell yeah, a kiss from you would be a start.* But I wasn't that kind of girl. I was a sleep deprived, jet lagged student with poor social skills and a disease that wasn't exactly high on the sexy list. Of course, I wasn't going to ask him for a kiss.

No matter how much the thought made my tummy flutter.

He studied me with a playful grin. "Going to tell me what it is?"

"A kiss." The word fell past my lips before I could stop it.

My face went cold as the blood drained from it. And then hot as all that blood rushed back into my cheeks just as fast. Holy shit, had I really said that aloud?

"A kiss?" he repeated, lifting an eyebrow.

Oh God, I *had* said it aloud. I stared at him, once again dumbstruck. What was I doing? Was I really *that* tired? Had to be. Why else would I say something so ... so ... *embarrassing*? I couldn't be flirting with him. I wasn't any good at it. I was an environmentalist dork with Parkinson's. As if I knew how to flirt.

Was I delusional? Was my brain finally betraying me compl—

Warm lips brushed over mine in a lingering caress of skin

on skin. I would have melted on the spot ... if it wasn't for the fact I yelped in shocked disbelief and stumbled back a step.

Mr. Broad Shoulders laughed. "Sorry. Didn't mean to freak you out."

Just to make it clear before I continue, I'm not a virgin. I lost my virginity four nights after my sixteenth birthday, to my high school boyfriend—the quarterback, no less. How's that for both an achievement and a cliché? But since I found out I have Parkinson's, I've pretty much shut down any and all notion of romance. Who wants to get romantic with someone who's going to be a shaky mess in a few years? I can't imagine there are many guys out there willing to roll with that kind of burden, so I stopped putting myself out there. Which *might* explain my very active fantasy obsession with a married Australian actor, now that I think about it. Hmmm. Desire the impossible to substitute the denied. Makes sense, right?

I gaped up at my mysterious kisser—again. Heart beating way too fast, I pressed my fingers to my lips. "Why did you do that?"

"You asked." His grin turned wickedly playful, hinting at a dimple in his right cheek, and he leaned a little closer to me, his brown eyes holding mine. "And you looked so damn sexy with your mussed-up hair and coffee-stained shirt."

A wave of embarrassment flooded my face. I slapped my hand to my left boob, hurting myself in a rather ridiculous attempt to hide the stain he'd already pointed out. Why do we do that, by the way? Try to conceal something once it's been pointed out? Like the way mining corporations plant rows of trees around the boundaries of their open-cut mines, as if some greenery will conceal the massive gaping wound gouged into the planet by their machinery.

His low chuckle drew a frown from me. "Are you mocking

me?" I asked, a distant part of my mind telling me I still needed to use the bathroom.

"No. Honest. The second you ran into me, I wanted to kiss you."

It was my turn to cock an eyebrow. I *love* that I can do that —it speaks volumes. Attitude from your waiter? Cock an eyebrow. Lip from your study partner? Cock an eyebrow. Absurd claim from a stranger in a public restroom? Cock an eyebrow.

"The second?" I echoed.

His lips twitched. Christ, he was hot. "Okay, maybe the second after the second. When you realized who you'd run into."

Who I'd run into? Didn't he mean *where* I'd run into? The men's toilet rather than the ladies'?

I frowned.

He frowned in return. "You *do* know who I am, right?" he asked, curious conviction in his deep voice. Have I mentioned the sexy Australian accent? "That's why you asked for the kiss. Because of the way my sister met the prince?"

My eyebrows shot up my forehead. I'd like to say I had a hand in their journey, but my brain was too busy being stunned by what I'd just heard for any conscious direction to body parts or facial features. What did he just say?

"Prince?" I echoed.

It was obvious I had no freaking clue what he was talking about. Clear enough for him to pull a grimace. A sexy grimace, if that's possible to visualize.

"You don't know who I am?"

I shook my head. Deep in the pit of my stomach, a twisting tension curled tighter. A sexual tension. Or maybe it was bladder tension, due to the fact I still hadn't peed.

He let out an amused sigh, dragging his hands through his

dark hair as he did so. "Fuck, 'eh? So you just asked for a kiss because ..."

The question hung on the air between us, looking for an answer. One I couldn't provide. What was I going to say? 'Cause you're really, really hot? Instead, I said, "Who *are* you?"

He flashed me that lopsided grin again, let out another laugh and ducked his head. "No one important," he said.

And then, before I could stop him, he closed the small distance between us, lowered his head to mine and kissed me again.

Longer this time.

Holy fuck, did he know how to kiss. He parted his lips, dipped his tongue into my mouth—when had *my* lips parted, I wonder?—and found mine with wicked ease, teasing it with a slow, lingering stroke.

The heat in the junction of my thighs fluttered and pulsed and throbbed in a way it never had before, and a soft little moan vibrated deep in my chest. Whoa.

And then someone cleared his throat behind us and I let out another yelp of surprise, this one a violent, full-body yelp involving jumping and spinning about.

A massive man wearing a dark blue suit and dark sunglasses was standing a few feet into the bathroom's entryway looking at Mr. Broad Shoulders. "It's time, Mr. Jones."

Behind me, Mr. Broad Shoulders—correct that, Mr. Jones —uttered an almost inaudible "Fuck".

He slid warm fingers up my arm, making me flinch, and I turned back to face him, completely mystified as to what the hell was going on.

"I have to go," he said, a grin playing on his lips. Lips that only a second ago had been on mine. "I'll make sure no one comes into the loo while you're in there, okay?"

And without another word, he strode past me, past the man in the dark blue suit, and out into the airport terminal.

Leaving me standing in a public restroom that obviously wasn't the ladies', with the moisture of his kiss a cool memory on my lips.

I gaped at the man in the suit, waiting for an explanation.

It didn't come.

The man pivoted on his heel and stood with his back to me, muttering something into his shirt cuff.

If that wasn't a WTF moment, I don't know what was.

I blinked. Took a step to follow the now-absent Mr. Jones —could that really be his name?—and was suddenly hit with the need to empty my bladder. Again. With all the force of a wrecking ball hitting an outhouse made of paper.

I let out a little cry, doubled over, rammed my thighs together and did that ridiculous sprint you do when you need to go to the bathroom in a hurry. The one where your knees are stuck together, your jaw is clenched shut and your hands are balled into fists.

I hit the door running, spun 180 degrees, slammed the door shut, locked it, dropped my bag, yanked down my jeans and panties in one go and made it without a second to lose.

If it weren't for the man in the suit only a few feet away, I would have let out an *ahhhh* of relief.

But there *was* a man in a suit only a few feet away. A mysterious man who seemed to be connected to an even more mysterious man who'd kissed me because I'd asked him to.

What the hell was up with that?

A few minutes later, with the sound of the toilet flush a loud roar in the surreal silence, I emerged from the cubicle only to discover I was completely alone.

"Huh. Weird."

By the time I finished washing my hands, a string of men was pouring into the bathroom. They all balked at the sight of me just as they were about to approach the urinal, hands on flies. No one said anything.

With heat flooding my face yet again, I hightailed it out of there as quickly as I could. I tried not to look around for the mysterious Mr. Jones and the man in the blue suit, but how could I not? There was no sign of them anywhere.

That was probably a good thing. My first few hours in Australia hadn't exactly gone to plan, and truth be told, if I *did* see Mr. Jones again, I'd probably make a fool of myself and ask him to kiss me again. It had been that good. I still had the tingles and a fluttering belly to prove it. But whoever he was, he was gone.

Life back to normal for me. Well, as normal as it could be given I was on the other side of the world from everything I knew and loved, in the country of my father's birth without a single person I could call a friend and—

Okay, let's stop right there and get off the self-pity bus. I was here, in Australia, about to start the most amazing experience of my student life. No need for dramatics.

Hitching up my bag, I took a deep breath, scanned the crowd one more time for any sight of Mr. Broad Shoulders and then headed out the exit. I had to catch a taxi to Sydney University, my home for the first half of my adventure.

Two steps outside, I was almost knocked over by a man running with a camera in his hand.

"Hey!" I protested, staggering to regain my footing. It was never fun to lose your balance, especially when the disease fighting to control your body liked to throw you *off* it just for shits and giggles.

The running man didn't slow down. Nor did the one following him. Or the one after that.

Suddenly, it dawned on me there were lots of hurrying, rushing, sprinting men with cameras, all heading toward a stretch black limousine parked at the curb a few feet away. A limo that Mr. Broad Shoulders, AKA Mr. Jones, AKA my mysterious kisser, was now climbing into, the man in the blue suit guiding his head as he glared at the approaching wave of frenzied photographers.

Confused by it all, I frowned. Who the hell *was* this guy to deserve so much manic attention?

Camera flashes detonated around the limo. The photographers shouted. Most of the calls sounded like, "Oi, Raphael." Which couldn't be right. Who had a name like Raphael these days? The crowd around me surged forward, sirens wailed from somewhere nearby and then, in a moment of surreal calm amongst it all, a gap in the madness formed between me and the limo, and Mr. Broad Shoulders' stare met mine.

Met.

Melded with.

Fixed on.

Pinned.

Our gazes held, and in that gaze, an entire conversation took place:

I liked kissing you.

I liked being kissed by you.

Shame it had to end.

Ditto.

And then the man in the dark blue suit shoved the photographers backward and slammed the limo door shut, ending my ocular correspondence with Mr. Broad Shoulders, just like that.

I blinked.

The limo engine roared, the man in the blue suit hurled some rather unpleasant words at the horde and then pulled open the front passenger door and disappeared into the cabin.

A chorus of boos rose from the paparazzi—it's safe to assume that's what they were—although I still didn't know who they were photographing. Someone famous, obviously.

Someone famous who'd kissed me. In the men's restroom, no less.

I tracked the limo's path as it sped past me and everyone else on the sidewalk, my tummy twisting and knotting and fluttering and generally being all manner of unsettled. It wasn't until the limousine vanished around the sweeping bend a few yards away that I finally found my brain and grabbed the photographer nearest to me.

"Who was that?" I asked the sneering man trying to disengage my grip on his wrist.

"In the limo?"

"Yes," I answered, trying not to sound agitated. Who else would I be talking about?

"You don't know?"

I shook my head.

"That was Raphael Jones." The man smirked.

"Who—"

But before I could finish asking who Raphael Jones was, the photographer had shaken off my hold and was hurrying away, studying the small screen on the back of his camera.

I stood and watched the dispersing photographers and crowd, racking my brain to find any clue as to why the name should mean anything worthy of such frenzied excitement.

Nothing.

I shrugged. "Must be an Australian celebrity."

Deciding to google the guy when I finally made it to my campus accommodation (my iPhone wasn't talking to the

Australian network yet, damn it), I headed for the first avail-able cab, climbed into the back and gave the driver the address I'd be staying at while I was a student of the University of Sydney.

The memory of Raphael Jones's kiss sent a delicious little thrill through me and I wriggled deeper into my seat. So I'd been kissed by an Australian celebrity not even a few hours in the country. Not bad for a college dork from Plenty, Ohio, even if I do say so myself. It kind of made up for the otherwise dismal start to my adventure. Pity I was never going to see him again or I'd show him how an American girl did things.

Okay, maybe not, given how much of a twitchy, emotional wreck I was, but a girl can kick ass in her fantasies, can't she? It's not like I *was* going to see him again. Australia's a big country, after all.

Right?

MORE ROMANCE FROM LEXXIE COUPER...

The Always Series

Unconditional
Unforgettable
Undeniable

The Outback Skies Series

Bound to You
Breathless for You
Burn for You
Bare for You
Better with You

The Heart of Fame Series

Love's Rhythm
Muscle for Hire
Guarded Desires
Steady Beat
Lead Me On
Blame it on the Bass
Getting Played
Blackthorne

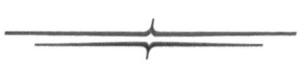

ABOUT LEXXIE COUPER

Lexxie Couper started writing when she was six and hasn't stopped since. She's not a deviant, but she does have a deviant's imagination and a desire to entertain readers with her words. Add the two together and you get erotic romances that can make you laugh, cry, shake with fear or tremble with desire. Sometimes all at once.

When she's not submerged in the worlds she creates, Lexxie's life revolves around her family, a husband who thinks she's insane, an indoor cat who likes to stalk shadows, and her daughters, who both utterly captured her heart and changed her life forever.

Lexxie lives by two simple rules – measure your success not by how much money you have, but by how often you laugh, and always try everything at least once. As a consequence, she's laughed her way through many an eyebrow raising adventure. You can find details of her writing at www.LexxieCouper.com

www.ingramcontent.com/pod-product-compliance
Lightning Source LLC
Chambersburg PA
CBHW050139120726
47903CB00002B/417